by Fritz Leiber

Author	Fritz Leiber
Cover Artist	Mike Mignola
Colorist	Sherilyn Van Valkenburg
Interior Artist	Mike Mignola
Series Editor	Stewart Wieck
Graphic Designer	Aaron Voss
Cover Designer	Richard Thomas
Art Director	Richard Thomas

More information and previews available at white–wolf.com

White Wolf Publishing
735 Park North Boulevard, Suite 128
Clarkston, GA 30021
www.white–wolf.com

First Edition: Aug 2000

10 9 8 7 6 5 4 3 2 1

Printed in Canada.

CONTENTS

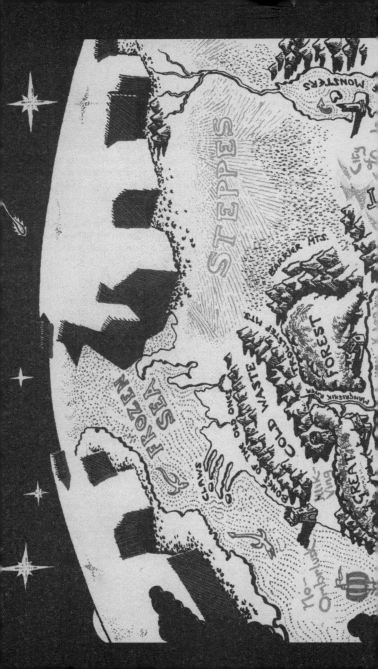

THE GRAY MOUSER: 1

The city lifts black roof-shields toward the stars
And shuts the jungle out with mortised stones
And seals the scent of flowers in glass jars
And locks Earth's secrets up in brass-clasped tomes.
No satyr may live there, no faun survive
The stench and clangor of each crowded street.
The white-fanged beasts of night cannot contrive
To gnaw an entrance through its black concrete.

Yet 'mongst the gargoyles on the slated roofs
One gray-masked face peers down with living grin
That mocks the scurry of the city's floor.
Two gray-gloved hands tease ope' the library's door
And break the ponderous books and scribble in
Footnotes that give the lie to all proud proofs.

THE GRAY MOUSER: 2

Soft-sandaled feet press lightly on the stones
That cobble Lankhmar's mazy alleyways;
A grayish cloak melts in the river mist
That billowing with many a darting twist
Fumes round the corner from the nighted bays
To chill with sorcery men's blood and bones;
Only a bat whose sharp ears caught one sound
Knows that the Mouser is on business bound.

A jewel from Quarmall or a girl from Kled,
A caravel said to be docking soon,
A rune that Sheelba magicked from the dead,
Or a dread whisper from beyond the moon
What man can name the thing the Mouser seeks
Or read the smile that links his sallow cheeks?

— Fritz Leiber

FRITZ LEIBER'S
LANKhMAR

INDUCTION

1

Sundered from us by gulfs of time and stranger
dimensions dreams the ancient world of Nehwon with
its towers and skulls and jewels, its swords and sorceries. Nehwon's known realms crowd about the Inner
Sea: northward the green-forested fierce Land of the
Eight Cities, eastward the steppe-dwelling Mingol
horsemen and the desert where caravans creep from
the rich Eastern Lands and the River Tilth. But southward, linked to the desert only by the Sinking Land
and further warded by the Great Dike and the Mountains of Hunger, are the rich grain fields and walled
cities of Lankhmar, eldest and chiefest of Nehwon's
lands. Dominating the Land of Lankhmar and crouching at the silty mouth of the River Hlal in a secure
corner between the grain fields, the Great Salt Marsh,
and the Inner Sea is the massive-walled and mazy-
alleyed metropolis of Lankhmar, thick with thieves and
shaven priests, lean-framed magicians and fat-bellied
merchants — Lankhmar the Imperishable, the City of
the Black Toga.

In Lankhmar on one murky night, if we can
believe the runic books of Sheelba of the Eyeless Face,
there met for the first time those two dubious heroes
and whimsical scoundrels, Fafhrd and the Gray Mouser.
Fafhrd's origins were easy to perceive in his near seven-
foot height and limber-looking ranginess, his
hammered ornaments and huge longsword: he was
clearly a barbarian from the Cold Waste north even of
the Eight Cities and the Trollstep Mountains. The
Mouser's antecedents were more cryptic and hardly to
be deduced from his childlike stature, gray garb,
mouseskin hood shadowing flat swart face, and decep-
tively dainty rapier; but somewhere about him was the
suggestion of cities and the south, the dark streets and
also the sun-drenched spaces. As the twain eyed each

other challengingly through the murky fog lit indirectly by distant torches, they were already dimly aware that they were two long-sundered, matching fragments of a greater hero and that each had found a comrade who would outlast a thousand quests and a lifetime—or a hundred lifetimes—of adventuring.

No one at that moment could have guessed that the Gray Mouser was once named Mouse, or that Fafhrd had recently been a youth whose voice was by training high-pitched, who wore white furs only, and who still slept in his mother's tent although he was eighteen.

FRITZ LEIBER'S
LANKhMAR

The SNOW WOMEN

II

AT COLD CORNER in midwinter, the women of the Snow Clan were waging a cold war against the men. They trudged about like ghosts in their whitest furs, almost invisible against the new-fallen snow, always together in female groups, silent or at most hissing like angry shades. They avoided Godshall with its trees for pillars and walls of laced leather and towering pine-needle roof.

They gathered in the big, oval Tent of the Women, which stood guard in front of the smaller home tents, for sessions of chanting and ominous moaning and various silent practices designed to create powerful enchantments that would tether their husbands' ankles to Cold Corner, tie up their loins, and give them sniveling, nose-dripping colds, with the threat of the Great Cough and Winter Fever held in reserve. Any man so unwise as to walk alone by day was apt to be set upon and snowballed and, if caught, thrashed—be he even skald or mighty hunter.

And a snowballing by Snow Clan women was nothing to laugh at. They threw overarm, it is true, but their muscles for that had been greatly strengthened by much splitting of firewood, lopping of high branches, and pounding of hides, including the iron-hard one of the snowy behemoth. And they sometimes froze their snowballs.

The sinewy, winter-hardened men took all of this with immense dignity, striding about like kings in their conspicuous black, russet, and rainbow-dyed ceremonial furs, drinking hugely but with discretion, and trading as shrewdly as Ilthmarts their bits of amber and ambergris, their snow-diamonds visible only by night, their glossy animal pelts, and their ice-herbs, in exchange for woven fabrics, hot spices, blued and

browned iron, honey, waxen candles, firepowders that
flared with a colored roar, and other products of the
civilized south. Nevertheless, they made a point of
keeping generally in groups, and there was many a
nose a-drip among them.

It was not the trading the women objected
to. Their men were good at that and they—the
women—were the chief beneficiaries. They greatly
preferred it to their husbands' occasional piratings,
which took those lusty men far down the eastern
coasts of the Outer Sea, out of reach of immediate
matriarchal supervision and even, the women sometimes feared, of their potent female magic. Cold
Corner was the farthest south ever got by the entire
Snow Clan, whose members spent most of their lives
on the Cold Waste and among the foothills of the
untopped Mountains of the Giants and the even
more northerly Bones of the Old Ones, and so this
midwinter camp was their one yearly chance to trade
peaceably with venturesome Mingols, Sarheenmarts,
Lankhmarts, and even an occasional Eastern desert-
man, heavily beturbaned, bundled up to the eyes, and
elephantinely gloved and booted.

Nor was it the guzzling which the women
opposed. Their husbands were great quaffers of mead
and ale at all times and even of the native white snow-
potato brandy, a headier drink than most of the wines
and boozes the traders hopefully dispensed.

No, what the Snow Women hated so ven-
omously and which each year caused them to wage
cold war with hardly any material or magical holds
barred, was the theatrical show which inevitably came
shivering north with the traders, its daring troupers
with faces chapped and legs chilblained, but hearts a-

beat for soft northern gold and easy if rampageous audiences—a show so blasphemous and obscene that the men preempted Godshall for its performance (God being unshockable) and refused to let the women and youths view it; a show whose actors were, according to the women, solely dirty old men and even dirtier scrawny southern girls, as loose in their morals as in the lacing of their skimpy garments, when they went clothed at all. It did not occur to the Snow Women that a scrawny wench, her dirty nakedness all blue goosebumps in the chill of drafty Godshall, would hardly be an object of erotic appeal, besides her risking permanent all-over frostbite.

So the Snow Women each midwinter hissed and magicked and sneaked and sniped with their crusty snowballs at huge men retreating with pomp, and frequently caught an old or crippled or foolish, young, drunken husband and beat him soundly.

This outwardly comic combat had sinister undertones. Particularly when working all together, the Snow Women were reputed to wield mighty magics, particularly through the element of cold and its consequences: slipperiness, the sudden freezing of flesh, the gluing of skin to metal, the frangibility of objects, the menacing mass of snow-laden trees and branches, and the vastly greater mass of avalanches. And there was no man wholly unafraid of the hypnotic power in their ice-blue eyes.

Each Snow Woman, usually with the aid of the rest, worked to maintain absolute control of her man, though leaving him seemingly free, and it was whispered that recalcitrant husbands had been injured and even slain, generally by some frigid instrumentality. While at the same time witchy cliques and individual sorceresses played against each other a power game in which the brawniest and boldest of men, even chiefs and priests, were but counters.

During the fortnight of trading and the two days of the Show, hags and great strapping girls guarded the Tent of the Women at all quarters, while from within came strong perfumes, stenches, flashes and intermittent glows by night, clashings and tinklings, cracklings and quenchings, and incantational chantings and whisperings that never quite stopped.

This morning one could imagine that the Snow Women's sorcery was working everywhere, for the weather was windless and overcast, and there were wisps of fog in the moist freezing air, so that crystals of ice were rapidly forming on every bush and branch, every twig and tip of any sort, including the ends of the men's moustaches and the eartips of the tamed lynxes. The crystals were as blue and flashing as the Snow Women's eyes and even mimicked in their forms, to an imaginative mind, the Snow Women's hooded, tall, and white-robed figures, for many of the crystals grew upright, like diamond flames.

And this morning the Snow Women had caught, or rather got a near certain chance of trapping, an almost unimaginably choice victim. For one of the Show girls, whether by ignorance or foolhardy daring, and perhaps tempted by the relatively mild, gem-begetting air, had strolled on the crusty snow away from the safety of the actors' tents, past Godshall on the precipice side, and from thence between two sky-thrusting copses of snow-laden evergreens, out onto the snow-carpeted natural rock bridge that had been the start of the Old Road south to Gnampf Nar until some five man-lengths of its central section had fallen three score years ago.

A short step from the up-curving, perilous brink she had paused and looked for a long while south through the wisps of mist that, in the distance, grew thin as pluckings of long-haired wool. Below her in the canyon's overhung slot, the snow-capped pines flooring Trollstep Canyon looked tiny as the white tents of an army of Ice Gnomes. Her gaze slowly traced Trollstep Canyon from its far eastern beginnings to where, narrowing, it passed directly beneath her and then, slowly widening, curved south, until the buttress opposite her with its matching, jutting section of the one-time rock bridge, cut off the view south. Then her gaze went back to trace the New Road from where it began its descent beyond the actors' tents and clung to the far wall of the canyon until, after many a switchback and many a swing into great gully and out again—unlike the far swifter, straighter descent of the Old Road—it plunged into the midst of the flooring pines and went with them south.

From her constant yearning look, one might have thought the actress a silly homesick soubrette, already regretting this freezing northern tour and pining for some hot, flea-bitten actors' alley beyond the Land of the Eight Cities and the Inner Sea—except for the quiet confidence of her movements, the proud set of her shoulders, and the perilous spot she had chosen for her peering. For this spot was not only physically dangerous, but also as near the Tent of the Snow Women as it was to Godshall, and in addition the spot was taboo because a chief and his children had plunged to their deaths when the central rock-span had cracked away three score years ago, and because the wooden replacement had fallen under the weight of a brandy-merchant's cart some two score

years later. Brandy of the fieriest, a loss fearsome
enough to justify the sternest of taboos, including one
against ever rebuilding the bridge.

And as if even those tragedies were not sufficient to glut the jealous gods and make taboo absolute,
only two years past the most skillful skier the Snow
Clan had produced in decades, one Skif, drunk with
snow brandy and an icy pride, had sought to jump the
gap from the Cold Corner side. Towed to a fast start
and thrusting furiously with his sticks, he had taken
off like a gliding hawk, yet missed the opposite snowy
verge by an arm's length; the prows of his skis had
crashed into rock, and he himself smashed in the rocky
depths of the canyon.

The bemused actress wore a long coat of au-
burn fox fur belted with a light, gold-washed brass
chain. Icy crystals had formed in her high-piled, fine,
dark brown hair.

From the narrowness of her coat, her figure
promised to be scrawny or at least thinly muscular
enough to satisfy the Snow Women's notion of female
players, but she was almost six feet tall—which was
not at all as actresses should be and definitely an added
affront to the tall Snow Women now approaching her
from behind in a silent white rank.

An over-hasty white fur boot sang against the
glazed snow.

The actress spun around and without hesitation raced back the way she had come. Her first three
steps broke the snow-crust, losing her time, but then
she learned the trick of running in a glide, feet graz-
ing the crust.

She hitched her russet coat high. She was
wearing black fur boots and bright scarlet stockings.

The Snow Women glided swiftly after her, pitching their hard-packed snowballs.

One struck her hard on the shoulder. She made the mistake of looking back.

By ill chance two snowballs took her in jaw and forehead, just beneath painted lip and on an arched black eyebrow.

She reeled then, turning fully back, and a snowball thrown almost with the force of a slinger's stone struck her in the midriff, doubling her up and driving the breath from her lungs in an open-mouthed *whoosh*.

She collapsed. The white women rushed forward, blue eyes a-glare.

A big, thinnish, black-moustached man in a drab quilted jacket and a low black turban stopped watching from beside a becrystalled, rough-barked living pillar of Godshall, and ran toward the fallen woman. His footsteps broke the crust, but his strong legs drove him powerfully on.

Then he slowed in amaze as he was passed almost as if he were at a standstill by a tall, white, slender figure glide-running so swiftly that it seemed for a moment it went on skis. Then for another instant, the turbaned man thought it was another Snow Woman, but then he noted that it wore a short fur jerkin rather than a long fur robe—and so was presumably a Snow Man or Snow Youth, though the black-turbaned man had never seen a Snow Clan male dressed in white.

The strange, swift figure glide-ran, with chin tucked down and eyes bent away from the Snow Women, as if fearing to meet their wrathful blue gaze. Then, as he swiftly knelt by the felled actress, long

reddish-blond hair spilled from his hood. From that
and the figure's slenderness, the black-turbaned man
knew an instant of fear that the intercomer was a very
tall Snow Girl, eager to strike the first blow at close
quarters.

But then he saw a jut of downy male chin
in the reddish-blond hair and also a pair of massive
silver bracelets of the sort one gained only by pirat-
ing. Next the youth picked up the actress and
glide-ran away from the Snow Women, who now
could see only their victim's scarlet-stockinged legs.
A volley of snowballs struck the rescuer's back. He
staggered a little, then sped determinedly on, still
ducking his head.

The biggest of the Snow Women, one with
the bearing of a queen and a haggard face still handsome, though the hair falling to either side of it was
white, stopped running and shouted in a deep voice,
"Come back, my son! You hear me, Fafhrd, come back
now!"

The youth nodded his ducked head slightly,
though he did not pause in his flight. Without turning his head, he called in a rather high voice, "I will
come back, revered Mor my mother . . . later on."

The other women took up the cry of "Come
back now!" Some of them added such epithets as "Dis-
solute youth!" "Curse of your good mother Mor!" and
"Chaser after whores!"

Mor silenced them with a curt, sidewise sweep
of her hands, palms down. "We will wait here," she
announced with authority.

The black-turbaned man paused a bit, then
strolled after the vanished pair, keeping a wary eye on
the Snow Women. They were supposed not to attack
traders, but with barbarian females, as with males, one

could never tell.

Fafhrd reached the actors' tents, which were pitched in a circle around a trampled stretch of snow at the altar end of Godshall. Farthest from the precipice was the tall, conical tent of the Master of the Show. Midway stretched the common actors' tent, somewhat fish-shaped, one-third for the girls, two-thirds for the men. Nearest Trollstep Canyon was a medium-size, hemicylindrical tent supported on half hoops. Across its middle, an evergreen sycamore thrust a great heavy branch balanced by two lesser branches on the opposite side, all spangled with crystals. In this tent's semicircular front was a laced entry-flap, which Fafhrd found difficult to open, since the long form in his arms was still limp.

A swag-bellied little old man came strutting toward him with something of the bounce of youth. This one wore ragged finery touched up with gilt. Even his long gray moustache and goatee glittered with specks of gold above and below his dirty-toothed mouth. His heavily pouched eyes were rheumy and red all around, but dark and darting at center. Above them was a purple turban supporting in turn a gilt crown set with battered gems of rock crystal, poorly aping diamonds.

Behind him came a skinny, one-armed Mingol, a fat Easterner with a vast black beard that stank of burning, and two scrawny girls who, despite their yawning and the heavy blankets huddled around them, looked watchful and evasive as alley cats.

"What's this now?" the leader demanded, his alert eyes taking in every detail of Fafhrd and his burden. "Vlana slain? Raped and slain, eh? Know, murderous youth, that you'll pay high for your fun. You may not know who I am, but you'll learn. I'll have reparations from your chiefs, I will! Vast reparations! I have influence, I have. You'll lose those pirate's bracelets of yours and that silver chain peeping from under your collar. Your family'll be beggared, and all your relatives, too. As for what *they'll* do to *you*—"

"You are Essedinex, Master of the Show," Fafhrd broke in dogmatically, his high tenor voice cutting like a trumpet through the other's hoarse, ranting baritone. "I am Fafhrd, son of Mor and of Nalgron the Legend-Breaker. Vlana the culture dancer is not raped or dead, but stunned with snowballs. This is her tent. Open it."

"We'll take care of her, barbarian," Essedinex asserted, though more quietly, appearing both surprised and somewhat intimidated by the youth's almost pedantic precision as to who was who, and what was what. "Hand her over. Then depart."

"I will lay her down," Fafhrd persisted. "Open the tent!"

Essedinex shrugged and motioned to the Mingol, who with a sardonic grin used his one hand and elbow to unlace and draw aside the entry-flap. An odor of sandalwood and closetberry came out. Stooping, Fafhrd entered. Midway down the length of the tent he noted a pallet of furs and a low table with a silver mirror propped against some jars and squat bottles. At the far end was a rack of costumes.

Stepping around a brazier from which a thread of pale smoke wreathed, Fafhrd carefully knelt and most gently deposited his burden on the pallet. Next he felt Vlana's pulse at jaw-hinge and wrist, rolled back a dark lid and peered into each eye, delicately explored with his fingertips the sizable bumps that were forming on jaw and forehead. Then he tweaked the lobe of her left ear and, when she did not react, shook his head and, drawing open her russet robe, began to unbutton the red dress under it.

Essedinex, who with the others had been watching the proceedings in a puzzled fashion, cried out, "Well, of all— Cease, lascivious youth!"

"Silence," Fafhrd commanded and continued unbuttoning.

The two blanketed girls giggled, then clapped hands to mouths, darting amused gazes at Essedinex and the rest.

Drawing aside his long hair from his right ear, Fafhrd laid that side of his face on Vlana's chest between her breasts, small as half pomegranates, their nipples rosy bronze in hue. He maintained a solemn expression. The girls smothered giggles again. Essedinex strangledly cleared his throat, preparing for large speech.

Fafhrd sat up and said, "Her spirit will shortly return. Her bruises should be dressed with snow-bandages, renewed when they begin to melt. Now I require a cup of your best brandy."

"My best brandy—!" Essedinex cried outragedly. "This goes too far. First you must have a help-yourself peep show, then strong drink! Presumptuous youth, depart at once!"

"I am merely seeking—" Fafhrd began in clear and at last slightly dangerous tones.

His patient interrupted the dispute by opening her eyes, shaking her head, wincing, then determindedly sitting up—whereupon she grew pale and her gaze wavered. Fafhrd helped her lie down again and put pillows under her feet. Then he looked at her face. Her eyes were still open and she was looking back at him curiously.

He saw a face small and sunken-cheeked, no longer girlish-young, but with a compact catlike beauty despite its lumps. Her eyes, being large, brown-irised and long-lashed, should have been melting, but were not. There was the look of the loner in them, and purpose, and a thoughtful weighing of what she saw.

She saw a handsome, fair-complexioned youth of about eighteen winters, wide-headed and long-jawed, as if he had not done growing. Fine red-gold hair cascaded down his cheeks. His eyes were green, cryptic, and as staring as a cat's. His lips were wide, but slightly compressed, as if they were a door that locked words in and opened only on the cryptic eyes' command.

One of the girls had poured a half cup of brandy from a bottle on the low table. Fafhrd took it and lifted Vlana's head for her to drink it in sips. The other girl came with powder snow folded in woolen cloths. Kneeling on the far side of the pallet, she bound them against the bruises.

After inquiring Fafhrd's name and confirming that he had rescued her from the Snow Women, Vlana asked, "Why do you speak in such a high voice?"

"I study with a singing skald," he answered. "They use that voice and are the true skalds, not the roaring ones who use deep tones."

"What reward do you expect for rescuing me?" she asked boldly.

"None," Fafhrd replied.

From the two girls came further giggles, quickly cut off at Vlana's glance.

Fafhrd added, "It was my personal obligation to rescue you, since the leader of the Snow Women was my mother. I must respect my mother's wishes, but I must also prevent her from performing wrong actions."

"Oh. Why do you act like a priest or healer?" Vlana continued. "Is that one of your mother's wishes?" She had not bothered to cover her breasts, but Fafhrd was not looking at them now, only at the actress's lips and eyes.

"Healing is part of the singing skald's art," he answered. "As for my mother, I do my duty toward her, nor less, nor more."

"Vlana, it is not politic that you talk thus with this youth," Essedinex interposed, now in a nervous voice. "He must—"

"Shut up!" Vlana snapped. Then, back to Fafhrd, "Why do you wear white?"

"It is proper garb for all Snow Folk. I do not follow the new custom of dark and dyed furs for males. My father always wore white."

"He is dead?"

"Yes. While climbing a tabooed mountain called White Fang."

"And your mother wishes you to wear white, as if you were your father returned?"

Fafhrd neither answered nor frowned at that shrewd question. Instead he asked, "How many languages can you speak—besides this pidgin-Lankhmarese?"

She smiled at last. "What a question! Why, I speak—though not too well—Mingol, Kvarchish, High and Low Lankhmarese, Quarmallian, Old Ghoulish, Desert-talk, and three Eastern tongues."

Fafhrd nodded. "That's good."

"Forever why?"

"Because it means you are very civilized," he answered.

"What's so great about that?" she demanded with a sour laugh.

"You should know, you're a culture dancer. In any case, I am interested in civilization."

"One comes," Essedinex hissed from the entry. "Vlana, the youth must—"

"He must not!"

"As it happens, I must indeed leave now," Fafhrd said, rising. "Keep up the snow-bandages," he instructed Vlana. "Rest until sundown. Then more brandy, with hot soup."

"Why must you leave?" Vlana demanded, rising on an elbow.

"I made a promise to my mother," Fafhrd said without looking back.

"Your mother!"

Stooping at the entry, Fafhrd finally did stop to look back. "I owe my mother many duties," he said. "I owe you none, as yet."

"Vlana, he *must* leave. It's *the* one," Essedinex stage-whispered hoarsely. Meanwhile he was shoving at Fafhrd, but for all the youth's slenderness, he might as well have been trying to push a tree off of its roots.

"Are you afraid of him who comes?" Vlana was buttoning up her dress now.

Fafhrd looked at her thoughtfully. Then, without replying in any way whatever to her question, he ducked through the entry and stood up, waiting the approach through the persistent mist of a man in whose face anger was gathering.

This man was as tall as Fafhrd, half again as thick and wide, and about twice as old. He was dressed in brown sealskin and amethyst-studded silver except for the two massive gold bracelets on his wrists and the gold chain about his neck, marks of a pirate chief.

Fafhrd felt a touch of fear, not at the approaching man, but at the crystals which were now thicker on the tents than he recalled them being when he had carried Vlana in. The element over which Mor and her sister witches had most power was cold—whether in a man's soup or loins, or in his sword or climbing rope, making them shatter. He often wondered whether it was Mor's magic that had made his own heart so cold. Now the cold would close in on the dancer. He should warn her, except she was civilized and would laugh at him.

The big man came up.

"Honorable Hringorl," Fafhrd greeted softly.

For reply, the big man aimed a backhanded uppercut at Fafhrd with his near arm.

Fafhrd leaned sharply away, slithering under the blow, and then simply walked off the way he had first come.

Hringorl, breathing heavily, glared after him for a couple of heartbeats, then plunged into the hemicylindrical tent.

Hringorl was certainly the most powerful man in the Snow Clan, Fafhrd reflected, though not one of its chiefs because of his bullying ways and defiances of custom. The Snow Women hated, but found it hard to get a hold of him, since his mother was dead and he had never taken a wife, satisfying himself with concubines he brought back from his piratings.

From wherever he'd been inconspicuously standing, the black-turbaned and black-moustached man came up quietly to Fafhrd. "That was well done, my friend. And when you brought in the dancer."

Fafhrd said impassively, "You are Vellix the Venturer."

The other nodded. "Bringing brandy from Kleg Nar to this mart. Will you sample the best with me?"

Fafhrd said, "I am sorry, but I have an engagement with my mother."

"Another time then," Vellix said easily.

"Fafhrd!"

It was Hringorl who called. His voice was no longer angry. Fafhrd turned. The big man stood by the tent, then came striding up when Fafhrd did not move. Meanwhile, Vellix faded back and away in a fashion as easy as his speech.

"I'm sorry, Fafhrd," Hringorl said gruffly. "I did not know you had saved the dancer's life. You have done me a great service. Here." He unclasped from his wrist one of the heavy gold bracelets and held it out.

Fafhrd kept his hands at his sides. "No service whatever," he said. "I was only saving my mother from committing a wrong action."

"You've sailed under me," Hringorl suddenly roared, his face reddening though he still grinned somewhat, or tried to. "So you'll take my gifts as well as my orders." He caught hold of Fafhrd's hand, pressed the weighty torus into it, closed Fafhrd's lax fingers on it, and stepped back.

Instantly Fafhrd knelt, saying swiftly, "I am sorry, but I may not take what I have not rightly won. And now I must keep an engagement with my mother." Then he swiftly rose, turned, and walked away. Behind him, on an unbroken crust of snow, the golden bracelet gleamed.

He heard Hringorl's snarl and choked-back curse, but did not look around to see whether or not Hringorl picked up his spurned gratuity, though he did find it a bit difficult not to weave in his stride or duck his head a trifle, in case Hringorl decided to throw the massive wristlet at his skull.

Shortly he came to the place where his mother was sitting amongst seven Snow Women, making eight in all. They stood up. He stopped a yard short. Ducking his head and looking to the side, he said, "Here I am, Mor."

"You took a long while," she said. "You took too long." Six heads around her nodded solemnly. Only Fafhrd noted, in the blurred edge of his vision, that the seventh and slenderest Snow Woman was moving silently backward.

"But here I am," Fafhrd said.

"You disobeyed my command," Mor pronounced coldly. Her haggard and once beautiful face would have looked very unhappy, had it not been so proud and masterful.

"But now I am obeying it," Fafhrd countered. He noted that the seventh Snow Woman was now silently running, her great white cloak a-stream, between the home tents toward the high, white forest that was Cold Corner's boundary everywhere that Trollstep Canyon wasn't.

"Very well," Mor said. "And now you will obey me by following me to the dream tent for ritual purification."

"I am not defiled," Fafhrd announced. "Moreover, I purify myself after my own fashion, one also agreeable to the gods."

There were clucks of shocked disapproval from all Mor's coven. Fafhrd had spoken boldly, but his head was still bent, so that he did not see their faces, and their entrapping eyes, but only their long-robed white forms, like a clump of great birches.

Mor said, "Look me in the eyes."

Fafhrd said, "I fulfill all the customary duties of a grown son, from food-winning to sword-guarding. But as far as I can ascertain, looking my mother in the eyes is not one of those duties."

"Your father always obeyed me," Mor said ominously.

"Whenever he saw a tall mountain, he climbed her, obeying no one but himself," Fafhrd contradicted.

"Yes, and died doing so!" Mor cried, her masterfulness controlling grief and anger without hiding them.

Fafhrd said hardly, "Whence came the great cold that shattered his rope and pick on White Fang?"

Amidst the gasps of her coven, Mor pronounced in her deepest voice, "A mother's curse, Fafhrd, on your disobedience and evil thinking!"

Fafhrd said with strange eagerness, "I dutifully accept your curse, Mother."

Mor said, "My curse is not on you, but on your evil imaginings."

"Nevertheless, I will forever treasure it," Fafhrd cut in. "And now, obeying myself, I must take leave of you, until the wrath-devil has let you go."

And with that, head still bent down and away, he walked rapidly toward a point in the forest east of the home tents, but west of the great tongue of forest that stretched south almost to Godshall. The angry hissings of Mor's coven followed him, but his mother did not cry out his name, nor any word at all. Fafhrd would almost rather that she had.

Youth heals swiftly, on the skin-side. By the time Fafhrd plunged into his beloved wood without jarring a single becrystalled twig, his senses were alert, his neck-joint supple, and the outward surface of his inner being as cleared for new experience as the unbroken snow ahead. He took the easiest path, avoiding bediamonded thorn bushes to left and huge pine-screened juttings of pale granite to right.

He saw bird tracks, squirrel tracks, day-old bear tracks; snow birds snapped their black beaks at red snowberries; a furred snow-snake hissed at him, and he would not have been startled by the emergence of a dragon with ice-crusted spines.

So he was in no wise amazed when a great high-branched pine opened its snow-plastered bark and showed him its dryad—a merry, blue-eyed, blonde-haired girl's face, a dryad no more than seventeen years old. In fact, he had been expecting such an apparition ever since he had noted the seventh Snow Woman in flight.

Yet he pretended to be amazed for almost two heartbeats. Then he sprang forward crying, "Mara, my witch," and with his two arms separated her white-cloaked self from her camouflaging background, and kept them wrapped around her while they stood like one white column, hood to hood and lips to lips for at least twenty heartbeats of the most thuddingly delightful sort.

Then she found his right hand and drew it into her cloak and, through a placket, under her long coat, and pressed it against her crisply-ringleted lower belly.

"Guess," she whispered, licking his ear.

"It's part of a girl. I do believe it's a—" he began most gayly, though his thoughts were already plunging wildly in a direly different direction.

"No, idiot, it's something that belongs to you," the wet whisper coached.

The dire direction became an iced chute leading toward certainty. Nevertheless he said bravely, "Well, I'd hoped you hadn't been trying out others, though that's your right. I must say I am vastly honored—"

"Silly beast! I meant it's something that belongs to *us*."

The dire direction was now a black icy tunnel, becoming a pit. Automatically and with an appropriately great heart-thump, Fafhrd said, "Not?"

"Yes! I'm certain, you monster. I've missed twice."

Better than ever in his life before, Fafhrd's lips performed their office of locking in words. When they opened at last, they and the tongue behind them were utterly under control of the great green eyes. There came forth in a joyous rush: "O gods! How wonderful! I am a father! How clever of you, Mara!"

"Very clever indeed," the girl admitted, "to have fashioned anything so delicate after your rude handling. But now I must pay you off for that ungracious remark about 'trying out others.'" Hitching up her skirt behind, she guided both his hands under her cloak to a knot of thongs at the base of her spine. (Snow Women wore fur hoods, fur boots, a high fur stocking on each leg gartered to a waist thong, and one or more fur coats and cloaks—it was a practical garb, not unlike the men's except for the longer coats.)

As he fingered the knot, from which three thongs led tightly off, Fafhrd said, "Truly, Mara dearest, I do not favor these chastity girdles. They are not a civilized device. Besides, they must interfere with the circulation of your blood."

"You and your fad for civilization! I'll love and belabor you out of it. Go on, untie the knot, making sure you and no other tied it."

Fafhrd complied and had to agree that it was his knot and no other man's. The task took some time and was a delightful one to Mara, judging from her soft squeals and moans, her gentle nips and bites. Fafhrd himself began to get interested. When the task was done, Fafhrd got the reward of all courteous liars: Mara loved him dearly because he had told her all the right lies and she showed it in her beguiling behavior, and his interest in her and his excitement became vast.

After certain handlings and other tokens of affection, they fell to the snow side by side, both mattressed and covered entirely by their white fur cloaks and hoods.

A passerby would have thought that a snowmound had come alive convulsively and was perhaps about to give birth to a snowman, elf, or demon.

After a while the snow-mound grew utterly quiescent and the hypothetical passerby would have had to lean very close to catch the voices coming from inside it.

MARA: Guess what I'm thinking.

FAFHRD: That you're the Queen of Bliss. Aaah!

MARA: Aaaah back at you, and ooooh! And that you're the King of Beasts. No, silly, I'll tell you. I was thinking of how glad I am that you've had your southward adventurings before marriage. I'm sure you've raped or even made indecent love to dozens of southern women, which perhaps accounts for your wrongheadedness about civilization. But I don't mind a bit. I'll love you out of it.

FAFHRD: Mara, you have a brilliant mind, but
just the same you greatly exaggerate that one pirate
cruise I made under Hringorl, and especially the op-
portunities it afforded for amorous adventures. In the
first place, all the inhabitants, and especially all the
young women of any shore town we sacked, ran away
to the hills before we'd even landed. And if there were
any women raped, I being youngest would have been
at the bottom of the list of rapists and so hardly
tempted. Truth to tell, the only interesting folk I met
on that dreary voyage were two old men held for ran-
som, from whom I learned a smattering of Quarmallian
and High Lankhmarese, and a scrawny youth appren-
ticed to a hedge-wizard. He was deft with the dagger,
that one, and had a legend-breaking mind, like mine
and my father's.

MARA: Do not grieve. Life will become more
exciting for you after we're married.

FAFHRD: That's where you're wrong, dearest
Mara. Hold, let me explain! I know my mother. Once
we're married, Mor will expect you to do all the cooking and tent-work. She'll treat you as seven-eighths
slave and—perhaps—one-eighth my concubine.

MARA: Ha! You really will have to learn to rule
your mother, Fafhrd. Yet do not fret, dearest, even
about that. It's clear you know nothing of the weapons a strong and untiring young wife has against an
old mother-in-law. I'll put her in her place, even if I
have to poison her—oh, not to kill, only to weaken
sufficiently. Before three moons have waxed, she'll be
trembling at my gaze and you'll feel yourself much more
a man. I know that you being an only child and your
wild father perishing young, she got an unnatural influence over you, but—

FAFHRD: I feel myself very much the man at this instant, you immoral and poisoning witchlet, you ice-tigress; and I intend to prove it on you without delay. Defend yourself! Ha, would you—!

Once more the snow-mound convulsed, like a giant ice-bear dying of fits. The bear died to a music of sistrums and triangles, as there clashed together and shattered the flashing ice crystals which had grown in unnatural numbers and size on Mara's and Fafhrd's cloaks during their dialogue.

The short day raced toward night, as if even the gods who govern the sun and stars were impatient to see the Show.

Hringorl conferred with his three chief henchmen, Hor, Harrax, and Hrey. There was scowling and nodding, and Fafhrd's name was mentioned.

The youngest husband of the Snow Clan, a vain and thoughtless cockerel, was ambushed and snowballed unconscious by a patrol of young Snow Wives who had seen him in brazen converse with a Mingol stage girl. Thereafter, a sure casualty for the two-day run of the Show, he was tenderly but slowly nursed back toward life by his wife, who had been the most enthusiastic of the snowballers.

Mara, happy as a snow dove, dropped in on this household and helped. But as she watched the husband so helpless and the wife so tender, her smiles and dreamy grace vanished. She grew tense and, for an athletic girl, fidgety. Thrice she opened her lips to speak, then pursed them, and finally left without saying a word.

In the Women's Tent, Mor and her coven put a spell on Fafhrd to bring him home and another to chill his loins, then went on to discuss weightier measures against the whole universe of sons, husbands, and actresses.

The second enchantment had no effect on Fafhrd, probably because he was taking a snow-bath at the time—it being a well-known fact that magic has little effect on those who are already inflicting upon themselves the same results which the spell is trying to cause. After parting with Mara, he had stripped, plunged into a snowbank, then rubbed every surface, crack and cranny of his body with the numbing powdery stuff. Thereafter he used thickly needled pine branches to dust himself off and beat his blood back into motion. Dressed, he felt the pull of the first enchantment, but opposed it and secretly made his way into the tent of two old Mingol traders, Zax and Effendrit, who had been his father's friends, and he snoozed amidst a pile of pelts until evening. Neither of his mother's spells was able to follow him into what was, by trading custom, a tiny area of Mingol territory, though the Mingols' tent did begin to sag with an unnaturally large number of ice crystals, which the Mingol oldsters, wizened and nimble as monkeys, beat off janglingiy with poles. The sound penetrated pleasantly into Fafhrd's dream without arousing him, which would have irked his mother had she known—she believed that both pleasure and rest were bad for men. His dream became one of Vlana dancing sinuously in a dress made of a net of fine silver wires, from the intersections of which hung myriads of tiny silver bells, a vision which would have irked Mor beyond endurance; fortunate indeed that she was not at that moment using her power of reading minds at a distance.

Vlana herself slumbered, while one of the Mingol girls, paid a half smerduk in advance by the injured actress, renewed the snow-bandages as necessary and, when they looked dry, wet Vlana's lips with sweet wine, of which a few drops trickled between. Vlana's mind was a-storm with anticipations and plots, but whenever she waked, she stilled it with an Eastern circle-charm that went something like, "Creep, sleep; rouse, drowse; browse, soughs; slumber, umber; raw, claw; burnt, earn'd; cumber, number; left, death; cunt, won't; count, fount; mount, down't; leap, deep; creep, sleep," and so on back around the incestuous loop. She knew that a woman can get wrinkles in her mind as well as her skin. She also knew that only a spinster looks after a spinster. And finally she knew that a trouper, like a soldier, does well to sleep whenever possible.

Vellix the Venturer, idly slipping about, overheard some of Hringorl's plottings, saw Fafhrd enter his tent of retreat, noted that Essedinex was drinking beyond his wont, and eavesdropped for a while on the Master of the Show.

In the girls' third of the actors' fish-shaped tent, Essedinex was arguing with the two Mingol girls, who were twins, and a barely nubile Ilthmarix, about the amount of grease they proposed to smear on their shaven bodies for tonight's performance.

"By the black bones, you'll beggar me," he wailingly expostulated. "And you'll look no more lascivious than lumps of lard."

"From what I know of Northerners, they like their women well larded, and why not outside as well as in?" the one Mingol girl demanded.

"What's more," her twin added sharply, "if you expect us to freeze off our toes and tits, to please an audience of smelly old bearskins, you've got your head on upside-down."

"Don't worry, Seddy," the Ilthmarix said, patting his flushed cheek and its sparse white hairs, "I always give my best performance when I'll all gooey. We'll have them chasing us up the walls, where we'll pop from their grabs like so many slippery melon seeds."

"Chasing—?" Essedinex gripped the Ilthmarix by her slim shoulder. "You'll provoke no orgies tonight, do you hear me? Teasing pays. Orgies don't. The point is to—"

"We know just how far to tease, daddy-pooh," one of the Mingol girls put in.

"We know how to control them," her sister continued.

"And if we don't, Vlana always does," the Ilthmarix finished.

As the almost imperceptible shadows lengthened and the mist-wreathed air grew dark, the omnipresent crystals seemed to be growing even a little more swiftly. The palaver at the trading tents, which the thick snowy tongue of the forest shut off from the home tents, grew softer-voiced, then ceased. The unending low chant from the Women's Tent became more noticeable, and also higher pitched. An evening breeze came from the north, making all the crystals tinkle. The chanting grew gruffer and the breeze and the tinkling ceased, as if on command. The mist came wreathing back from east and west, and the crystals were growing again. The women's chanting faded to a murmur. All of Cold Corner grew tautly and expectantly silent with the approach of night.

Day ran away over the ice-fanged western horizon, as if she were afraid of the dark.

In the narrow space between the actors' tents and Godshall there was movement, a glimmer, a bright spark that sputtered for nine, ten, eleven heartbeats, then a flash, a flaring, and there rose up—slowly at first, then swifter and swifter—a comet with a brushy tail of orange fire that dribbled sparks. High above the pines, almost on the edge of heaven—twenty-one, twenty-two, twenty-three—the comet's tail faded and it burst with a thunderclap into nine white stars.

It was the rocket signaling the first performance of the Show.

Godshall on the inside was a tall, crazy longship of chill blackness, inadequately lit and warmed by an arc of candles in the prow, which all the rest of the year was an altar, but now a stage. Its masts were eleven vast living pines thrusting up from the ship's bow, stern, and sides. Its sails—in sober fact, its walls—were stitched hides laced tautly to the masts. Instead of sky overhead, there were thickly interthrusting pine branches, white with drifting snow, beginning a good five man's-heights above the deck.

The stern and waist of this weird ship, which moved only on the winds of imagination, were crowded with Snow Men in their darkly colorful furs and seated on stumps and thick blanket rolls. They were laughing with drink and growling out short talk and jokes at each other, but not very loudly. Religious awe and fear touched them on entering Godshall, or more properly, God's Ship, despite or more likely because of the profane use to which it was being put tonight.

There came a rhythmic drumming, sinister as the padding of a snow-leopard and at first so soft that no man might say exactly when it began, except that one moment there was talk and movement in the audience and the next none at all, only so many pairs of hands gripping or lightly resting on knees, and so many pairs of eyes scanning the candlelit stage between two screens painted with black and gray whorls.

The drumming grew louder, quickened, complicated itself into weaving arabesques of tapped sound, and returned to the leopard's padding.

There loped onto the stage, precisely in time with the drum beats, a silver-furred, short-bodied, slender feline with long legs, long ears a-prick, long whiskers, and long, white fangs. It stood about a yard high at the shoulder and rump. The only human feature was a glossy mop of long, straight black hair falling down the back of its neck and thence forward over its right shoulder.

It circled the stage thrice, ducking its head and sniffing as if on a scent and growling deep in its throat.

Then it noticed the audience and with a scream crouched back from them rampant, menacing them with the long, glittering claws which terminated its forelegs.

Two members of the audience were so taken in by the illusion that they had to be restrained by neighbors from pitching a knife or hurling a short-handled axe at what they were certain was a genuine and dangerous beast.

The beast scanned them, writhing its black lips back from its fangs and lesser teeth. As it swiftly swung its muzzle from side to side, inspecting them with its great brown eyes, its short-furred tail lashed back and forth in time.

Then it danced a leopardly dance of life, love, and death, sometimes on hind legs, but mostly on all fours. It scampered and investigated, it menaced and shrank, it attacked and fled, it caterwauled and writhed cat-lasciviously.

Despite the long black hair, it became no easier for the audience to think of it as a human female in a close-fitting suit of fur. For one thing, its forelegs were as long as its hind legs and appeared to have an extra joint in them.

Something white squawked and came fluttering upward from behind one of the screens. With a swift leap and slash of foreleg, the great silvery cat struck.

Everyone in Godshall heard the scream of the snow pigeon and the crack of its neck.

Holding the dead bird to its fangs, the great cat, standing womanly now, gave the audience a long look, then walked without haste behind the nearest screen. There came from the audience a sigh compounded of loathing and longing, of a wonder as to what would happen next, and of a wish to see what was going on now.

Fafhrd, however, did not sigh. For one thing, the slightest movement might have revealed his hiding place. For another, he could clearly see all that was going on behind both whorl-marked screens.

Being barred from the Show by his youth, let alone by Mor's wishes and witcheries, half an hour before showtime he had mounted one of the trunk-pillars of Godshall on the precipice side when no one was looking. The strong lacings of the hide walls made it the easiest of climbs. Then he had cautiously crawled out onto two of several stout pine branches growing inward close together over the hall, being very careful to disturb neither browning needles nor drifted snow, until he had found a good viewing hole, one opening toward the stage, but mostly hidden from the audience. Thereafter, it had been simply a matter of holding still enough so that no betraying needles or snow dropped down. Anyone looking up through the gloom and chancing to see parts of his white garb would take it for snow, he hoped.

Now he watched the two Mingol girls rapidly pull off from Vlana's arms the tight fur sleeves together with the fur-covered, claw-tipped, rigid extra lengths in which they ended and which her hands had been gripping. Next they dragged from Vlana's legs their fur coverings, while she sat on a stool and, after drawing her fangs off her teeth, speedily unhooked her leopard mask and shoulder piece.

A moment later she slouched back on stage— a cave woman in a brief sarong of silvery fur and lazily gnawing at the end of a long, thick bone. She mimed a cave woman's day: fire-and-baby-tending, brat-slapping, hide-chewing, and laborious sewing. Things got a bit more exciting with the return of her husband, an unseen presence made visible by her miming.

Her audience followed the story easily, grinning when she demanded what meat her husband had brought, showed dissatisfaction with his meager kill, and refused him an embrace. They guffawed when she tried to clobber him with her chewing bone and got knocked sprawling in return, her children cowering around her.

From that position she scuttled off stage behind the other screen, which hid the actors' doorway (normally the Snow Priest's) and also concealed the one-armed Mingol, whose flickering five fingers did all the drum music on the instrument clutched between his feet. Vlana whipped off the rest of her fur, changed the slant of her eyes and eyebrows by four deft strokes of makeup, seemingly in one movement shouldered into a long gray gown with hood, and was back on stage in the persona of a Mingol woman of the Steppes.

After another brief session of miming, she squatted gracefully down at a low, jar-stocked table stage front, and began carefully to make up her face and do her hair, the audience serving as her mirror. She dropped back hood and gown, revealing the briefer red silk garment her fur one had hidden. It was most fascinating to watch her apply the variously colored salves and powders and glittering dusts to her lips, cheeks, and eyes, and see her comb up her dark hair into a high structure kept in place by long, gem-headed pins.

Just then Fafhrd's composure was tested to the uttermost, when a large handful of snow was clapped to his eyes and held there.

He stayed perfectly still for three heartbeats. Then he captured a rather slender wrist and dragged it down a short distance, meantime gently shaking his head and blinking his eyes.

The trapped wrist twisted free and the clot of snow fell down the neck of the wolfskin coat of Hringorl's man Hor seated immediately below. Hor gave a strange low cry and started to glare upward, but fortunately at that moment Vlana pulled down her red silk sarong and began to anoint her nipples with a coral salve.

Fafhrd looked around and saw Mara grinning fiercely at him from where she lay outstretched on the two branches next his, her head level with his shoulder.

"If I'd been an Ice Gnome, you'd be dead," she hissed at him. "Or if I'd set my four brothers to trap you, as I should have. Your ears *were* dead, your

mind all in your eyes straining toward that skinny har-
lot. I've heard how you challenged Hringorl for her!
And refused his gift of a gold bracelet!"

"I admit, dear, that you slithered up behind
me most skillfully and silently," Fafhrd breathed at her
softly, "while you seem to have eyes and ears for all
things that transpire—and some that don't—at Cold
Corner. But I must say, Mara—"

"Hah! Now you'll tell me I shouldn't be here,
being a woman. Male prerogatives, intersexual sacrilege, and so forth. Well, neither should you be here."

Fafhrd gravely considered part of that. "No, I
think all the women should be here. What they would
learn would be much to their interest and advantage."

"To caper like a cat in heat? To slouch about
like a silly slave? Yes, I saw those acts too—while you
were drooling dumb and deaf! You men will laugh at
anything, especially when your stupid, gasping, red-
faced lust's been aroused by a shameless bitch making
a show of her scrawny nakedness!"

Mara's heated hissings were getting danger-
ously loud and might well have attracted the attention
of Hor and others, but once again good fortune inter-
vened, in that there was a ripple of drumming as Vlana
streaked off the stage, and then there began a wild,
somewhat thin, but galloping music, the one-armed
Mingol being joined by the little Ilthmarix playing a
nose flute.

"I did not laugh, my dear," Fafhrd breathed
somewhat loftily, "nor did I drool or flush or speed my
breath, as I am sure you noted. No, Mara, my sole purpose in being here is to learn more about civilization."

She glared at him, grinned, then of a sudden
smiled tenderly. "You know, I honestly think you believe that, you incredible infant," she breathed back

wonderingly. "Granting that the decadence called civilization could possibly be of interest to anyone, and a capering whore able to carry its message, or rather absence of message."

"I neither think nor believe, I *know* it," Fafhrd replied, ignoring Mara's other remarks. "A whole world calls and have we eyes only for Cold Corner? Watch with me, Mara, and gain wisdom. The actress dances the cultures of all lands and ages. Now she is a woman of the Eight Cities."

Perhaps Mara was in some small part persuaded. Or perhaps it was that Vlana's new costume covered her thoroughly—sleeved, green bodice; full, blue skirt; red stockings; and yellow shoes—and that the culture dancer was panting a trifle and showing the cords in her neck from the stamping and whirling dance she was doing. At any rate, the Snow Girl shrugged and smiled indulgently and whispered, "Well, I must admit it all has a certain disgusting interest."

"I knew you'd understand, dearest. You have twice the mind of any woman of our tribe, aye, or of any man," Fafhrd cooed, caressing her tenderly but somewhat absently as he peered at the stage.

In succession, always making lightning costume changes, Vlana became a houri of the Eastern Lands, a custom-hobbled Quarmallian queen, a languorous concubine of the King of Kings, and a haughty Lankhmar lady wearing a black toga. This last was theatrical license: only the men of Lankhmar wear the toga, but the garment was Lankhmar's chiefest symbol across the world of Nehwon.

Meanwhile Mara did her best to share the eccentric whim of her husband-to-be. At first she was genuinely intrigued and made mental notes on details of Vlana's dress styles and tricks of behavior which she might herself adopt to advantage. But then she was gradually overwhelmed by a realization of the older woman's superiority in training, knowledge and experience. Vlana's dancing and miming clearly couldn't be learned except with much coaching and drill. And how, and especially where, could a Snow Girl ever wear such clothes? Feelings of inferiority gave way to jealousy and that to hatred.

Civilization was nasty, Vlana ought to be whipped out of Cold Corner, and Fafhrd needed a woman to run his life and keep his mad imagination in check. Not his mother, of course—that awful and incestuous eater of her own son—but a glamorous and shrewd young wife. Herself.

She began to watch Fafhrd intently. He didn't look like an infatuated male, he looked cold as ice, but he was certainly utterly intent on the scene below. She reminded herself that a few men were adept at hiding their true feelings.

Vlana shed her toga and stood in a wide-meshed tunic of fine silver wires. At each crossing of the wires a tiny silver bell stood out. She shimmied and the bells tinkled, like a tree of tiny birds all chirruping together a hymn to her body. Now her slenderness seemed that of adolescence, while from between the strands of her sleekly cascading hair, her large eyes gleamed with mysterious hints and invitations.

Fafhrd's controlled breathing quickened. So his dream in the Mingols' tent had been true! His attention, which had half been off to the lands and ages Vlana had danced, centered wholly on her and became desire.

This time his composure was put to an even sorer test for, without warning, Mara's hand clutched his crotch.

But he had little time in which to demonstrate his composure. She let go and crying, "Filthy beast! You are lusting!" struck him in the side, below the ribs.

He tried to catch her wrists, while staying on his branches. She kept trying to hit him. The pine boughs creaked and shed snow and needles.

In landing a clout on Fafhrd's ear, Mara's upper body overbalanced, though her feet kept hooked to branchlets.

Growling, "God freeze you, you bitch!" Fafhrd gripped his stoutest bough with one hand and lunged down with the other to catch Mara's arm just beneath the shoulder.

Those looking up from below—and by now there were some, despite the strong counter-attraction of the stage—saw two struggling, white-clad torsos and fair-haired heads dipping out of the branchy roof, as if about to descend in swan dives. Then, still struggling, the figures withdrew upward.

An older Snow Man cried out, "Sacrilege!" A younger, "Peepers! Let's thrash 'em!" He might have been obeyed, for a quarter of the Snow Men were on their feet by now, if it hadn't been that Essedinex was keeping a close eye on things through a peephole in one of the screens and that he was wise in the ways of handling unruly audiences. He shot a finger at the Mingol behind him, then sharply raised that hand, palm upward.

The music surged. Cymbals clashed. The two Mingol girls and the Ilthmarix bounded on stage stark naked and began to caper around Vlana. The fat Easterner clumped past them and set fire to his great black beard. Blue flames crawled up and flickered before his face and around his ears. He didn't put the fire out—

with a wet towel he carried—until Essedinex hoarsely stage-whispered from his peephole, "That's enough. We've got 'em again." The length of the black beard had been halved. Actors make great sacrifices, which the yokels and even their co-mates rarely appreciate.

Fafhrd, dropping the last dozen feet, lighted in the high drift outside Godshall at the same instant Mara finished her downward climb. They faced each other calf-deep in crusted snow, across which the rising, slightly gibbous moon threw streaks of white glimmer and made shadow between them.

Fafhrd asked, "Mara, where did you hear that lie about me challenging Hringorl for the actress?"

"Faithless lecher!" she cried, punched him in the eye, and ran off toward the Tent of the Women, sobbing and crying, "I will tell my brothers! You'll see!"

Fafhrd jumped up and down, smothering a howl of pain, sprinted after her three steps, stopped, clapped snow to his pain-stabbed eye and, as soon as it was only throbbing, began to think.

He looked around with the other eye, saw no one, made his way to a clump of snow-laden evergreens on the edge of the precipice, concealed himself among them, and continued to think.

His ears told him that the Show was still going at a hot pace inside Godshall. There were laughs and cheers, sometimes drowning the wild drumming and fluting. His eyes—the hit one was working again—told him there was no one near him. They swiveled to the actors' tents at that end of Godshall which lay nearest the new road south, and at the stables beyond them, and at the traders' tents beyond the stables. Then they came back to the nearest tent: Vlana's hemicylindrical one. Crystals clothed it, twinkling in the moonlight, and a giant crystal flatworm seemed to be crawling across its middle just below the evergreen sycamore bough.

He slitheringly walked toward it across the bediamonded snow crust. The knot joining the lacings of its doorway was hidden in shadow and felt complex and foreign. He went to the back of the tent, loosened two pegs, went on belly through the crack like a snake, found himself amongst the hems of the skirts of Vlana's racked garments, loosely replaced the pegs, stood up, shook himself, took four steps and lay down on the pallet. A little heat radiated from a banked brazier. After a while he reached to the table and poured himself a cup of brandy.

At last he heard voices. They grew louder. As the lacings of the door were being unknotted and loosened, he felt for his knife and also prepared to draw a large fur rug over him.

Saying with laughter but also decision, "No, no, *no*," Vlana swiftly stepped in backward over the slack lashings, held the door closed with one hand while she gave the lashings a tightening pull with the other, and glanced over her shoulder.

Her look of stark surprise was gone almost before Fafhrd marked it, to be replaced by a quick welcoming grin that wrinkled her nose comically. She turned away from him, carefully drew the lacings tight, and spent some time tying a knot on the inside. Then she came over and knelt beside him where he lay, her body erect from her knees. There was no grin now as she looked down at him, only a composed, enigmatic thoughtfulness, which he sought to match. She was wearing the hooded robe of her Mingol costume.

"So you changed your mind about a reward," she said quietly but matter-of-factly. "How do you know that I too may not have changed mine since?"

Fafhrd shook his head, replying to her first statement. Then, after a pause, he said, "Nevertheless, I have discovered that I desire you."

Vlana said, "I saw you watching the show from the gallery. You almost stole it, you know—I mean the show—Who was the girl with you? Or was it a youth? I couldn't be quite sure."

Fafhrd did not answer her inquiries. Instead he said, "I also wish to ask you questions about your supremely skillful dancing and...and acting in loneliness."

"Miming." She supplied the word.

"Miming, yes. *And* I want to talk to you about civilization."

"That's right, this morning you asked me how many languages I knew," she said, looking straight across him at the wall of the tent. It was clear that she too was a thinker. She took the cup of brandy out of his hand, swallowed half of what was left, and returned it to him.

"Very well," she said, at last looking down at him, but with unchanged expression. "I will give you your desire, my dear boy. But now is not the time. First, I must rest and gather strength. Go away and return when the star Shadah sets. Wake me if I slumber."

"That's an hour before dawn," he said, looking up at her. "It will be a chilly wait for me in the snow."

"Don't do that," she said quickly. "I don't want you three-quarters frozen. Go where it's warm. To stay awake, think of me. Don't drink too much wine. Now go."

He got up and made to embrace her. She drew back a step, saying, "Later. Later—everything." He started toward the door. She shook her head, saying, "You might be seen. As you came."

Passing her again, his head brushed something hard. Between the hoops supporting the tent's middle, the supple hide of the tent bulged down, while the hoops themselves were bowed out and somewhat flattened bearing the weight. He cringed down for an instant, ready to grab Vlana and jump any way, then began methodically to punch and sweep at the bulges, always striking outward. There was a crashing and a loud tinkling as the massed crystals, which outside had reminded him of a giant flatworm—must be a giant snow serpent by now!—broke up and showered off.

Meanwhile he said, "The Snow Women do not love you. Nor is Mor my mother your friend."

"Do they think to frighten me with ice crystals?" Vlana demanded contemptuously. "Why, I know of Eastern fire sorceries compared to which their feeble magickings—"

"But you are in *their* territory now, at the mercy of *their* element, which is crueler and subtler than fire," Fafhrd interposed, brushing away the last of the bulgings, so that the hoops stood up again and the leather stretched almost flat between them. "Do not underrate their powers."

"Thank you for saving my tent from being crumpled. But now—and swiftly—go."

She spoke as if of trivial matters, but her large eyes were thoughtful.

Just before snaking under the back wall, Fafhrd looked over his shoulder. Vlana was gazing at the side wall again, holding the empty cup he had given her, but she caught his movement and, now smiling tenderly, put a kiss on her palm and blew it toward him.

Outside the cold had grown bitter. Nevertheless, Fafhrd went to his clump of evergreens, drew his cloak closely around him, dropped its hood over his forehead, tightened the hood's drawstring, and sat himself facing Vlana's tent.

When the cold began to penetrate his furs, he thought of Vlana.

Suddenly he was crouching and had loosened his knife in its sheath.

A figure was approaching Vlana's tent, keeping to the shadows when it could. It appeared to be clad in black.

Fafhrd silently advanced.

Through the still air came the faint sound of fingernails scratching leather.

There was a flash of dim light as the doorway was opened.

It was bright enough to show the face of Vellix the Venturer. He stepped inside and there was the sound of lacings being drawn tight.

Fafhrd stopped ten paces from the tent and stood there for perhaps two dozen breaths. Then he softly walked past the tent, keeping the same distance.

There was a glow in the doorway of the high, conical tent of Essedinex. From the stables beyond, a horse whickered twice.

Fafhrd crouched and peered through the low, glowing doorway a knife-cast away. He moved from side to side. He saw a table crowded with jugs and cups set against the sloping wall of the tent opposite the doorway.

To one side of the table sat Essedinex. To the other, Hringorl.

On the watch for Hor, Harrax, or Hrey, Fafhrd circled the tent. He approached it where the table and the two men were faintly silhouetted. Drawing aside his hood and hair, he set his ear against the leather.

"Three gold bars—that's my top," Hringorl was saying surlily. The leather made his voice hollow.

"Five," Essedinex answered, and there was the *slup* of wine mouthed and swallowed.

"Look here, old man," Hringorl countered, his voice at its most gruffly menacing, "I don't need you. I can snatch the girl and pay you nothing."

"Oh no, that won't do, Master Hringorl." Essedinex sounded merry. "For then the Show would never return again to Cold Corner, and how would your tribesmen like that? Nor would there be any more girls brought you by me."

"What matter?" the other answered carelessly. The words were muffled by a gulp of wine, yet Fafhrd could hear the bluff in them. "I have my ship. I can cut your throat this instant and snatch the girl to-night."

"Then do so," Essedinex said brightly. "Only give me a moment for one more quaff."

"Very well, you old miser. Four gold bars."

"Five."

Hringorl cursed sulfurously. "Some night, you ancient pimp, you will provoke me too far. Besides, the girl is old."

"Aye, in the ways of pleasure. Did I tell you that she once became an acolyte of the Wizards of Azorkah?—so that she might be trained by them to become a concubine of the King of Kings and their spy in the court at Horborixen. Aye, and eluded those dread necromancers most cleverly when she had gained the erotic knowledge she desired."

Hringorl laughed with a forced lightness. "Why should I pay even one silver bar for a girl who has been possessed by dozens? Every man's plaything."

"By hundreds," Essedinex corrected. "Skill is gained only by experience, as you know well. And the greater the experience, the greater the skill. Yet this girl is never a plaything. She is the instructress, the revelator; she plays with a man for his pleasure, she can make a man feel king of the universe and per-chance—who knows?—even *be* that. What is impossible to a girl who knows the pleasure-ways of the gods themselves—aye, and of the arch-demons? And yet—you won't believe this, but it's true—she remains in her fashion forever virginal. For no man has ever mastered her."

"That will be seen to!" Hringorl's words were almost a laughing shout. There was the sound of wine gulped. Then his voice dropped. "Very well, five gold bars it is, you usurer. Delivery after tomorrow night's Show. The gold paid against the girl."

"Three hours after the Show, when the girl's drugged and all's quiet. No need to rouse the jealousy of your fellow tribesmen so soon."

"Make it two hours. Agreed? And now let's talk of next year. I'll want a black girl, a full-blooded Kleshite. And no five-gold-bar deal ever again. I'll not want a witchy wonder, only youth and great beauty."

Essedinex answered, "Believe me, you won't ever again desire another woman, once you've known and—I wish you luck—mastered Vlana. Oh, of course, I suppose—"

Fafhrd reeled back from the tent a half dozen paces and there planted his feet firm and wide, feeling strangely dizzy, or was it drunk? He had early guessed they were almost certainly talking of Vlana, but hearing her name spoken made a much greater difference than he'd expected.

The two revelations, coming so close, filled him with a mixed feeling he'd never known before; an overmastering rage and also a desire to laugh hugely. He wanted a sword long enough to slash open the sky and tumble the dwellers in paradise from their beds. He wanted to find and fire off all the Show's sky-rockets into the tent of Essedinex. He wanted to topple Godshall with its pines and drag it across all the actors' tents. He wanted—

He turned around and swiftly made for the stable tent. The one groom was snoring on the straw beside an empty jug and near the light sleigh of Essedinex. Fafhrd noted with a fiendish grin that the horse he knew best happened to be one of Hringorl's. He found a horse collar and a long coil of light, strong rope. Then, making reassuring mumbles behind half-closed lips, he led out the chosen horse—a white mare—from the rest. The groom only snored louder.

He again noted the light sleigh. A risk-devil seized him and he unlaced the stiff, pitchy tarpaulin covering the storage space behind the two seats. Beneath it among other things was the Show's supply of rockets. He selected three of the biggest—with their stout ash tails they were long as ski sticks—and then took time to relace the tarpaulin. He still felt the mad desire for destruction, but now it was under a measure of control.

Outside he put the collar on the mare and firmly knotted to it one end of the rope. The other end he fashioned into a roomy noose. Then, coiling the rest of the rope and gripping the rockets under his left elbow, he nimbly mounted the mare and walked it near the tent of Essedinex. The two dim silhouettes still confronted each other across the table.

He whirled the noose above his head and cast. It settled around the apex of the tent with hardly a sound, for he was quick to draw in the slack before it rattled against the tent's wall.

The noose tightened around the top of the tent's central mast. Containing his excitement, he walked the mare toward the forest across the moon-bright snow, paying out the rope. When there were only four coils of it left, he urged the mare into a lope. He crouched over the collar, holding it firm, his heels clamped to the mare's sides. The rope tightened. The mare strained. There was a satisfying, muffled *crack* behind him. He shouted a triumphant laugh. The mare plunged on against the rope's irregular restraint. Looking back, he saw the tent dragging after them. He saw fire and heard yells of surprise and anger. Again he shouted his laughter.

At the edge of the forest he drew his knife and slashed the rope. Vaulting down, he buzzed approvingly in the mare's ear and gave her a slap on the flank that set her cantering toward the stable. He considered firing off the rockets toward the fallen tent, but decided it would be anticlimactic. With them still clamped under his elbow, he walked into the edge of the woods. So hidden, he started home. He walked lightly to minimize footprints, found a branch of fringe pine and dragged it behind him and, when he could, he walked on rock.

His mountainous humor was gone and his rage too, replaced by black depression. He no longer hated Vellix or even Vlana, but civilization seemed a tawdry thing, unworthy of his interest. He was glad he had spilled Hringorl and Essedinex, but they were woodlice. He himself was a lonely ghost, doomed to roam the Cold Waste.

He thought of walking north through the woods until he found a new life or froze, of fetching and strapping on his skis and attempting to leap the tabooed gap that had been the death of Skif, of getting sword and challenging Hringorl's henchmen all at once, and of a hundred other doom-treadings.

The tents of the Snow Clan looked like pale mushrooms in the light of the crazily glaring moon. Some were cones topping a squat cylinder; others, bloated hemispheres, turnip shapes. Like mushrooms, they did not quite touch the ground at the edges. Their floors of packed branches, carpeted with hides and supported by heavier boughs, stood on and overhung chunky posts, so that a tent's heat would not turn the frozen ground below it to a mush.

The huge, silvery trunk of a dead snow oak, ending in what looked like a giant's split fingernails, where an old lightning bolt had shattered it midway up, marked the site of Mor's and Fafhrd's tent —and also of his father's grave, which the tent overlay. Each year it was pitched just so.

There were lights in a few of the tents and in the great Tent of the Women lying beyond in the direction of Godshall, but Fafhrd could see no one abroad. With a dispirited grunt he headed for his home door then, remembering the rockets, he veered toward the dead oak. It was smooth surfaced, the bark long gone. The few remaining branches were likewise bare and broken off short, the lowest of them appearing well out of reach.

A few paces away he paused for another look around. Assured of secrecy, he raced toward the oak and making a vertical leap more like a leopard's than a man's, he caught hold of the lowest branch with his free hand and whipped himself up onto it before his upward impetus was altogether spent.

Standing lightly on the dead branch with a finger touching the trunk, he made a final scan for peepers and late walkers, then with pressure of fingers and tease of fingernails, opened in the seemingly seamless gray wood a doorway tall as himself but scarcely half as wide. Feeling past skis and ski sticks, he found a long thin shape wrapped thrice around with lightly oiled sealskin. Undoing it, he uncovered a powerful-looking bow and a quiver of long arrows. He added the rockets to it, replaced the wrappings, then shut the queer door of his treesafe and dropped to the snow below, which he brushed smooth.

Entering his home tent, he felt again like a ghost and made as little noise as one. The odors of home comforted him uncomfortably and against his will; smells of meat, cooking, old smoke, hides, sweat, the chamber pot, Mor's faint, sour-sweet stench. He crossed the springy floor and, fully clad, he stretched himself in his sleeping furs. He felt tired as death. The silence was profound. He couldn't hear Mor's breathing. He thought of his last sight of his father, blue and shut-eyed, his broken limbs straightened, his best sword naked at his side with his slate-colored fingers fitted around the hilt. He thought of Nalgron now in the earth under the tent, worm-gnawed to a skeleton, the sword black rust, the eyes open now—sockets staring upward through solid dirt. He remembered his last sight of his father alive: a tall wolfskin cloak striding away with Mor's warnings and threats spattering against it. Then the skeleton came back into his mind. It was a night for ghosts.

"Fafhrd?" Mor called softly from across the tent.

Fafhrd stiffened and held his breath. When he could no longer, he began to let it out and draw it in, open-mouthed, in noiseless draughts.

"Fafhrd?" The voice was a little louder, though still like a ghost cry. "I heard you come in. You're not asleep."

No use keeping silent. "You haven't slept either, Mother?"

"The old sleep little."

That wasn't true, he thought. Mor wasn't old, even by the Cold Waste's merciless measure. At the same time, it *was* the truth. Mor was as old as the tribe, the Waste itself, as old as death.

Mor said composedly—Fafhrd knew she had to be lying on her back, staring straight upward—"I am willing that you should take Mara to wife. Not pleased, but willing. There is need for a strong back here, so long as you daydream, shooting your thoughts like arrows loosed high and at random, and prank about and gad after actresses and such gilded dirt. Besides, you have got Mara with child and her family does not altogether lack status."

"Mara spoke to you tonight?" Fafhrd asked. He tried to keep his voice dispassionate, but the words came out strangledly.

"As any Snow Girl should. Except she ought to have told me earlier. And you earlier still. But you have inherited threefold your father's secretiveness along with his urge to neglect his family and indulge himself in useless adventurings. Except that in you the sickness takes a more repulsive form. Cold mountaintops were his mistresses, while you are

drawn to civilization, that putrid festering of the hot
south, where there is no natural stern cold to punish
the foolish and luxurious and to see that the decen-
cies are kept. But you will discover that there is a
witchy cold that can follow you anywhere in
Nehwon. Ice once went down and covered all the
hot lands, in punishment for an earlier cycle of lech-
erous evil. And wherever ice once went, witchery
can send it again. You will come to believe that, and
shed your sickness, or else you will learn as your father learned."

Fafhrd tried to make the accusation of hus-
band-murder that he had hinted at so easily this
morning, but the words stuck, not in his throat, but
in his very mind, which felt invaded. Mor had long
ago made his heart cold. Now, up in his brain, she was
creating among his most private thoughts crystals
which distorted everything and prevented him from
using against her the weapons of duty coldly performed
and joined by a cold reason which let him keep his
integrity. He felt as if there were closing in on him
forever the whole world of cold, in which the rigidity
of ice and the rigidity of morals and the rigidity of
thought were all one.

As if sensing her victory and permitting herself to joy in it a little, Mor said in the same dead,
reflective tones, "Aye, your father now bitterly regrets
Gran Hanack, White Fang, the Ice Queen, and all his
other mountain paramours. They cannot help him
now. They have forgotten him. He stares up endlessly
from lidless sockets at the home he despised and now
yearns for, so near, yet so impossibly far. His fingerbones
scrabble feebly against the frozen earth, he tries futilely to twist under its weight...."

Fafhrd heard a faint scratching, perhaps of icy twigs against tent leather, but his hair rose. Yet he could move no other part of him, he discovered as he tried to lift himself. The blackness all around him was a vast weight. He wondered if Mor had magicked him down under the ground beside his father. Yet it was a greater weight than that of eight feet of frozen earth that pressed on him. It was the weight of the entire Cold Waste and its killingness, of the taboos and contempts and shut-mindedness of the Snow Clan, of the pirate greed and loutish lust of Hringorl, of even Mara's merry self-absorption and bright, half-blind mind, and atop them all Mor with ice crystals forming on her fingertips as she wove them in a binding spell.

And then he thought of Vlana.

It may not have been the thought of Vlana that did it. A star may have chanced to crawl across the tent's tiny smoke-hole and shoot its tiny silver arrow into the pupil of one of his eyes. It may have been that his held breath suddenly puffed out and his lungs automatically sucked another breath in, showing him that his muscles *could* move.

At any rate he shot up and dashed for the doorway. He dared not stop for the lashings, because Mor's ice-jagged fingers were clutching at him. Instead he ripped the brittle, old leather with one downward sweep of his clawed right hand and then *leaped* from the door, because Nalgron's skeletal arms were straining toward him from the narrow black space between the frozen ground and the tent's elevated floor.

And then he ran as he had never run before. He ran as if all the ghosts of the Cold Waste were at his heels—and in some fashion they were. He passed the last of the Snow Clan's tents, all dark, and the faintly tinkling Tent of the Women, and sprinted out onto the gentle slope, all silvered by the moon, leading down to the upcurving lip of Trollstep Canyon. He felt the urge to dash off that verge, challenging the air to uphold him and bear him south or else hurl him to instant oblivion—and for a moment there seemed nothing to choose between those two fates.

Then he was running not so much away from the cold and its crippling, supernatural horrors, as toward civilization, which was once again a bright emblem in his brain, an answer to all small-mindedness.

He slowed down a little and some sense came back into his head, so that he peered for living late-walkers as well as for demons and fetches.

He noted Shadah twinkling blue in the western treetops.

He was walking by the time he reached Godshall.

He went between it and the canyon's rim, which no longer tugged him.

He noted that Essedinex's tent had been set up again and was once more lit. No new snow worm crawled across Vlana's tent. The snow sycamore bough above it glittered with crystals in the moonlight.

He entered without warning by the back door, silently drawing out the loosened pegs and then thrusting together under the wall and the hems of the racked costumes his head and right fist, the latter gripping his drawn knife.

Vlana lay asleep alone on her back on the pallet, a light red woolen blanket drawn up to her naked armpits. The lamp burned yellow and small, yet brightly enough to show all the interior and no one but her. The unbanked and newly stoked brazier radiated heat.

Fafhrd came all the way in, sheathed his knife, and stood looking down at the actress. Her arms seemed very slender, her hands long-fingered and a shade large. With her big eyes shut, her face seemed rather small at the center of its glory of outspread, dark brown hair. Yet it looked both noble and knowing and its moist, long, generous lips, newly and carefully carmined, roused and tempted him. Her skin had a faint sheen of oil. He could smell its perfume.

For a moment Vlana's supine posture reminded him of both Mor and Nalgron, but this thought was instantly swept away by the brazier's fierce heat, like that of a small wrought-iron sun, by the rich textures and graceful instruments of civilization all around him, and by Vlana's beauty and couth grace, which seemed self-aware even in sleep. She was civilization's sigil.

He moved back toward the rack and began to strip off his clothes and neatly fold and pile them. Vlana did not wake, or at least her eyes did not open.

Getting back under the red blanket again some time later, after crawling out to relieve himself, Fafhrd said, "Now tell me about civilization and your part in it."

Vlana drank half of the wine Fafhrd had fetched her on his way back, then stretched luxuriously, her head resting on her intertwined hands.

"Well, to begin with, I'm not a princess, though I liked being called one," she said lightly. "I must inform you that you have not got yourself even a lady, darlingest boy. As for civilization, it stinks."

"No," Fafhrd agreed, "I have got myself the skillfullest and most glamorous actress in all Nehwon. But why has civilization an ill odor for you?"

"I think I must disillusion you still further, beloved," Vlana said, somewhat absently rubbing her side against his. "Otherwise you might get silly notions about me and even devise silly plans."

"If you're talking about pretending to be a whore in order to gain erotic knowledge and other wisdoms—" Fafhrd began.

She glanced at him in considerable surprise and interrupted rather sharply: "I'm worse than a whore, by some standards. I'm a thief. Yes, Red Ringlets, a cutpurse and filchpocket, a roller of drunks, a burglar and alleybasher. I was born a farm girl, which I suppose makes me lower still to a hunter, who lives by the death of animals and keeps his hands out of the dirt and reaps no harvest except with the sword. When my parents' plot of land was confiscated by the law's trickery to make a tiny corner of one of the new, vast, slave-worked, Lankhmar-owned grain farms, and they in consequence starved to death, I determined to get my own back from the grain merchants. Lankhmar City would feed me, aye, feed me well—and be paid only with lumps and perhaps a deep scratch or two. So to Lankhmar I went. Falling in there with a clever girl of the same turn of mind and some experience, I did well for two full rounds of moons and a few more. We worked only in black garb, and called ourselves to ourselves the Dark Duo.

"For a cover, we danced, chiefly in the twilight hours, to fill in the time before the big-name entertainers. A little later we began to mime too, taught by one Hinerio, a famous actor fallen by wine on evil days, the darlingest and courtliest old trembler who ever begged for a drink at dawn or contrived to fondle a girl one quarter his age at dusk. And so, as I say, I did quite well...until I fell afoul, as my parents had, of the law. No, not the Overlord's courts, dear boy, and his prisons and racks and head-and-hand-chopping blocks, though they are a shame crying to the stars. No, I ran afoul of a law older even than Lankhmar's and a court less merciful. In short, my friend's and my own cover was finally blown by the Thieves' Guild, a most ancient organization with locals in every city of the civilized world with a hidebound law against female membership and with a deep detestation of all freelance pilferers. Back on the farm I had heard of the Guild and hoped in my innocence to become worthy to join it, but soon learned their byword, 'Sooner give a cobra a kiss, than a secret to a woman.' Incidentally, sweet scholar of civilization's arts, such women as the Guild must use as lures and attention-shifters and such, they hire by the half hour from the Whores' Guild.

"I was lucky. At the moment when I was supposed to be slowly strangling somewhere else, I was stumbling over my friend's body, having looped swiftly home to get a key I'd forgot. I lit a lamp in our close-shuttered abode and saw the long agony in Vilis' face and the red silken cord buried deep in her neck. But what filled me with the hottest rage and coldest hate—besides a second measure of knee-melting fear—was that they had strangled old Hinerio too. Vilis and I were at least competitors and so perhaps fair game by civilization's malodorous standards, but he had never even suspected us of thievery. He had assumed merely that we had other lovers or else—and also—erotic clients.

"So I scuttled out of Lankhmar as swiftly as a spied crab, eyes behind me for pursuit, and in Ilthmar encountered Essedinex' troupe, headed north for the off-season. By good fortune they needed a leading mime and my skill was sufficient to satisfy old Seddy.

"But at the same time, I swore an oath by the morning star to avenge the deaths of Vilis and Hinerio. And some day I shall! With proper plans and help and a new cover. More than one high potentate of the Thieves' Guild will learn how it feels to have his weasand narrowed a fingerclip's breadth at a time, aye, and worse things!

"But this is a hellish topic for a comfy morning, lover, and I raise it only to show you why you must not get deeply involved with a dirty and vicious one such as me."

Vlana turned her body then so that it leaned against Fafhrd's and she kissed him from the corner of the lip to the lobe of the ear, but when he would have returned these courtesies in full measure and more, she carried away his groping hands and, bracing herself on his arms, thereby confining them, pushed herself up and gazed at him with her enigmatic look, saying, "Dearest boy, it is the gray of dawn and soon comes the pink and you must leave me at once, or at most after a last engagement. Go home, marry that lovely and nimble treegirl—I'm sure now it was not a male youth—and live your proper, arrow-straight life far from the stinks and snares of civilization. The Show packs up and leaves early, day after tomorrow, and I have my crooked destiny to tread. When your blood has cooled, you will feel only contempt for me. Nay, deny it not—I know men! Though there is a tiny chance that you, being you, will recall me with a little pleasure. In which case I advise one thing only: never hint of it to your wife!"

Fafhrd matched her enigmatic look and answered, "Princess, I've been a pirate, which is nothing but a water thief, who often raids folk poor as your parents. Barbarism can match civilization's every stench. Not one move in our frostbit lives but is strictured by a mad god's laws, which we call customs, and by black-handed irrationalities from which there is no escape. My own father was condemned to death by bone-breaking by a court I dare not name. His offense: climbing a mountain. And there are murders and thievings and pimpings and—Oh, there are tales I could tell you if—"

He broke off to lift his hands so that he was holding her half above him, grasping her gently below the armpits, rather than she propped on her arms. "Let me come south with you, Vlana," he said eagerly, "whether as member of your troupe or moving alone—though I *am* a singing skald, I can also sword dance, juggle four whirling daggers, and hit with one at ten paces a mark the size of my thumbnail. And when we get to Lankhmar City, perhaps disguised as two Northerners, for you are tall, I'll be your good right arm of vengeance. I can thieve by land, too, believe me, and stalk a victim through alleys, I should think, as sightlessly and silently as through forests. I can—"

Vlana, supported by his hands, laid a palm across his lips while her other hand wandered idly under the long hair at the back of his neck. "Darling," she said, "I doubt not that you are brave and loyal and skillful for a lad of eighteen. And you make love well enough for a youth—quite well enough to hold your white-furred girl and mayhap a few more wenches, if you choose. But, despite your ferocious words—forgive my frankness—I sense in you honesty, nobility even, a love of fair play, and a hatred of torture. The lieutenant I seek for my revenge must be cruel and treacherous and fell as a serpent, while knowing at least as much as I of the fantastically twisty ways of the great cities and the ancient guilds. And, to be blunt, he must be old as I, which you miss by almost the fingers of two hands. So come kiss me, dear boy, and pleasure me once more and—"

Fafhrd suddenly sat up, and lifted her a little and sat her down, so that she sat sideways on his thighs, he shifting his grasp to her shoulders.

"No," he said firmly. "I see nothing to be gained by subjecting you once more to my inexpert caresses. But—"

"I was afraid you would take it that way," she interrupted unhappily. "I did not mean—"

"But," he continued with cool authority, "I want to ask you one question. Have you already chosen your lieutenant?"

"I will not answer that," she replied, eyeing him as coolly and confidently.

"Is he—?" he began and then pressed his lips together, catching the name "Vellix" before it was uttered.

She looked at him with undisguised curiosity as to what his next move would be. "Very well," he said at last, dropping his hands from her shoulders and propping himself with them. "You have tried, I think, to act in what you believe to be my best interests, so I will return like with like. What I have to reveal indicts barbarism and civilization equally." And he told her of Essedinex' and Hringorl's plan for her.

She laughed heartily when he was done, though he fancied she had turned a shade pale.

"I must be slipping," she commented. "So that was why my somewhat subtle mimings so easily pleased Seddy's rough and ready tastes, and why there was a place open for me in the troupe, and why he did not insist I whore for him after the Show, as the other girls must." She looked at Fafhrd sharply. "Some prank-sters overset Seddy's tent this midnight. Was it—?"

He nodded. "I was in a strange humor, last night, merry yet furious."

Honest, delighted laughter from her then, followed by another of the sharp looks. "So you did not go home when I sent you away after the Show?"

"Not until afterward," he said. "No, I stayed and watched."

She looked at him in a tender, mocking, won-dering way which asked quite plainly, "And what did you see?" But this time he found it very easy not to name Vellix.

"So you're a gentleman, too," she joked. "But why didn't you tell me about Hringorl's base scheme earlier? Did you think I'd become too frightened to be amorous?"

"A little of that," he admitted, "but it was chiefly that I did not decide until this moment to warn you. Truth to tell, I only came back to you to-night because I was frightened by ghosts, though later I found other good reasons. Indeed, just before I came to your tent, fear and loneliness—yes, and a certain jealousy too—had me minded to hurl myself into Trollstep Canyon, or else don skis and attempt the next-to-impossible leap which has teased my cour-age for years...."

She clutched his upper arm, digging in fin-gers. "Never do that," she said very seriously. "Hold onto life. Think only of yourself. The worst always changes for the better—or oblivion."

"Yes, so I was thinking when I would have let the air over the canyon decide my destiny. Would it cradle me or dash me down? But selfishness, of which I've a plenty whatever you think—that and a certain leeriness of all miracles—quashed that whim. Also, I was earlier half minded to trample your tent before pulling down the Show Master's. So there is some evil in me, you see. Aye, and a shut-mouthed deceitfulness."

She did not laugh, but studied his face most thoughtfully. Then for a time the enigma-look came back into her eyes. For a moment Fafhrd thought he could peer past it, and he was troubled, for what he thought he glimpsed behind those large, brown-irised pupils was not a sibyl surveying the universe from a mountaintop, but a merchant with scales in which he weighed objects most carefully, at whiles noting down in a little book old debts and new bribes and alternate plans for gain.

But it was only one troubling glimpse, so his heart joyed when Vlana, whom his big hands still held tilted above him, smiled down into his eyes and said, "I will now answer your question, which I would and could not earlier. For I have only this instant decided that my lieutenant will be...you. Hug me on it!"

Fafhrd grappled her with eager warmth and a strength that made her squeal, but then just before his body had fired unendurably, she pushed up from him, saying breathlessly, "Wait, wait! We must first lay our plans."

"Afterward, my love. Afterward," he pleaded, straining her down.

"No!" she protested sharply. "Afterward loses too many battles to Too Late. If you are lieutenant, I am captain and give directions."

"Harkening in obedience," he said, giving way. "Only be swift."

"We must be well away from Cold Corner before kidnap time," she said. "Today I must gather my things together and provide us with sleigh, swift horses, and a store of food. Leave all that to me. You behave today exactly as is your wont, keeping well away from me, in case our enemies set spies on you, as both Seddy and Hringorl are most like to do—"

"Very well, very well," Fafhrd agreed hurriedly. "And now, my sweetest—"

"Hush and have patience! To cap your deception, climb into the roof of Godshall well before the Show, just as you did last night. There just might be an attempt to kidnap me during the Show—Hringorl or his men becoming overeager, or Hringorl seeking to cheat Seddy of his gold—and I'll feel safest with you on watch. Then when I exit after wearing the toga and the silver bells, come you down swiftly and meet me at the stable. We'll escape during the break between the first and second halves of the Show, when one way or another all are too intent on what more's coming, to take note of us. You've got that? Stay far away today? Hide in the roof? Join me at the halves break? Very well! And now, darlingest lieutenant, banish all discipline. Forget every atom of respect you owe your captain and—"

But now it was Fafhrd's turn to delay. Vlana's talk had allowed time for his own worries to rouse and he held her away from him although she had knit her hands behind his neck and was straining to draw their two bodies together.

He said, "I will obey you in every particular. Only one warning more, which it's vital you heed. Think as little as you can today about our plans, even while performing actions vital to them. Keep them hid behind the scenery of your other thoughts. As I shall mine, you may be sure. For Mor my mother is a great reader of minds."

"Your mother! Truly she has overawed you inordinately, darling, in a fashion which makes me itch to set you wholly free—oh, do not hold me off! Why, you speak of her as if she were the Queen of Witches."

"And so she is, make no mistake," Fafhrd assured her dourly. "She is the great white spider, while the whole Cold Waste, both above and below, is her web, on which we flies must go tippy-toe, o'erstepping sticky stretches. You *will* heed me?"

"Yes, yes, yes! And now—"

He brought her slowly down toward him, as a man might put a wineskin to his mouth, tantalizing himself. Their skins met. Their lips poised.

Fafhrd became aware of a profound silence above, around, below, as if the very earth were holding her breath. It frightened him.

They kissed, drinking deeply of each other, and his fear was drowned.

They parted for breath. Fafhrd reached out and pinched the lamp's wick so that the flame fled and the tent was dark except for the cold silver of dawn seeping in by cranny and crack. His fingers stung. He wondered why he'd done it—they'd loved by lamplight before. Again fear came.

He clasped Vlana tightly in the hug that banishes all fears.

And then of a sudden—he could not possibly have told why—he was rolling over and over with her toward the back of the tent. His hands gripping her shoulders, his legs clamping hers together, he was hurling her sideways over him and then himself over her in swiftest alteration.

There was a *crack* like thunder and the jolt of a giant's fist hammered against the granite-frozen ground behind them, where the middle of the tent became nothing high, while the hoops above them leaned sharply that way, drawing the tent's leather skin after.

They rolled into the racked garments spilling down. There was a second monster *crack* followed by a crashing and a crunching like some super-giant beast snapping up a behemoth and crunching it between its jaws. Earth quivered for a space.

Then all was silent after that great noise and ground-shaking, except for the astonishment and fear buzzing in their ears. They clutched each other like terrified children.

Fafhrd recovered himself first. "Dress!" he told Vlana and squirmed under the back of the tent and stood up naked in the biting cold under the pinkening sky.

The great bough of the snow sycamore, its crystals dashed off in a vast heap, lay athwart the middle of the tent, pressing it and the pallet beneath into the frozen earth.

The rest of the sycamore, robbed of its great balancing bough, had fallen entire in the opposite direction and lay mounded around with shaken-off crystals. Its black, hairy, broken-off roots were nakedly exposed.

All the crystals shone with a pale flesh-pink from the sun.

Nothing moved anywhere, not even a wisp of breakfast smoke. Sorcery had struck a great hammerstroke and none had noted it except the intended victims.

Fafhrd, beginning to shake, slithered under again. Vlana had obeyed his word and was dressing with an actress's swiftness. Fafhrd hurried into his own garments, piled so providentially at this end of the tent. He wondered if he had been under a god's directions in doing that and in snuffing out the lamp, which else by now would have had the crushed tent flaming.

His clothes felt colder than the icy air, but he knew that would change.

He crawled with Vlana outside once more. As they stood up, he faced her toward the fallen bough with the great crystal heap around it and said, "Now laugh at the witchy powers of my mother and her coven and all the Snow Women."

Vlana said doubtfully, "I see only a bough that was overweighted with ice."

Fafhrd said, "Compare the mass of crystals and snow that was shaken off that bough with those elsewhere. Remember: hide your thoughts!"

Vlana was silent.

A black figure was racing toward them from the traders' tents. It grew in size as it grotesquely bounded.

Vellix the Venturer was gasping as he stamped to a stop and seized Vlana's arms. Controlling his breathing, he said, "I dreamed a dream of you struck down and pashed. Then a thunderclap waked me."

Vlana answered, "You dreamed the beginning of the truth, but in a matter like this, almost is as good as not at all."

Vellix at last saw Fafhrd. Lines of jealous anger engraved his face and his hand went to the dagger at his belt.

"Hold!" Vlana commanded sharply. "I had indeed been mashed to a mummy, except that this youth's senses, which ought to have been utterly engrossed in something else, caught the first cues of the bough's fall, and he whipped me out of death's way in the very nick. Fafhrd's his name."

Vellix changed his hand's movement into part of a low bow, sweeping his other arm out wide.

"I am much indebted to you, young man," he said warmly, and then after a pause, "for saving the life of a notable *artiste*."

By now other figures were in view, some hurrying toward them from the nearby actors' tents, others at the doors of the far-off Snow Tribe's tents and not moving at all.

Pressing her cheek to Fafhrd's, as if in formal gratitude, Vlana whispered rapidly, "Remember my plan for tonight and for all our future rapture. Do not depart a jot from it. Efface yourself."

Fafhrd managed, "Beware ice and snow. Act without thought."

To Vellix, Vlana said more distantly, though with courtesy and kindness, "Thank you, sir, for your concern for me, both in your dreams and your wakings."

From out a fur robe, whose collar topped his ears, Essedinex greeted with gruff humor, "It's been a hard night on tents." Vlana shrugged.

The women of the troupe gathered around her with anxious questions and she talked with them privately as they walked to the actors' tent and went in through the girls' door-flap.

Vellix frowned after her and pulled at his black moustache.

The male actors stared and shook their heads at the beating the hemicylindrical tent had taken.

Vellix said to Fafhrd with warm friendliness, "I offered you brandy before and now I'd guess you need it. Also, since yestermorning I've had a great desire to talk with you."

"Your pardon, but once I sit I will not be able to stay awake for a word, were they wise as owls', nor for even a brandy swig," Fafhrd answered politely, hiding a great yawn, which was only half feigned. "But I thank you."

"It appears I am fated always to ask at the wrong time," Vellix commented with a shrug. "Perhaps at noon? Or midafternoon?" he added swiftly.

"The latter, if it please you," Fafhrd replied and rapidly walked off, taking great strides toward the trading tents. Vellix did not seek to keep up with him.

Fafhrd felt more satisfied than he ever had in his life. The thought that tonight he would forever escape this stupid snow world and its man-chaining women almost made him nostalgic about Cold Corner. Thought-guard! he told himself. Feelings of eerie menace or else his hunger for sleep turned his surroundings spectral, like a childhood scene revisited.

He drained a white porcelain tankard of wine given him by his Mingol friends Zax and Effendrit, let them conduct him to a glossy pallet hidden by piles of other furs, and fell at once into a deep sleep.

After eons of absolute, pillowy darkness, lights came softly on. Fafhrd sat beside Nalgron his father at a stout banquet table crowded with all savory foods smoking hot and all fortified wines in jugs of earthenware, stone, silver, crystal and gold. There were other feasters lining the table, but Fafhrd could make nothing of them except their dark silhouettes and the sleepy sound of their unceasing talk too soft to be understood, like many streams of murmuring water, though with occasional bursts of low laughter, like small waves running up and returning down a gravelly beach. While the dull clash of knife and spoon against plate and each other was like the clank of the pebbles in that surf.

Nalgron was clad and cloaked in ice-bear furs of the whitest with pins and chains and wristlets and rings of purest silver, and there was silver also in his hair, which troubled Fafhrd. In his left hand he held a silver goblet, which at intervals he touched to his lips, but he kept his eating hand under his cloak.

Nalgron was discoursing wisely, tolerantly, almost tenderly of many matters. He directed his gaze here and there around the table, yet spoke so quietly that Fafhrd knew his conversation was directed at his son alone.

Fafhrd also knew he should be listening intently to every word and carefully stowing away each aphorism, for Nalgron was speaking of courage, of honor, of prudence, of thoughtfulness in giving and punctilio in keeping your word, of following your heart, of setting and unswervingly striving toward a high, romantic goal, of self-honesty in all these things but especially in recognizing your aversions and desires, of the need to close your ears to the fears and naggings of women, yet freely forgive them all their jealousies, attempted trammelings, and even extremest wickednesses, since those all sprang from their ungovernable love, for you or another, and of many a different matter most useful to know for a youth on manhood's verge.

But although he knew this much, Fafhrd heard his father only in snatches, for he was so troubled by the gauntness of Nalgron's cheek and by the leanness of the strong fingers lightly holding the silver goblet and by the silver in his hair, and a faint overlay of blue on his ruddy lips, although Nalgron was most sure and even sprightly in every movement, gesture, and word, that he was compelled to be forever searching the steaming platters and bowls around him for especially succulent portions to spoon or fork onto Nalgron's wide, silver plate to tempt his appetite.

Whenever he did this, Nalgron would look toward him with a smile and a courteous nod, and with love in his eyes, and then touch his goblet to his lips and return to his discoursings, but never would he uncover his eating hand.

As the banquet progressed, Nalgron began to speak of matters yet more important, but now Fafhrd heard hardly one of the precious words, so greatly agitated was he by his concern for his father's health. Now the thin skin seemed stretched to bursting on the jutting cheekbone, the bright eyes ever more sunken and dark-ringed, the blue veins more bulgingly a-crawl across the stout tendons of the hand lightly holding the silver goblet—and Fafhrd had begun to suspect that although Nalgron often let the wine touch his lips he drank never a drop.

"Eat, father," Fafhrd pleaded in a low voice taut with concern. "At least drink."

Again the look, the smile, the agreeable nod, the bright eyes warmer still with love, the brief tipping of goblet against unparted lips, the looking away, the tranquil, unattendable discourse resumed.

And now Fafhrd knew fear, for the lights were growing blue and he realized that none of the black, unfeatured fellow-feasters were or had all the while been lifting so much as hand, let alone cup-rim, to mouth, though making an unceasing dull clatter with their cutlery. His concern for his father became an agony and before he rightly knew what he was doing, he had brushed back his father's cloak and gripped his father's right arm at forearm and wrist and so shoved his eating hand toward his high-piled plate.

Then Nalgron was not nodding, but thrusting his head at Fafhrd, and not smiling, but grinning in such fashion as to show all his teeth of old ivory hue, whilst his eyes were cold, cold, cold.

The hand and arm that Fafhrd gripped felt like, looked like, *were* bare brown bone.

Of a sudden shaking violently in all his parts, but chiefly in his arms, Fafhrd recoiled swift as a serpent down the bench.

Then Fafhrd was not shaking, but being shaken by strong hands of flesh on his shoulders, and instead of the dark there was the faintly translucent hide of the Mingols' tent-roof, and in place of his father's face the sallow-cheeked, black-moustached one, somber yet concerned, of Vellix the Venturer.

Fafhrd stared dazedly, then shook his shoulders and head to bring a quicker-tempoed life back into his body and throw off the gripping hands.

But Vellix had already let go and seated himself on the next pile of furs.

"Your pardon, young warrior," he said gravely. "You appeared to be having a dream no man would care to continue."

His manner and the tone of his voice were

like the nightmare-Nalgron's. Fafhrd pushed up on an elbow, yawned, and with a shuddery grimace shook himself again.

"You're chilled in body, mind, or both," Vellix said. "So we've good excuse for the brandy I promised."

He brought up from beside him two small silver mugs in one hand and in the other a brown jug of brandy which he now uncorked with that forefinger and thumb.

Fafhrd frowned inwardly at the dark tarnish on the mugs and at the thought of what might be crusted or dusted in their bottoms, or perhaps that of one only. With a troubled twinge, he reminded himself that this man was his rival for Vlana's affections.

"Hold," he said as Vellix prepared to pour. "A silver cup played a nasty role in my dream. Zax!" he called to the Mingol looking out the tent door. "A porcelain mug, if you please!"

"You take the dream as a warning against drinking from silver?" Vellix inquired softly with an ambiguous smile.

"No," Fafhrd answered, "but it instilled an antipathy into my flesh, which still crawls." He wondered a little that the Mingols had so casually let in Vellix to sit beside him. Perhaps the three were old acquaintances from the trading camps. Or perhaps there'd been bribery.

Vellix chuckled and became freer of manner. "Also, I've fallen into filthy ways, living without a woman or servant. Effendrit! Make that two porcelain mugs, clean as newly-debarked birch!"

It was indeed the other Mingol who had been standing by the door—Vellix knew them better than

Fafhrd did. The Venturer immediately handed over one of the gleaming white mugs. He poured a little of the nose-tickling drink into his own porcelain mug, then a generous gush for Fafhrd, then more for him-self—as if to demonstrate that Fafhrd's drink could not possibly be poisoned or drugged. And Fafhrd, who had been watching closely, could find no fault in the demonstration. They lightly clinked mugs and when Vellix drank deeply, Fafhrd took a large though care-fully slow sip. The stuff burned gently.

"It's my last jug," Vellix said cheerfully. "I've traded my whole stock for amber, snow-gems, and other smalls—aye, and my tent and cart too, every-thing but my two horses and our gear and winter rations."

"I've heard your horses are the swiftest and hardiest on the Steppes," Fafhrd remarked.

"That's too large a claim. Here they rank well, no doubt."

"Here!" Fafhrd said contemptuously.

Vellix eyed him as Nalgron had in all but the last part of the dream. Then he said, "Fafhrd—I may call you that? Call me Vellix. May I make a sugges-tion? May I give you advice such as I might give a son of mine?"

"Surely," Fafhrd answered, feeling not only uncomfortable now but wary.

"You're clearly restless and dissatisfied here. So is any sound young man, anywhere, at your age. The wide world calls you. You've an itching foot. Yet let me say this: it takes more than wit and prudence—aye, and wisdom, too—to cope with civilization and find any comfort. That requires low cunning, a smirch-ing of yourself as civilization is smirched. You cannot climb to success there as you climb a mountain, no matter how icy and treacherous. The latter demands all your best. The former, much of your worst: a calculated self-evil you have yet to experience, and need not. I was born a renegade. My father was a man of the Eight Cities who rode with the Mingols. I wish now I had stuck to the Steppes myself, cruel as they are, nor harkened to the corrupting call of Lankhmar and the Eastern Lands.

"I know, I know, the folk here are narrow-visioned, custom-bound. But matched with the twisted minds of civilization, they're straight as pines. With your natural gifts you'll easily be a chief here—more, in sooth, a chief paramount, weld a dozen clans together, make the Northerners a power for nations to reckon with. Then, if you wish, you can challenge civilization. On your terms, not hers."

Fafhrd's thoughts and feelings were like choppy water, though he had outwardly become almost preternaturally calm. There was even a current of glee in him, that Vellix rated a youth's chances with Vlana so high that he would ply him with flattery as well as brandy.

But across all other currents, making the chop sharp and high, was the impression, hard to shake, that the Venturer was not altogether dissimulating, that he did feel like a father toward Fafhrd, that he was truly seeking to save him hurt, that what he said of civilization had an honest core. Of course that might be because Vellix felt so sure of Vlana that he could afford to be kind to a rival. Nevertheless...

Nevertheless, Fafhrd now once again felt more uncomfortable than anything else.

He drained his mug. "Your advice is worth thought, sir—Vellix, I mean. I'll ponder it."

Refusing another drink with a headshake and smile, he stood up and straightened his clothes.

"I had hoped for a longer chat," Vellix said, not rising.

"I've business to attend," Fafhrd answered. "My hearty thanks."

Vellix smiled thoughtfully as he departed.

The concourse of trodden snow winding amongst the traders' tents was racketty with noise and crowdedly a-bustle. While Fafhrd slept, the men of the Ice Tribe and fully half of the Frost Companions had come in and now many of these were gathered around two sunfires—so called for their bigness, heat, and the height of their leaping flames—quaffing steaming mead and laughing and scuffling together. To either side were oases of buying and bargaining, encroached on by the merrymakers or given careful berth according to the rank of those involved in the business doings. Old comrades spotted one another and shouted and sometimes drove through the press to embrace. Food and drink were spilled, challenges made and accepted, or more often laughed down. Skalds sang and roared.

The tumult irked Fafhrd, who wanted quiet in which to disentangle Vellix from Nalgron in his feelings, and banish his vague doubts of Vlana, and unsmirch civilization. He walked as a troubled dreamer, frowning yet unmindful of elbowings and other shoves.

Then all at once he was tinglingly alert, for he glimpsed angling toward him through the crowd Hor and Harrax, and he read the purpose in their eyes. Letting an eddy in the crush spin him around, he noted Hrey, one other of Hringorl's creatures, close behind him.

The purpose of the three was clear. Under guise of comradely scuffling, they would give him a vicious beating or worse.

In his moody concern with Vellix, he had forgotten his more certain enemy and rival, the brutally direct yet cunning Hringorl.

Then the three were upon him. In a frozen instant he noted that Hor bore a small bludgeon and that Harrax' fists were overly large, as if they gripped stone or metal to heavy their blows.

He lunged backward, as if he meant to dodge between that couple and Hrey; then as suddenly reversed course and with a shocking bellow raced toward the sunfire ahead. Heads turned at his yell and a startled few dodged from his way. But the Ice Tribesmen and Frost Companions had time to take in what was happening: a tall youth pursued by three huskies. This promised sport. They sprang to either side of the sunfire to block his passage past it. Fafhrd veered first to left, then to right. Jeering, they bunched more closely.

Holding his breath and throwing up an arm to guard his eyes, Fafhrd leaped straight through the flames. They lifted his fur cloak from his back and blew it high. He felt the stab of heat on hand and neck.

He came out with his furs a-smolder, blue flames running up his hair. There was more crowd ahead except for a swept, carpeted, and canopied space between two tents, where chiefs and priests sat intently around a low table where a merchant weighed gold dust in a pair of scales.

He heard bump and yell behind, someone cried, "Run, coward," another, "A fight, a fight"; he saw Mara's face ahead, red and excited.

Then the future chief paramount of Northland—for so he happened at that instant to think of himself—half sprang, half dived a-flame across the canopied table, unavoidably tumbling the merchant and two chiefs, banging aside the scales, and knocking the gold dust to the winds before he landed with a steaming zizzle in the great, soft snow-bank beyond.

He swiftly rolled over twice to make sure all his fires were quenched, then scrambled to his feet and ran like a deer into the woods, followed by gusts of curses and gales of laughter.

Fifty big trees later he stopped abruptly in the snowy gloom and held his breath while he listened. Through the soft pounding of his blood, there came not the faintest sound of pursuit. Ruefully he combed with his fingers his stinking, diminished hair and sketchily brushed his now patchy, equally fire-stinking furs.

Then he waited for his breath to quiet and his awareness to expand. It was during this pause that he made a disconcerting discovery. For the first time in his life the forest, which had always been his retreat, his continent-spanning tent, his great private needle-roofed room, seemed hostile to him, as if the very trees and the cold-fleshed, warm-boweled mother-earth in which they were rooted knew of his apostasy, his spurning, jilting and intended divorce of his native land.

It was not the unusual silence, nor the sinister and suspicious quality of the faint sounds he at last began to hear: scratch on bark of small claw, pitter of tiny paw-steps, hoot of a distant owl anticipating night. Those were effects, or at most concomitants. It was something unnamable, intangible, yet profound, like the frown of a god. Or goddess.

He was greatly depressed. At the same time he had never known his heart feel as hard.

When at last he set out again, it was as silently as might be, and not with his unusual relaxed and wide-open awareness, but rather the naked-nerved sensitivity and bent-bow readiness of a scout in enemy territory.

And it was well for him that he did so, since otherwise he might not have dodged the nearly soundless fall of an icicle, sharp, heavy, and long as a siege-catapult's missile, nor the down-clubbing of a huge snow-weighted dead branch that broke with a single thunderous crack, nor the venomous dart of a snow-adder's head from its unaccustomed white coil in the open, nor the sidewise slash of the narrow, cruel claws of a snow-leopard that seemed almost to materialize a-spring in the frigid air and that vanished as strangely when Fafhrd slipped aside from its first attack and faced it with dirk drawn. Nor might he have spotted in time the up-whipping, slip-knotted snare, set against all custom in this home-area of the forest and big enough to strangle not a hare but a bear.

He wondered where Mor was and what she might be muttering or chanting. Had his mistake been simply to dream of Nalgron? Despite yesterday's curse—and others before it—and last night's naked threats, he had never truly and wholly imagined his mother seeking to kill him. But now the hair on his neck was lifted in apprehension and horror, the watchful glare in his eyes was febrile and wild, while a little blood dripped unheeded from the cut in his cheek where the great icicle down-dropping had grazed it.

So intent had he become on spying dangers that it was with a little surprise that he found himself standing in the glade where he and Mara had embraced only yesterday, his feet on the short trail leading to the home tents. He relaxed a little then, sheathing his dirk and pressing a handful of snow to his bleeding cheek—but he relaxed only a little, with the result that he was aware of one coming to meet him before he consciously heard footsteps.

So silently and completely did he then melt into the snowy background that Mara was three paces away before she saw him.

"They hurt you," she exclaimed.

"No," he answered curtly, still intent on dangers in the forest.

"But the red snow on your cheek. There was a fight?"

"Only a nick got in the woods. I outran 'em."

Her look of concern faded. "First time I saw you run from a quarrel."

"I had no mind to take on three or more," he said flatly.

"Why do you look behind? They're trailing you?"

"No."

Her expression hardened. "The elders are outraged. The younger men call you scareling. My brothers among them. I didn't know what to say."

"Your brothers!" Fafhrd exclaimed. "Let the stinking Snow Clan call me what they will. I care not."

Mara planted her fists on her hips. "You've grown very free with your insults of late. I'll not have my family berated, do you hear? Nor myself insulted, now that I think of it." She was breathing hard. "Last

night you went back to that shriveled old whore of a
dancer. You were in her tent for hours."

"I was not!" Fafhrd denied, thinking *An hour
and a half at most.* The bickering was warming his blood
and quelling his supernatural dread.

"You lie! The story's all around the camp. Any
other girl would have set her brothers on you ere this."

Fafhrd came back to his schemy self almost
with a jerk. On this eve of all eves he must not risk
needless trouble—the chance of being crippled, it
might even be, or dead.

Tactics, man, tactics, he told himself as he
moved eagerly toward Mara, exclaiming in hurt, hon-
eyed tones, "Mara, my queen, how can you believe
such of me, who love you more than—"

"Keep off me, liar and cheat!"

"And you carrying my son," he persisted, still
trying to embrace her. "How does the bonny babe?"

"Spits at his father. Keep off me, I say."

"But I yearn to touch your ticklesome skin,
than which there is no other balm for me this side of
Hell, oh most beauteous made more beautiful by moth-
erhood."

"Go to Hell, then. And stop these sickening
pretenses. Your acting wouldn't deceive a drunken she-
scullion. Hamfatter!"

Stung to his blood, which instantly grew hot,
Fafhrd retorted, "And what of your own lies? Yesterday you boasted of how you'd cow and control my
mother. Instanter you went sniveling to tell her you
were with child by me."

"Only after I knew you lusted after the actress. And was it anything but the complete truth?
Oh, you twister!"

Fafhrd stood back and folded his arms. He pronounced, "Wife of mine must be true to me, must trust me, must ask me first before she acts, must comport herself like the mate of a chief paramount to-be. It appears to me that in all of these you fall short."

"True to you? You're one to talk!" Her fair face grew unpleasantly red and strained with rage. "Chief paramount! Set your sights merely on being called a man by the Snow Clan, which they've not done yet. Hear me now, sneak and dissembler. You will instantly plead for my pardon on your knees and then come with me to ask my mother and aunts for my hand, or else—"

"I'd sooner kneel to a snake! Or wed a she-bear!" Fafhrd cried out, all thoughts of tactics vanished.

"I'll set my brothers on you," she screamed back. "Cowardly boor!"

Fafhrd lifted his fist, dropped it, set his hands to his head and rocked it in a gesture of maniacal desperation, then suddenly ran past her toward the camp.

"I'll set the whole tribe on you! I'll tell it in the Tent of the Women. I'll tell your mother..." Mara shrieked after him, her voice fading fast with the intervening boughs, snow, and distance.

Barely pausing to note that none were abroad amongst the Snow Clan's tents, either because they were still at the trading fair or inside preparing supper, Fafhrd bounded up his treasure tree and flipped open the door of his hidey hole. Cursing the fingernail he broke doing so, he got out the sealskin-wrapped bow and arrows and rockets and added thereto his best pair of skis and ski sticks, a somewhat shorter package holding his father's second-best sword well-oiled, and

a pouch of smaller gear. Dropping to the snow, he
swiftly bound the longer items into a single pack,
which he slung over shoulder.

After a moment of indecision, he hurtled inside Mor's tent, snatching from his pouch a small
fire-pot of bubblestone, and filled it with glowing embers from the hearth, sprinkled ashes over them, laced
the pot tight shut, and returned it to his pouch.

Then turning in frantic haste toward the
doorway, he stopped dead. Mor stood in it, a tall silhouette white-edged and shadow-faced.

"So you're deserting me and the Waste. Not
to return. You think."

Fafhrd was speechless.

"Yet you will return. If you wish it to be a-
crawl on four feet, or blessedly on two, and not
stretched lifeless on a litter of spears, weigh soon your
duties and your birth."

Fafhrd framed a bitter answer, but the very
words were a gag in his gullet. He stalked toward Mor.

"Make way, Mother," he managed in a whisper.

She did not move.

His jaws clamped in a horrid grimace of tension, he shot forth his hands, gripped her under the
armpits—his flesh crawling—and set her to one side.
She seemed as stiff and cold as ice. She made no pro-
test. He could not look her in the face.

Outside, he started at a brisk pace for
Godshall, but there were men in his way—four hulking young blond ones flanked by a dozen others.

Mara had brought not only her brothers from
the fair, but all her available kinsmen.

Yet now she appeared to have repented of her
act, for she was dragging at her eldest brother's arm

and talking earnestly to him, to judge by her expression and the movements of her lips.

Her eldest brother marched on as if she weren't there. And now as his gaze hit Fafhrd he gave a joyous shout, jerked from her grasp, and came on a-rush followed by the rest. All waved clubs or their scabbarded swords.

Mara's agonized, "Fly, my love!" was anticipated by Fafhrd by at least two heartbeats. He turned and raced for the woods, his long, stiff pack banging his back. When the path of his flight joined the trail of footprints he'd made running out of the woods, he took care to set a foot in each without slackening speed.

Behind him they cried, "Coward!" He ran faster.

When he reached the juttings of granite a short way inside the forest, he turned sharply to the right and leaping from bare rock to rock, making not one additional print, he reached a low cliff of granite and mounted it with only two hand-grabs, then darted on until the cliff's edge hid him from anyone below.

He heard the pursuit enter the woods, angry cries as in veering around trees they bumped each other, then a masterful voice crying for silence.

He carefully lobbed three stones so that they fell along his false trail well ahead of Mara's human hounds. The thud of the stones and the rustle of branches they made falling drew cries of "There he goes!" and another demand for silence.

Lifting a larger rock, he hurled it two-handed so that it struck solidly the trunk of a stout tree on the nearer side of the trail, jarring down great branchfuls of snow and ice. There were muffled cries of startlement, confusion, and rage from the showered and likely three-quarters buried men. Fafhrd grinned,

then his face sobered and his eyes grew dartingly
watchful as he set off at a lope through the darkening
woods.

But this time he felt no inimical presences
and the living and the lifeless, whether rock or ghost,
held off their assaults. Perhaps Mor, deeming him sufficiently harried by Mara's kinsmen, had ceased to
energize her charms. Or perhaps Fafhrd left off thinking and devoted all of himself to silent speeding. Vlana
and civilization lay ahead. His mother and barbarism
behind—but he endeavored not to think of her.

Night was near when Fafhrd left the wood.
He had made the fullest possible circuit through them,
coming out next to the drop into Trollstep Canyon.
The strap of his long pack chafed his shoulder.

There were the lights and sounds of feasting
amongst the traders' tents. Godshall and the actors'
tents were dark. Still nearer loomed the dark bulk of
the stable tent.

He silently crossed the frosty, rutted gravel
of the New Road leading south into the canyon.

Then he saw that the stable tent was not altogether dark. A ghostly glow moved inside it. He
approached its door cautiously and saw the silhouette
of Hor peering in. Still the soul of silence, he came up
behind Hor and peered over his shoulder.

Vlana and Vellix were harnessing the latter's
two horses to Essedinex' sleigh, from which Fafhrd had
stolen the three rockets.

Hor tipped up his head and lifted a hand to
his lips to make some sort of owl or wolf cry.

Fafhrd whipped out his knife and, as he was
about to slash Hor's throat, reversed his intent and
his knife too, and struck him senseless with a blow of

the pommel against the side of his head. As Hor collapsed, Fafhrd hauled him to one side of the doorway.

Vlana and Vellix sprang into the sleigh, the latter touched his horses with the reins, and they came thud-slithering out. Fafhrd gripped his knife fiercely...then sheathed it and shrank back into the shadows.

The sleigh went gliding off down the New Road. Fafhrd stared after it, standing tall, his arms as straight down his sides as those of a corpse laid out, but with his fingers and thumbs gripped into tightest fists.

He suddenly turned and fled toward Godshall.

There came an owl-hooting from behind the stable tent. Fafhrd skidded to a stop in the snow and turned around, his hands still fists.

Out of the dark, two forms, one trailing fire, raced toward Trollstep Canyon. The tall form was unmistakably Hringorl's. They stopped at the brink. Hringorl swung his torch in a great circle of flame. The light showed the face of Harrax beside him. Once, twice, thrice, as if in signal to someone far south down the canyon. Then they raced for the stable.

Fafhrd ran for Godshall. There was a harsh cry behind him. He stopped and turned again. Out of the stable galloped a big horse. Hringorl rode it. He dragged by rope a man on skis: Harrax. The pair careened down the New Road in a flaring upswirl of snow.

Fafhrd raced on until he was past Godshall and a quarter way up the slope leading to the Tent of the Women. He cast off his pack, opened it, drew his skis from it and strapped them to his feet. Next he unwrapped his father's sword and belted it to his left side, balancing his pouch on right.

Then he faced Trollstep Canyon where the Old Road had gone. He took up two of his ski sticks, crouched, and dug them in. His face was a skull, the visage of one who casts dice with Death.

At that instant, beyond Godshall, the way he had come, there was a tiny yellow sputtering. He paused for it, counting heartbeats, he knew not why.

Nine, ten, eleven—there was a great flare of flame. The rocket rose, signaling tonight's Show. Twenty-one, twenty-two, twenty-three—and the tail-flame faded and the nine white stars burst out.

Fafhrd dropped his ski sticks, picked up one of the three rockets he'd stolen, and drew its fuse from its end, pulling just hard enough to break the cementing tar without breaking the fuse.

Holding the slender, finger-long, tarry cylinder delicately between his teeth, he took his fire-pot out of his pouch. The bubblestone was barely warm. He unlaced the top and brushed away the ashes below until he saw—and was stung by—a red glow.

He took the fuse from between his teeth and placed it so that one end leaned on the edge of the fire-pot while the other end touched the red glow. There was a sputtering. Seven, eight, nine, ten, eleven, twelve—and the sputtering became a flaring jet, then was done.

Setting his fire-pot on the snow, he took up the two remaining rockets, and hugged their thick bodies under his arms and dug their tails into the snow, testing them against the ground. The tails were truly as stiff and strong as ski sticks.

He held the rockets propped parallel in one hand and blew hard on the glowing fire-patch in his fire-pot and brought it up toward the two fuses.

Mara ran out of the dark and said, "Darling, I'm so glad my kin didn't catch you!"

The glow of the fire-pot showed the beauty of her face.

Staring at her across it, Fafhrd said, "I'm leaving Cold Corner. I'm leaving the Snow Tribe. I'm leaving you."

Mara said, "You can't."

Fafhrd set down the fire-pot and the rockets.

Mara stretched out her hands.

Fafhrd took the silver bracelets off his wrists and put them in Mara's palms.

Mara clenched them and cried, "I don't ask for these. I don't ask for anything. You're the father of my child. You're mine!"

Fafhrd whipped the heavy silver chain off his neck, laid it across her wrists, and said, "Yes. You're mine forever, and I'm yours. Your son is mine. I'll never have another Snow Clan wife. We're married."

Meanwhile he had taken up the two rockets again and held their fuses to the fire-pot. They sputtered simultaneously. He set them down, thonged shut the fire-pot and thrust it in his pouch. Three, four...

Mor looked over Mara's shoulder and said, "I witness your words, my son. Stop!"

Fafhrd grabbed up the rockets, each by its sputtering body, dug in the stick ends and took off down the slope with a great shove. Six, seven...

Mara screamed, "Fafhrd! Husband!" As Mor shouted, "No son of mine!"

Fafhrd shoved again with the sputtering rockets. Cold air whipped his face. He barely felt it. The moonlit lip of the jump was close ahead. He felt its up-curve. Beyond it, darkness. Eight, nine...

He hugged the rockets fiercely to his sides, under his elbows, and was flying through darkness. Eleven, twelve...

The rockets did not fire. The moonlight showed the opposite wall of the canyon rushing toward him. His skis were directed at a point just beneath its top and that point was steadily falling. He tilted the rockets down and hugged them more fiercely still.

They fired. It was as if he were clinging to two great wrists that were dragging him up. His elbows and sides were warm. In the sudden glare the rock wall showed close, but now below. Sixteen, seventeen...

He touched down smoothly on the fair crust of snow covering the Old Road and hurled the rockets to either side. There was a double thunderclap and white stars were shooting around him. One smote and stung, then tortured his cheek as it died. There was time for the one great laughing thought, *I depart in a burst of glory.*

Then no time for large thoughts at all, as he gave all his attention to skiing down the steep slope of the Old Road, now bright in the moonlight, now pitch black as it curved, crags to the right, a precipice to his left. Crouching and keeping his skis locked side to side, he steered by swaying his hips. His face and his hands grew numb. Reality was the Old Road hurled at him. Tiny bumps became great jolts. White rims came close. Black shoulders threatened.

Deep, deep down there were thoughts nevertheless. Even as he strained to keep all his attention on his skiing, they were there. *Idiot, you should have grabbed a pair of sticks with the rockets. But how would you have held them when casting aside the rockets? In your pack?—then they'd be doing you no good now. Will*

the fire-pot in your pouch prove more worthwhile than
sticks? You should have stayed with Mara. Such loveli-
ness you'll never see again. But it's Vlana you want. Or
is it? How, with Vellix? If you weren't so cold-hearted
and good, you'd have killed Vellix in the stable, instead
of speeding to— Did you truly intend killing yourself?
What do you intend now? Can Mor's charms outspeed
your skiing? Were the rocket wrists really Nalgron's,
reaching from Hell? What's that ahead?

That was a hulking shoulder skidded around.
He lay over on his right side as the white edge to his
left narrowed. The edge held. Beyond it, on the opposite wall of the widening canyon, he saw a tiny streak
of flame. Hringorl still had his torch, as he galloped
down the New Road dragging Harrax? Fafhrd lay over
again to his right as the Old Road curved farther that
way in a tightening turn. The sky reeled. Life demanded that he lie still farther over, braking to a stop.
But Death was still an equal player in this game. Ahead
was the intersection where Old and New Road met.
He must reach it as soon as Vellix and Vlana in their
sleigh. Speed was the essence. Why? He was uncertain. New curves ahead.

By infinitesimal stages the slope grew less.
Snow-freighted treetops thrust from the sinister
depths—to the left—then shot up to either side.
He was in a flat black tunnel. His progress became
soundless as a ghost's. He coasted to a stop just at
the tunnel's end. His numb fingers went up and
feather-touched the bulge of the star-born blister
on his cheek. Ice needles crackled very faintly inside the blister.

No other sound but the faint tinkle of the
crystals growing all around in the still, damp air.

Five paces ahead of him, down a sudden slope, was a bulbous roll bush weighted with snow. Behind it crouched Hringorl's chief lieutenant Hrey—no mistaking that pointed beard, though its red was gray in the moonlight. He held a strung bow in his left hand.

Beyond him, two dozen paces down slope, was the fork where New and Old Road met. The tunnel going south through the trees was blocked by a pair of roll bushes higher than a man's head. Vellix' and Vlana's sleigh was stopped short of the pile, its two horses great loomings. Moonlight struck silvery manes and silvery bushes. Vlana sat hunched in the sleigh, her head fur-hooded. Vellix had got down and was casting the roll bushes out of the way.

Torchlight came streaking down the New Road from Cold Corner. Vellix gave up his work and drew his sword. Vlana looked over her shoulder.

Hringorl galloped into the clearing with a laughing cry of triumph, and threw his torch high in the air, reined his horse to a stop behind the sleigh. The skier he towed—Harrax—shot past him and half-way up the slope. There Harrax braked to a stop and stooped to unlace his skis. The torch came down and went out sizzling.

Hringorl dropped from his horse, a fighting axe ready in his right hand.

Vellix ran toward Hringorl. Clearly he understood that he must dispose of the giant pirate before Harrax got off his skis or he would be fighting two at once. Vlana's face was a small white mask in the moonlight as she half lifted from her seat to stare after him. The hood fell back from her head.

Fafhrd could have helped Vellix, but he still hadn't made a move to unlash his skis. With a pang—

or was it relief?—he remembered he'd left his bow and arrows behind. He told himself that he should help Vellix. Hadn't he skied down here at incalculable risk to save the Venturer and Vlana, or at least warn them of the ambush he had suspected ever since he'd seen Hringorl whirl his torch on the precipice's edge? And didn't Vellix look like Nalgron, now more than ever in his moment of bravery? But the phantom Death still stood at Fafhrd's side, inhibiting all action.

Besides, Fafhrd felt there was a spell on the clearing, making all action inside it futile. As if a giant spider, white-furred, had already spun a web around it, shutting it off from the rest of the universe, making it a volume inscribed, "This space belongs to the White Spider of Death." No matter that this giant spider spun not silk, but crystals—the result was the same.

Hringorl aimed a great axe swipe at Vellix. The Venturer evaded it and thrust his sword into Hringorl's forearm. With a howl of rage, Hringorl shifted his axe to his left hand, lunged forward and struck again.

Taken by surprise, Vellix barely dodged back out of the way of the hissing curve of steel, bright in the moonlight. Yet he was nimbly on guard again, while Hringorl advanced more warily, axe-head high and a little ahead of him, ready to make short chops.

Vlana stood up in the sleigh, steel flashing in her hand. She made as if to hurl it, then paused uncertainly.

Hrey rose from his bush, an arrow nocked to his bow.

Fafhrd could have killed him, by hurling his sword spearwise if in no other way. But the sense of Death beside him was still paralyzingly strong, and the sense of being in the White Ice Spider's great womblike trap. Besides, what did he really feel toward Vellix, or even Nalgron?

The bowstring twanged. Vellix paused in his fencing, transfixed. The arrow had struck him in the back, to one side of his spine, and protruded from his chest, just below the breastbone.

With a chop of the axe, Hringorl knocked the sword from the dying man's grip as he started to fall. He gave another of his great, harsh laughs. He turned toward the sleigh.

Vlana screamed.

Before he quite realized it, Fafhrd had silently drawn his sword from its well-oiled sheath and, using it as a stick, pushed off down the white slope. His skis sang very faintly, though very high-pitched, against the snow crust.

Death no longer stood at his side. Death had stepped inside him. It was Death's feet that were lashed to the skis. It was Death who felt the White Spider's trap to be home.

Hrey turned, just in convenient time for Fafhrd's blade to open the side of his neck in a deep, slicing thrust that slit gullet as well as jugular. His sword came away almost before the gushing blood, black in the moonlight, had wet it, and certainly before Hrey had lifted his great hands in a futile effort to stop the great choking flow. It all happened very easily. His skis had thrust, Fafhrd told himself, not he. His skis, that had their own life, Death's life, and were carrying him on a most doomful journey.

Harrax, too, as if a very puppet of the gods, finished unlacing his skis and rose and turned just in time for Fafhrd's thrust, made upward from a crouch, to take him high in the guts, just as his arrow had taken Vellix, but in reverse direction.

The sword grated against Harrax' spine, but came out easily. Fafhrd sped downhill with hardly a check. Harrax stared wide-eyed after him. The great brute's mouth was wide open, too, but no sound came from it. Likely the thrust had sliced a lung and his heart as well, or else some of the great vessels springing from it.

And now Fafhrd's sword was pointed straight at the back of Hringorl, who was preparing to mount into the sleigh, and the skis were speeding the bloody blade faster and faster.

Vlana stared at Fafhrd over Hringorl's shoulder, as if she were looking at the approach of Death himself, and she screamed.

Hringorl swung around and instantly raised his axe to strike Fafhrd's sword aside. His wide face had the alert, yet sleepy look of one who has stared at Death many times and is never surprised by the sudden appearance of the Killer of All.

Fafhrd braked and turned so that, his rush slowing, he went past the back end of the sleigh. His sword strained all the while toward Hringorl without quite reaching him. It evaded the chop Hringorl made at it.

Then Fafhrd saw, just ahead, the sprawled body of Vellix. He made a right-angle turn, braking instantly, even thrusting his sword into the snow so that it struck sparks from the rock below, to keep from tumbling over the corpse.

He wrenched his body around then, as far as he could when his feet were still lashed to the skis, just in time to see Hringorl rushing down on him, out of the snow thrown up by the skis, and aiming his axe in a great blow at Fafhrd's neck.

Fafhrd parried the blow with his sword. Held at right angle to the sweep of the axe, the blade would have been shattered, but Fafhrd held his sword at just the proper angle for the axe to be deflected with a screech of steel and go whistling over his head.

Hringorl louted past him, unable to stop his rush.

Fafhrd again wrenched around his body, cursing the skis that now nailed his feet to the earth. His thrust was too late to reach Hringorl.

The thicker man turned and came rushing back, aiming another axe-swipe. This time the only way Fafhrd could dodge it was by falling flat on the ground.

He glimpsed two streakings of moonlit steel. Then he used his sword to thrust himself to his feet, ready for another blow at Hringorl, or another dodge, if there was time.

The big man had dropped his axe and was clawing at his own face.

Lunging by making a clumsy sidewise step with his ski—no place this for style!—Fafhrd ran him through the heart.

Hringorl dropped his hands as his body pitched over backward. From his right eye socket protruded the silver pommel and black grip of a dagger. Fafhrd wrenched out his sword. Hringorl hit with a great soft thud and an out-blow of snow around him, writhed violently twice, and was still.

Fafhrd poised his sword and his gaze darted around. He was ready for any other attack, by anyone at all.

But not one of the five bodies moved—the two at his feet, the two sprawled on the slope, nor

Vlana's erect in the sleigh. With a little surprise he realized that the gasping he heard was his own breath. Otherwise the only sound was a faint, high tinkling, which for the present he ignored. Even Vellix' two horses hitched to the sleigh and Hringorl's big mount, standing a short way up the Old Road, were unaccountably silent.

He leaned back against the sleigh, resting his left arm on the icy tarpaulin covering the rockets and other gear. His right hand still held his sword poised, a little negligently now, but ready.

He inspected the bodies once more, ending at Vlana's. Still none of them had moved. Each of the first four was surrounded by its blotches of blood-blackened snow, huge for Hrey, Harrax, and Hringorl, tiny for the arrow-slain Vellix.

He fixed his gaze on Vlana's staring, white-rimmed eyes. Controlling his breath, he said, "I owe you thanks for slaying Hringorl. Perhaps. I doubt I could have bested him, he on his feet, I on my back. But was your knife aimed at Hringorl, or at my back? And did I 'scape death simply by falling, while the knife passed over me to strike down another man?"

She answered not a word. Instead her hands flew up to press her cheeks and lips. She continued to stare, now over her fingers, at Fafhrd.

He continued, his voice growing still more casual, "You chose Vellix over me, after making me a promise. Why not Hringorl then over Vellix—and over me—when Hringorl seemed the likelier man to win? Why didn't you help Vellix with your knife, when he so bravely tackled Hringorl? Why did you scream when you saw me, spoiling my chance to kill Hringorl with one silent thrust?"

He emphasized each question by idly poking his sword in her direction. His breath was coming easily now, weariness departing from his body even as black depression filled his mind.

Vlana slowly took her hands from her lips and swallowed twice. Then she said, her voice harsh, but clear, and not very loud, "A woman must always keep all ways open, can you understand that? Only by being ready to league with any man, and discard one for another as fortune shifts the plan, can she begin to counter men's great advantage. I chose Vellix over you because his experience was greater and because—believe this or not, as you will—I did not think a partner of mine would have much chance for long life and I wanted you to live. I did not help Vellix here at the roadblock because I thought then that he and I were doomed. The roadblock and from it the knowledge that there must be ambushers around it cowed me—though Vellix seemed not to think so, or to care. As for my screaming when I saw you, I did not recognize you. I thought you were Death himself."

"Well, it appears I was," Fafhrd commented softly, looking around for a third time at the scattered corpses. He unlashed his skis. Then, after stamping his feet, he kneeled by Hringorl and jerked the dagger from his eye and wiped it on the dead man's furs.

Vlana continued, "And I fear death even more than I detested Hringorl. Yes, I would eagerly flee with Hringorl, if it were away from death."

"This time Hringorl was headed in the wrong direction," Fafhrd commented, hefting the dagger. It balanced well for thrusting or throwing.

Vlana said, "Now of course I'm yours. Eagerly and happily—again believe it or not. If you'll have me. Perhaps you still think I tried to kill you."

Fafhrd turned toward her and tossed the dagger. "Catch," he said. She caught.

He laughed and said, "No, a showgirl who's also been a thief would be apt to be expert at knifethrowing. And I doubt that Hringorl was struck in his brains through his eye by accident. Are you still minded to have revenge on the Thieves' Guild?"

"I am," she answered.

Fafhrd said, "Women are horrible. I mean, quite as horrible as men. Oh, is there anyone in the wide world that has aught but ice water in his or her veins?"

And he laughed again, more loudly, as if knowing there could be no answer to that question. Then he wiped his sword on Hringorl's furs, thrust it in his scabbard, and without looking at Vlana strode past her and the silent horses to the pile of roll bushes and began to cast their remainder aside. They were frozen to each other and he had to tug and twist to get them loose, putting more effort into it, fighting the bushes more than he recalled Vellix having to do.

Vlana did not look at him, even as he passed. She was gazing straight up the slope with its sinuous ski track leading to the black tunnel-mouth of the Old Road. Her white gaze was not fixed on Harrax and Hrey, nor on the tunnel mouth. It went higher.

There was a faint tinkling that never stopped.

Then there was a crystal clatter and Fafhrd wrenched loose and hurled aside the last of the ice-weighted roll bushes.

He looked down the road leading south. To civilization, whatever that was worth now.

This road was a tunnel, too, between snow-shouldered pines.

And it was filled, the moonlight showed, with a web of crystals that seemed to go on forever, strands of ice stretching from twig to twig and bough to bough, depth beyond icy depth.

Fafhrd recalled his mother's words, *There is a witchy cold that can follow you anywhere in Nehwon. Wherever ice once went, witchery can send it again. Your father now bitterly regrets...*

He thought of a great white spider, spinning its frigid way around this clearing.

He saw Mor's face, beside Mara's, atop the precipice, the other side of the great leap.

He wondered what was being chanted now in the Tent of the Women, and if Mara was chanting too. Somehow he thought not.

Vlana cried out softly, "Women indeed are horrible. Look. Look. Look!"

At that instant, Hringorl's horse gave a great whinny. There was the pound of hooves as he fled up the Old Road.

An instant later, Vellix' horses reared and screamed.

Fafhrd smote the neck of the nearest horse with the outside of his arm. Then he looked toward the small, big-eyed, triangular white mask of Vlana's face and followed her gaze.

Growing up out of the slope that led to the Old Road were a half dozen tenuous forms high as trees. They looked like hooded women. They got solider and solider as Fafhrd watched.

He crouched down in terror. This movement caught his pouch between his belly and his thigh. He felt a faint warmth.

He sprang up and dashed back the way he had come. He ripped the tarpaulin off the back of the sleigh. He grabbed the eight remaining rockets one by one and thrust the tail of each into the snow so that their heads pointed at the vast, thickening ice-figures.

Then he reached in his pouch, took out his fire-pot, unthonged its top, shook off its gray ashes, shook its red ashes to one side of the bowl, and rapidly touched them to the fuses of the rockets.

Their multiple spluttering in his ears, he sprang into the sleigh.

Vlana did not move as he brushed her. But she chinked. She seemed to have put on a translucent cloak of ice crystals that held her where she stood. Reflected moonlight shone stolidly from the crystals. He felt it would move only as the moon moved.

He grabbed the reins. They stung his fingers like frozen iron. He could not stir them. The ice web ahead had grown around the horses. They were part of it—great equine statues enclosed in a greater crystal. One stood on four legs, one reared on two. The walls of the ice womb were closing in. *There is a witchy cold that can follow you....*

The first rocket roared, then the second. He felt their warmth. He heard the mighty tinkling as they struck their up-slope targets.

The reins moved, slapped the backs of the horses. There was a glassy smashing as they plunged forward. He ducked his head and, holding the reins in his left hand, swung up his right and dragged Vlana down into the seat. Her ice-cloak jingled madly and vanished. Four, five...

There was a continuous jangling as horses and sleigh shot forward through the ice web. Crystals showered onto and glanced off his ducked head. The jangling grew fainter. Seven, eight...

All icy constraints fell away. Hooves pounded. A great north wind sprang up, ending the calm of days. Ahead the sky was faintly pink with dawn. Behind, it was faintly red with fire of pine-needles ignited by the rockets. It seemed to Fafhrd that the north wind brought the roaring of flames.

He shouted, "Gnamph Nar, Mlurg Nar, great Kvarch Nar—we'll see them all! All the cities of the Forest Land! All the Land of the Eight Cities."

Beside him Vlana stirred warm under his embracing arm and took up his cry with, "Sarheenmar, Ilthmar, Lankhmar! All the cities of the south! Quarmall! Horborixen! Slim-spired Tislinilit! The Rising Land."

It seemed to Fafhrd that mirages of all those unknown cities and places filled the brightening horizon. "Travel, love, adventure, the world!" he shouted, hugging Vlana to him with his right arm while his left slapped the horses with the reins.

He wondered why, although his imagination was roaringly aflame like the canyon behind him, his heart was still so cold.

FRITZ LEIBER'S LANKHMAR

THE UNHOLY GRAIL

III

THREE THINGS WARNED the wizard's apprentice that something was wrong: first the deep-trodden prints of iron-shod hooves along the forest path—he sensed them through his boots before stooping to feel them out in the dark; next, the eerie drone of a bee unnaturally abroad by night; and finally, a faint aromatic odor of burning. Mouse raced ahead, dodging treetrunks and skipping over twisted roots by memory and by a bat's feeling for rebounding whispers of sound. Gray leggings, tunic, peaked hood and streaming cloak made the slight youth, skinny with asceticism, seem like a rushing shadow.

The exaltation Mouse had felt at the successful completion of his long quest and his triumphal return to this sorcerous master, Glavas Rho, now vanished from his mind and gave way to a fear he hardly dared put into thoughts. Harm to the great wizard, whose mere apprentice he was?—"My Gray Mouse, still midway in his allegiance between white magic and black," Glavas Rho had once put it—no, it was unthinkable that that great figure of wisdom and spiritual might should come to harm. The great magician…(There was something hysterical about the way Mouse insisted on that "great," for to the world Glavas Rho was but a hedge-wizard, no better than a Mingol necromancer with his second-sighted spotted dog or a conjurer beggar of Quarmall)…the great magician and his dwelling were alike protected by strong enchantments no impious outsider could breach—not even (the heart of Mouse skipped a beat) the lord paramount of these forests, Duke Janarrl, who hated all magic, but white worse than black.

And yet the smell of burning was stronger now and Glavas Rho's low cottage was built of resinous wood.

There also vanished from Mouse's mind the vision of a girl's face, perpetually frightened yet sweet—that of Duke Janarrl's daughter Ivrian, who came secretly to study under Glavas Rho, figuratively sipping the milk of his white wisdom side by side with Mouse. Indeed, they had privately come to call each other Mouse and Misling, while under his tunic Mouse carried a plain green glove he had teased from Ivrian when he set forth on his quest, as if he were her armored and beweaponed knight and not a swordless wizardling.

By the time Mouse reached the hilltop clearing he was breathing hard, not from exertion.

There the gathering light showed him at a glance the hoof-hacked garden of magic herbs, the overturned straw beehive, the great flare of soot sweeping up the smooth surface of the vast granite boulder that sheltered the wizard's tiny house.

But even without the dawn light he would have seen the fire-shrunken beams and fire-gnawed posts a-creep with red ember-worms and the wraith-like green flame where some stubborn sorcerous ointment still burned. He would have smelled the confusion of precious odors of burned drugs and balms and the horribly appetizing kitchen-odor of burned flesh.

His whole lean body winced. Then, like a hound getting the scent, he darted forward.

The wizard lay just inside the buckled door. And he had fared as his house: the beams of his body bared and blackened; the priceless juices and subtle substances boiled, burned, destroyed forever or streamed upward to some cold hell beyond the moon.

From all around came very faintly a low sad hum, as the unhoused bees mourned.

Memories fled horror-stricken through Mouse's mind: these shriveled lips softly chanting incantations, those charred fingers pointing at the stars or stroking a small woodland animal.

Trembling, Mouse drew from the leather pouch at his belt a flat green stone, engraved on the one side with deep-cut alien hieroglyphs, on the other with an armored, many-jointed monster, like a giant ant, that trod among tiny fleeing human figures. That stone had been the object of the quest on which Glavas Rho had sent him. For sake of it, he had rafted across the Lakes of Pleea, tramped the foothills of the Mountains of Hunger, hidden from a raiding party of red-bearded pirates, tricked lumpish peasant-fishermen, flattered and flirted with an elderly odorous witch, robbed a tribal shrine, and eluded hounds set on his trail. His winning the green stone without shedding blood meant that he had advanced another grade in his apprenticeship. Now he gazed dully at its ancient surface and then, his trembling controlled, laid it carefully on his master's blackened palm. As he stooped he realized that the soles of his feet were painfully hot, his boots smoldering a little at the edges, yet he did not hurry his steps as he moved away.

It was lighter now and he noticed little things, such as the anthill by the threshold. The master had studied the black-armored creatures as intently as he had their cousin bees. Now it was deeply dented by a great heelmark showing a semicircle of pits made by spikes—yet something was moving. Peering closely he saw a tiny heat-maimed warrior struggling over the sand-grains. He remembered the monster on the green stone and shrugged at a thought that led nowhere.

He crossed the clearing through the mourning bees to where pale light showed between the treetrunks and soon was standing, hand resting on a gnarly bole, at a point where the hillside sloped sharply away. In the wooded valley below was a serpent of milky mist, indicating the course of the stream that wound through it. The air was heavy with the dissipating smoke of darkness. The horizon was edged to the right with red from the coming sun. Beyond it, Mouse knew, lay more forest and then the interminable grain fields and marshes of Lankhmar and beyond even those the ancient world-center of Lankhmar city, which Mouse had never seen, yet whose Overlord ruled in theory even this far.

But near at hand, outlined by the sunrise red, was a bundle of jagged-topped towers—the stronghold of Duke Janarrl. A wary animation came into Mouse's masklike face. He thought of the spiked heelmark, the hacked turf, the trail of hoofmarks leading down this slope. Everything pointed to the wizard-hating Janarrl as the author of the atrocity behind him, except that, still revering his master's skills as matchless, Mouse did not understand how the Duke had broken through the enchantments, strong enough to dizzy the keenest woodsman, which had protected Glavas Rho's abode for many a year.

He bowed his head...and saw, lying lightly on the springing grassblades, a plain green glove. He snatched it up and digging in his tunic drew forth another glove, darkly mottled and streakily bleached by sweat, and held them side by side. They were mates.

His lips writhed back from his teeth and his gaze went again to the distant stronghold. Then he unseated a thick round of scraggy bark from the treetrunk he'd been touching and delved shoulder-deep in the black cavity revealed. As he did these things with a slow tense automatism, the words came back to him of a reading Glavas Rho had smilingly given him over a meal of milkless gruel.

"Mouse," the mage had said, firelight dancing on his short white beard, "when you stare your eyes like that and flare your nostrils, you are too much like a cat for me to credit you will ever be a sheepdog of the truth. You are a middling dutiful scholar, but secretly you favor swords over wands. You are more tempted by the hot lips of black magic than the chaste slim fingers of white, no matter to how pretty a misling the latter belong—no, do not deny it! You are more drawn to the beguiling sinuosities of the left-hand path than the straight steep road of the right. I fear me you will never be mouse in the end but mouser. And never white but gray—oh well, that's better than black. Now, wash up these bowls and go breathe an hour on the newborn ague-plant, for 'tis a chill night, and remember to talk kindly to the thorn bush."

The remembered words grew faint, but did not fade, as Mouse drew from the hole a leather belt furred green with mold and dangling from it a moldy scabbard. From the latter he drew, seizing it by the thong-wrapped grip, a tapering bronze sword showing more verdigris than metal. His eyes grew wide, but pinpoint-pupiled, and his face yet more masklike, as he held the pale-green, brown-edged blade against the red hump of the rising sun.

From across the valley came faintly the high, clear, ringing note of a hunting horn, calling men to the chase.

Abruptly Mouse strode off down the slope, cutting over to the trail of the hooves, moving with long hasty strides and a little stiff-leggedly, as if drunk, and buckling around his waist as he went the mold-furred sword-belt.

A dark four-footed shape rushed across the sun-specked forest glade, bearing down the underbrush with its broad low chest and trampling it with its narrow cloven hooves. From behind sounded the notes of a horn and the harsh shouts of men. At the far edge of the glade, the boar turned. Breath whistled through its nostrils and it swayed. Then its half-glazed little eyes fixed on the figure of a man on horseback. It turned toward him and some trick of the sunlight made its pelt grow blacker. Then it charged. But before the terrible up-turning tusks could find flesh to slash, a heavy-bladed spear bent like a bow against the knob of its shoulder and it went crashing over half backward, its blood spattering the greenery.

Huntsmen clad in brown and green appeared in the glade, some surrounding the fallen boar with a wall of spear points, others hurrying up to the man on the horse. He was clad in rich garments of yellow and brown. He laughed, tossed one of his huntsmen the bloodied spear and accepted a silver-worked leather wine flask from another.

A second rider appeared in the glade and the Duke's small yellow eyes clouded under the tangled brows. He drank deep and wiped his lips with the back of his sleeve. The huntsmen were warily closing their spear-wall on the boar, which lay rigid but with head lifted a finger's breadth off the turf, its only movements the darting of its gaze from side to side and the pulse of bright blood from its shoulder. The spear-wall was about to close when Janarrl waved the huntsmen to a halt.

"Ivrian!" he called harshly to the newcomer. "You had two chances at the beast, but you flinched. Your cursed dead mother would already have sliced thin and tasted the beast's raw heart."

His daughter stared at him miserably. She was dressed as the huntsmen and rode astride with a sword at her side and a spear in her hand, but it only made her seem more the thin-faced, spindle-armed girl.

"You are a milksop, a wizard-loving coward," Janarrl continued. "Your abominable mother would have faced the boar a-foot and laughed when its blood gushed in her face. Look here, this boar is scotched. It cannot harm you. Drive your spear into it now! I command you!"

The huntsmen broke their spear-wall and drew back to either side, making a path between the boar and the girl. They sniggered openly at her and the Duke smiled at them approvingly. The girl hesitated, sucking at her underlip, staring with fear and fascination too at the beast which eyed her, head still just a-lift.

"Drive in your spear!" Janarrl repeated, sucking quickly at the flask. "Do so, or I will whip you here and now."

Then she touched her heels to the horse's flanks and cantered down the glade, her body bent low, the spear trained at its target. But at the last instant its point swerved aside and gouged the dirt. The boar had not moved. The huntsmen laughed raucously.

Janarrl's wide face reddened with anger as he whipped out suddenly and trapped her wrist, tightened on it. "Your damned mother could cut men's throats and not change color. I'll see you flesh your spear in that carcass, or I'll make you dance, here and now, as I did last night, when you told me the wizard's spells and the place of his den."

He leaned closer and his voice sank to a whisper. "Know, chit, that I've long suspected that your mother, fierce as she could be, was perhaps ensorceled against her will—a wizard-lover like yourself...and you the whelp of that burned charmer."

Her eyes widened and she started to pull away from him, but he drew her closer. "Have no fear, chit, I'll work the taint out of your flesh one way or another. For a beginning, prick me that boar!"

She did not move. Her face was a cream-colored mask of fear. He raised his hand. But at that moment there was an interruption.

A figure appeared at the edge of the glade at the point where the boar had turned to make its last charge. It was that of a slim youth, dressed all in gray. Like one drugged or in a trance, he walked straight toward Janarrl. The three huntsmen who had been attending the Duke drew swords and moved leisurely toward him.

The youth's face was white and tensed, his forehead beaded with sweat under the gray hood half thrown back. Jaw muscles made ivory knobs. His eyes, fixed on the Duke, squinted as if they looked at the blinding sun.

His lips parted wide, showing his teeth. "Slayer of Glavas Rho! Wizard-killer!"

Then his bronze sword was out of its moldy scabbard. Two of the huntsmen moved in his way, one of them crying, "Beware poison!" at the green of the newcomer's blade. The youth aimed a terrific blow at him, handling his sword as if it were a sledge. The huntsman parried it with ease, so that it whistled over his head, and the youth almost fell with the force of his own blow. The huntsman stepped forward and with a snappy stroke rapped the youth's sword near the hilt to disarm him, and the fight was done before begun—almost. For the glazed look left the youth's eyes and his features twitched like those of a cat and, recovering his grip on his sword, he lunged forward with a twisting motion at the wrist that captured the huntsman's blade in his own green one and whipped it out of its startled owner's grasp. Then he continued his lunge straight toward the heart of the second huntsman, who escaped only by collapsing backward to the turf.

Janarrl leaned forward tensely in his saddle, muttering, "The whelp has fangs," but at that instant the third huntsman, who had circled past, struck the youth with sword-pommel on the back of his neck. The youth dropped his sword, swayed and started to fall, but the first huntsman grabbed him by the neck of his tunic and hurled him toward his companions. They received him in their own jocular fashion with cuffs and slaps, slashing his head and ribs with sheathed daggers, eventually letting him fall to the ground, kicking him, worrying him like a pack of hounds.

Janarrl sat motionless, watching his daughter. He had not missed her frightened start of recognition when the youth appeared. Now he saw her lean forward, lips twitching. Twice she started to speak. Her horse moved uneasily and whinnied. Finally she hung her head and cowered back while low retching sobs came from her throat. Then Janarrl gave a satisfied grunt and called out, "Enough for the present! Bring him here!"

Two huntsmen dragged between them the half-fainting youth clad now in red-spattered gray.

"Coward," said the Duke. "This sport will not kill you. They were only gentling you in preparation for other sports. But I forget you are a pawky wizardling, an effeminate creature who babbles spells in the dark and curses behind the back, a craven who fondles animals and would make the forests mawkish places. Faught! My teeth are on edge. And yet you sought to corrupt my daughter and— Hearken to me, wizardling, I say!" And leaning low from his saddle he caught the youth's sagging head by the hair, tangling in his fingers. The youth's eyes rolled wildly and he gave a convulsive jerk that took the huntsmen by surprise and almost tumbled Janarrl out of the saddle.

Just then there was an ominous crackling of underbrush and the rapid thud of hooves. Someone cried, "Have a care, master! Oh Gods, guard the Duke!"

The wounded boar had lurched to its feet and was charging the group by Janarrl's horse.

The huntsmen scattered back, snatching for their weapons.

Janarrl's horse shied, further overbalancing its rider. The boar thundered past, like red-smeared midnight. Janarrl almost fell atop it. The boar swung sharply around for a return charge, evading three thrown spears that thudded into the earth just beside it. Janarrl tried to stand, but one of his feet was snagged in a stirrup and his horse, jerking clear, tumbled him again.

The boar came on, but other hooves were thudding now. Another horse swept past Janarrl and a firmly-held spear entered near the boar's shoulder and buried itself deep. The black beast, jarred backward, slashed once at the spear with its tusk, fell heavily on its side and was still.

Then Ivrian let go the spear. The arm with which she had been holding it dangled unnaturally. She slumped in her saddle, catching its pommel with her other hand.

Janarrl scrambled to his feet, eyed his daughter and the boar. Then his gaze traveled slowly around the glade, full circle.

Glavas Rho's apprentice was gone.

"North be south, east be west. Copse be glade and gully crest. Dizziness all paths invest. Leaves and grasses, do the rest."

Mouse mumbled the chant through swollen lips almost as though he were talking into the ground on which he lay. His fingers arranging themselves into cabalistic symbols, he thumbed a pinch of green powder from a tiny pouch and tossed it into the air with a wrist-flick that made him wince. "Know it, hound, you are wolf-born, enemy to whip and horn. Horse, think of the unicorn, uncaught since the primal morn. Weave off from me, by the Norn!"

The charm completed, he lay still and the pains in his bruised flesh and bones became more bearable. He listened to the sounds of the hunt trail off in the distance.

His face was pushed close to a patch of grass. He saw an ant laboriously climb a blade, fall to the ground, and then continue on its way. For a moment he felt a bond of kinship between himself and the tiny insect. He remembered the black boar whose unexpected charge had given him a chance to escape and for a strange moment his mind linked it with the ant.

Vaguely he thought of the pirates who had threatened his life in the west. But their gay ruthlessness had been a different thing from the premeditated and presavored brutality of Janarrl's huntsmen.

Gradually anger and hate began to swirl in him. He saw the gods of Glavas Rho, their formerly serene faces white and sneering. He heard the words of the old incantations, but they twanged with a new meaning. Then these visions receded, and he saw only a whirl of grinning faces and cruel hands. Somewhere in it the white, guilt-stricken face of a girl. Swords, sticks, whips. All spinning. And at the center, like the hub of a wheel on which men are broken, the thick strong form of the Duke.

What was the teaching of Glavas Rho to that wheel? It had rolled over him and crushed him. What was white magic to Janarrl and his henchmen? Only a priceless parchment to be besmirched. Magic gems to be trampled in filth. Thoughts of deep wisdom to be pulped with their encasing brain.

But there was the other magic. The magic Glavas Rho had forbidden, sometimes smilingly but always with an underlying seriousness. The magic Mouse had learned of only by hints and warnings. The magic which stemmed from death and hate and pain and decay, which dealt in poisons and night-shrieks, which trickled down from the black spaces between the stars, which, as Janarrl himself had said, cursed in the dark behind the back.

It was as if all Mouse's former knowledge—of small creatures and stars and beneficial sorceries and Nature's codes of courtesy—burned in one swift sudden holocaust. And the black ashes took life and began to stir, and from them crept a host of night shapes, resembling those which had been burned, but all distorted. Creeping, skulking, scurrying shapes. Heartless, all hate and terror, but as lovely to look on as black spiders swinging along their geometrical webs.

To sound a hunting horn for that pack! To set them on the track of Janarrl!

Deep in his brain an evil voice began to whisper, "The Duke must die. The Duke must die." And he knew that he would always hear that voice, until its purpose was fulfilled.

Laboriously he pushed himself up, feeling a stabbing pain that told of broken ribs; he wondered how he had managed to flee this far. Grinding his teeth, he stumbled across a clearing. By the time he had gotten into the shelter of the trees again, the pain had forced him to his hands and knees. He crawled on a little way, then collapsed.

Near evening of the third day after the hunt, Ivrian stole down from her tower room, ordered the smirking groom to fetch her horse, and rode through the valley and across the stream and up the opposite hill until she reached the rock-sheltered house of Glavas Rho. The destruction she saw brought new misery to her white taut face. She dismounted and went close to the fire-gutted ruin, trembling lest she come upon the body of Glavas Rho. But it was not there. She could see that the ashes had been disturbed, as though someone had been searching through them and sifting them for any objects that might have escaped the flames. Everything was very quiet.

An inequality in the ground off toward the side of the clearing caught her eye and she walked in that direction. It was a new-made grave, and in place of a headstone was, set around with gray pebbles, a small flat greenish stone with strange carvings on its surface.

A sudden little sound from the forest set her trembling and made her realize that she was very much afraid, only that up to this point her misery had outweighed her terror. She looked up and gave a gasping cry, for a face was peering at her through a hole in the leaves. It was a wild face, smeared with dirt and grass stains, smirched here and there with old patches of dried blood, shadowed by a stubble of beard. Then she recognized it.

"Mouse," she called haltingly.

She hardly knew the answering voice.

"So you have returned to gloat over the wreckage caused by your treachery."

"No, Mouse, no!" she cried. "I did not intend this. You must believe me."

"Liar! It was your father's men who killed him and burned his house."

"But I never thought they would!"

"Never thought they would—as if that's any excuse. You are so afraid of your father that you would tell him anything. You live by fear."

"Not always, Mouse. In the end I killed the boar."

"So much the worse—killing the beast the gods had sent to kill your father."

"But truly I never killed the boar. I was only boasting when I said so—I thought you liked me brave. I have no memory of that killing. My mind went black. I think my dead mother entered me and drove the spear."

"Liar and changer of lies! But I'll amend my judgment: you live by fear except when your father whips you to courage. I should have realized that and warned Glavas Rho against you. But I had dreams about you."

"You called me Misling," she said faintly.

"Aye, we played at being mice, forgetting cats are real. And then while I was away, you were fright-

ened by mere whippings into betraying Glavas Rho
to your father!"

"Mouse, do not condemn me." Ivrian was sobbing. "I know that my life has been nothing but fear.
Ever since I was a child my father has tried to force
me to believe that cruelty and hate are the laws of the
universe. He has tortured and tormented me. There
was no one to whom I could turn, until I found Glavas
Rho and learned that the universe has laws of sympathy and love that shape even death and the seeming
hates. But now Glavas Rho is dead and I am more
frightened and alone than ever. I need your help,
Mouse. You studied under Glavas Rho. You know his
teachings. Come and help me."

His laughter mocked her. "Come out and be
betrayed? Be whipped again while you look on? Listen to your sweet lying voice, while your father's
huntsmen creep closer? No, I have other plans."

"Plans?" she questioned. Her voice was apprehensive. "Mouse, your life is in danger so long as
you lurk here. My father's men are sworn to slay you
on sight. I would die, I tell you, if they caught you.
Don't delay, get away. Only tell me first that you do
not hate me." And she moved toward him.

Again his laughter mocked her.

"You are beneath my hate," came the stinging words. "I feel only contempt for your cowardly
weakness. Glavas Rho talked too much of love.
There are laws of hate in the universe, shaping even
its loves, and it is time I made them work for me.
Come no closer! I do not intend to betray my plans
to you, or my new hidey holes. But this much I will
tell you, and listen well. In seven days your father's
torment begins."

"My father's torments——? Mouse, Mouse, listen to me. I want to question you about more than Glavas Rho's teachings. I want to question you about Glavas Rho. My father hinted to me that he knew my mother, that he was perchance my very father."

This time there was a pause before the mocking laughter, but when it came, it was doubled. "Good, good, good! It pleasures me to think that Old White-beard enjoyed life a little before he became so wise, wise, wise. I dearly hope he did tumble your mother. That would explain his nobility. Where so much love was—love for each creature ever born—there must have been lust and guilt before. Out of that encounter—and all your mother's evil—his white magic grew. It is true! Guilt and white magic side by side—and the gods never lied! Which leaves you the daughter of Glavas Rho, betraying your true father to his sooty death."

And then his face was gone and the leaves framed only a dark hole. She blundered into the forest after him, calling out "Mouse! Mouse!" and trying to follow the receding laughter. But it died away, and she found herself in a gloomy hollow, and she began to realize how evil the apprentice's laughter had sounded, as if he laughed at the death of all love, or even its unbirth. Then panic seized her, and she fled back through the undergrowth, brambles catching at her clothes and twigs stinging her cheeks, until she had regained the clearing and was galloping back through the dusk, a thousand fears besetting her and her heart sick with the thought there was now no one in the wide world who did not hate and despise her.

When she reached the stronghold, it seemed to crouch above her like an ugly jag-crested monster, and when she passed through the great gateway, it seemed to her that the monster had gobbled her up forever.

Come nightfall on the seventh day, when dinner was being served in the great banquet hall, with much loud talk and crunching of rushes and clashing of silver plates, Janarrl stifled a cry of pain and clapped his hand to his heart.

"It is nothing," he said a moment later to the thin-faced henchman sitting at his side. "Give me a cup of wine! That will stop it twinging."

But he continued to look pale and ill at ease, and he ate little of the meat that was served up in great smoking slices. His eyes kept roving about the table, finally settling on his daughter.

"Stop staring at me in that gloomy way, girl!" he called. "One would think that you had poisoned my wine and were watching to see green spots come out on me. Or red ones edged with black, belike."

This bought a general guffaw of laughter which seemed to please the Duke, for he tore off the wing of a fowl and gnawed at it hungrily, but the next moment he gave another sudden cry of pain, louder than the first, staggered to his feet, clawed convulsively at his chest, and then pitched over on the table, where he lay groaning and writhing in his pain.

"The Duke is stricken," the thin-faced henchman announced quite unnecessarily and yet most portentously after bending over him. "Carry him to bed. One of you loosen his shirt. He gasps for air."

A flurry of whispering went up and down the table. As the great door to his private apartments was opened for the Duke, a heavy gust of chill air made the torches flicker and turn blue, so that shadows crowded into the hall. Then one torch flared white-bright as a star, showing the face of a girl. Ivrian felt the others draw away from her with suspicious glances and mutterings, as if they were certain there had been truth in the Duke's jest. She did not look up. After a while someone came and told her that the Duke commanded her presence. Without a word she rose and followed.

The Duke's face was gray and furrowed with pain, but he had control of himself, though with each breath his hand tightened convulsively on the edge of the bed until his knuckles were like knobs of rock. He was propped up with pillows and a furred robe had been tucked closely about his shoulders and long-legged braziers glowed around the bed. In spite of all he was shivering convulsively.

"Come here, girl," he ordered in a low, labored voice that hissed against his drawn lips. "You know what has happened. My heart pains as though there were a fire under it and yet my skin is cased in ice. There is a stabbing in my joints as if long needles pierced clear through the marrow. It is wizard's work."

"Wizard's work, beyond doubt," confirmed Giscorl, the thin-faced henchman, who stood at the head of the bed. "And there is no need to guess who. That young serpent whom you did not kill quickly enough ten days ago! He's been reported skulking in the woods, aye, and talking to…certain ones," he added, eyeing Ivrian narrowly, suspiciously.

A spasm of agony shook the Duke. "I should have stamped out whelp with sire," he groaned. Then his eyes shifted back to Ivrian. "Look, girl, you've been seen poking about in the forest where the old wizard was killed. It's believed you talked with his cub."

Ivrian wet her lips, tried to speak, shook her head. She could feel her father's eyes probing into her. Then his fingers reached out and twisted themselves in her hair.

"I believe you're in league with him!" His whisper was like a rusty knife. "You're helping him do this to me. Admit it! Admit!" And he thrust her cheek against the nearest brazier so that her hair smoked and her "No!" became a shuddering scream. The brazier swayed and Giscorl steadied it. Through Ivrian's scream the Duke snarled, "Your mother once held red coals to prove her honor."

A ghostly blue flame ran up Ivrian's hair. The Duke jerked her from the brazier and fell back against the pillows.

"Send her away," he finally whispered faintly, each word an effort. "She's a coward and wouldn't dare to hurt even me. Meantime, Giscorl, send out more men to hunt through the woods. They must find his lair before dawn, or I'll rupture my heart withstanding the pain."

Curtly Giscorl motioned Ivrian toward the door. She cringed, and slunk from the room, fighting down tears. Her cheek pulsed with pain. She was not aware of the strangely speculative smile with which the hawk-faced henchman watched her out.

Ivrian stood at the narrow window of her room watching the little bands of horsemen come and go, their torches glowing like will-o'-the-wisps in the woods. The stronghold was full of mysterious movement. The very stones seemed restlessly alive, as if they shared the torment of their master.

She felt herself drawn toward a certain point out there in the darkness. A memory kept recurring to her of how one day Glavas Rho had showed her a small cavern in the hillside and had warned her that it was an evil place, where much baneful sorcery had been done in the past. Her fingertips moved around the crescent-shaped blister on her cheek and over the rough streak in her hair.

Finally her uneasiness and the pull from the night became too strong for her. She dressed in the dark and edged open the door of her chamber. The corridor seemed for the moment deserted. She hurried along it, keeping close to the wall, and darted down the worn rounded hummocks of the stone stair. The tramp of footsteps sent her hurrying into a niche, where she cowered while two huntsmen strode glum-faced toward the Duke's chamber. They were dust-stained and stiff from riding.

"No one'll find him in all that dark," one of them muttered. "It's like hunting an ant in a cellar."

The other nodded. "And wizards can change landmarks and make forest paths turn on themselves, so that all searchers are befuddled."

As soon as they were past Ivrian hastened into the banquet hall, now dark and empty, and through the kitchen with its high brick ovens and its huge copper kettles glinting in the shadows.

Outside in the courtyard torches were flaring and there was a bustle of activity as grooms brought fresh horses or led off spent ones, but she trusted to her huntsman's costume to let her pass unrecognized. Keeping to the shadows, she worked her way around to the stables. Her horse moved restlessly and neighed when she slipped into the stall but quieted at her low whisper. A few moments and it was saddled, and she was leading it around to the open fields at the back.

No searching parties seemed to be near, so she mounted and rode swiftly toward the wood.

Her mind was a storm of anxieties. She could not explain to herself how she had dared come this far, except that the attraction toward that point in the night—the cavern against which Glavas Rho had warned her—possessed a sorcerous insistence not to be denied.

Then, when the forest engulfed her, she suddenly felt that she was committing herself to the arms of darkness and putting behind forever the grim stronghold and its cruel occupants. The ceiling of leaves blotted out most of the stars. She trusted to a light rein on her horse to guide her straight. And in this she was successful, for within a half hour she reached a shallow ravine which led past the cavern she sought.

Now, for the first time, her horse became uneasy. It balked and uttered little whinnying cries of fear and tried repeatedly to turn off as she urged it along the ravine. Its pace slowed to a walk. Finally it refused to move further. Its ears were laid back and it was trembling all over.

Ivrian dismounted and moved on. The forest was portentously quiet, as if all animals and birds—even the insects—had gone. The darkness ahead was almost tangible, as if built of black bricks just beyond her hand.

Then Ivrian became aware of the green glow, vague and faint at first as the ghosts of an aurora. Gradually it grew brighter and acquired a flickering quality, as the leafy curtains between her and it became fewer. Suddenly she found herself staring directly at it—a thick, heavy, soot-edge flame that writhed instead of danced. If green slime could be transmuted to fire, it would have that look. It burned in the mouth of a shallow cavern.

Then, beside the flame, she saw the face of the apprentice of Glavas Rho, and in that instant an agony of horror and sympathy tore at her mind.

The face seemed inhuman—more a green mask of torment than anything alive. The cheeks were drawn in; the eyes were unnaturally wild; it was very pale, and dripping with cold sweat induced by intense inward effort. There was much suffering in it, but also much power—power to control the thick twisting shadows that seemed to crowd around the green flame, power to master the forces of hate that were being marshaled. At regular intervals the cracked lips moved and the arms and hands made set gestures.

It seemed to Ivrian that she heard the mellow voice of Glavas Rho repeating a statement he had once made to Mouse and to her. "None can use black magic without straining the soul to the uttermost—and staining it into the bargain. None can inflict suffering without enduring the same. None can send death by spells and sorcery without walking on the brink of death's own abyss, aye, and dripping his own blood into it. The forces black magic evokes are like two-edged poisoned swords with grips studded with scorpion stings. Only a strong man, leather-handed, in whom hate and evil are very powerful, can wield them, and he only for a space."

In Mouse's face Ivrian saw the living example of those words. Step by step she moved toward him, feeling no more power to control her movements than if she were in a nightmare. She became aware of shadowy presences, as if she were pushing her way through cobweb veils. She came so near that she could have reached out her hand and touched him, and still he did not notice her, as if his spirit were out beyond the stars, grappling the blackness there.

Then a twig snapped under her foot and Mouse sprang up with terrifying swiftness, the energy of every taut muscle released. He snatched up his sword and lunged at the intruder. But when the green blade was within a hand's breadth of Ivrian's throat, he checked it with an effort. He glared, lips drawn back from his teeth. Although he had checked his sword, he seemed only half to recognize her.

At that instant Ivrian was buffeted by a mighty gust of wind, which came from the mouth of the cavern, a strange wind, carrying shadows. The green fire burned low, running rapidly along the sticks that were its fuel, and almost snuffing out.

Then the wind ceased and the thick darkness lifted, to be replaced by a wan gray light heralding the dawn. The fire turned from green to yellow. The wizard's apprentice staggered, and the sword dropped from his fingers.

"Why did you come here?" he questioned thickly.

She saw how his face was wasted with hunger and hate, how his clothing bore the signs of many nights spent in the forest like an animal, under no roof. Then suddenly she realized that she knew the answer to his question.

"Oh, Mouse," she whispered, "let us go away from this place. Here is only horror." He swayed, and she caught hold of him. "Take me with you, Mouse," she said.

He stared frowningly into her eyes. "You do not hate me then, for what I have done to your father? Or what I have done to the teachings of Glavas

Rho?" he questioned puzzledly. "You are not afraid of me?"

"I am afraid of everything," she whispered, clinging to him. "I am afraid of you, yes, a great deal afraid. But that fear can be unlearned. Oh, Mouse, will you take me away?—to Lankhmar or to Earth's End?"

He took her by the shoulders. "I have dreamed of that," he said slowly. "But you..."

"Apprentice of Glavas Rho!" thundered a stern, triumphant voice. "I apprehend you in the name of Duke Janarrl for sorceries practiced on the Duke's body!"

Four huntsmen were springing forward from the undergrowth with swords drawn and Giscorl three paces behind them. Mouse met them halfway. They soon found that this time they were not dealing with a youth blinded by anger, but with a cold and cunning swordsman. There was a kind of magic in his primitive blade. He ripped up the arm of his first assailant with a well-judged thrust, disarmed the second with an unexpected twist, then coolly warded off the blows of the other two, retreating slowly. But other huntsmen followed the first four and circled around. Still fighting with terrible intensity and giving blow for blow, Mouse went down under the sheer weight of their attack. They pinioned his arms and dragged him to his feet. He was bleeding from a cut in the cheek, but he carried his head high, though it was beast-shaggy. His bloodshot eyes sought out Ivrian.

"I should have known," he said evenly, "that having betrayed Glavas Rho you would not rest until you had betrayed me. You did your work well, girl. I trust you take much pleasure in my death."

Giscorl laughed. Like a whip, the words of Mouse stung Ivrian. She could not meet his eyes. Then she became aware that there was a man on horseback behind Giscorl and, looking up, she saw that it was her father. His wide body was bent by pain. His face was a death's mask. It seemed a miracle that he managed to cling to the saddle.

"Quick, Giscorl!" he hissed.

But the thin-faced henchman was already sniffing around in the cavern's mouth like a well-trained ferret. He gave a cry of satisfaction and lifted down a little figure from a ledge above the fire, which he next stamped out. He carried the figure as gingerly as if it were made of cobweb. As he passed by her, Ivrian saw that it was a clay doll wide as it was tall and dressed in brown and yellow leaves, and that its features were a grotesque copy of her father's. It was pierced in several places by long bone needles.

"This is the thing, oh Master," said Giscorl, holding it up, but the Duke only repeated, "Quick, Giscorl!" The henchman started to withdraw the largest needle which pierced the doll's middle, but the Duke gasped in agony and cried, "Forget not the balm!" Whereupon Giscorl uncorked with his teeth and poured a large vial of sirupy liquid over the doll's body and the Duke sighed a little with relief. Then Giscorl very carefully withdrew the needles, one by one, and as each needle was withdrawn the Duke's breath whistled and he clapped his hand to his shoulder or thigh, as if it were from his own body that the needles were being drawn. After the last one was out, he sat slumped in his saddle for a long time. When he finally looked up the transformation that had taken place was astonishing. There was color in his face, and the lines of pain had vanished, and his voice was loud and ringing.

"Take the prisoner back to our stronghold to await our judgment," he cried. "Let this be a warning to all who would practice wizardry in our domain. Giscorl, you have proved yourself a faithful servant." His eyes rested on Ivrian. "You have played with witchcraft too often, girl, and need other instruction. As a beginning you will witness the punishment I shall visit on this foul wizardling."

"A small boon, oh Duke!" Mouse cried. He had been hoisted onto a saddle and his legs tied under the horse's belly. "Keep your foul, spying daughter out of my sight. And let her not look at me in my pain."

"Strike him in the lips, one of you," the Duke ordered. "Ivrian, ride close behind him—I command it."

Slowly the little cavalcade rode off toward the stronghold through the brightening dawn. Ivrian's horse had been brought to her and she took her place as bidden, sunk in a nightmare of misery and defeat. She seemed to see the pattern of her whole life laid out before her—past, present, and future—and it consisted of nothing but fear, loneliness, and pain. Even the memory of her mother, who had died when she was a little girl, was something that still brought a palpitation of panic to her heart: a bold, handsome woman, who always had a whip in her hand, and whom even her father had feared. Ivrian remembered how when the servants had brought word that her mother had broken her neck in a fall from a horse, her only emotion had been fear that they were lying to her, and that this was some new trick of her mother's to put her off guard, and that some new punishment would follow.

Then, from the day of her mother's death, her father had shown her nothing but a strangely perverse cruelty. Perhaps it was his disgust at not having a son that made him treat her like a cowardly boy instead of a girl and encourage his lowliest followers to maltreat her—from the maids who played at ghosts around her bed to the kitchen wenches who put frogs in her milk and nettles in her salad.

Sometimes it seemed to her that anger at not having a son was too weak an explanation for her father's cruelties, and that he was revenging himself through Ivrian on his dead wife, whom he had certainly feared and who still influenced his actions, since he had never married again or openly taken mistresses. Or perhaps there was truth in what he had said of her mother and Glavas Rho—no, surely that must be a wild imagining of his anger. Or perhaps, as he sometimes told her, he was trying to make her live up to her mother's vicious and blood-thirsty example, trying to recreate his hated and adored wife in the person of her daughter, and finding a queer pleasure in the refractoriness of the material on which he worked and the grotesquerie of the whole endeavor.

Then in Glavas Rho Ivrian had found a refuge. When she had first chanced upon the white-bearded old man in her lonely wanderings through the forest, he had been mending the broken leg of a fawn and he had spoken to her softly of the ways of kindness and of the brotherhood of all life, human and animal. And she had come back day after day to hear her own vague intuitions revealed to her as deep truths and to take refuge in his wide sympathy. . . and to explore her timid friendship with his clever little apprentice. But now Glavas Rho was dead and Mouse had taken the spider's way, or the snake's track, or the cat's path, as the old wizard had some-times referred to bale magic.

She looked up and saw Mouse riding a little ahead and to one side of her, his hands bound behind him, his head and body bowed forward. Conscience smote her, for she knew she had been responsible for his capture. But worse than conscience was the pang of lost opportunity, for there ahead of her rode, doomed, the one man who might have saved her from her life.

A narrowing of the path brought her close beside him. She said hurriedly, ashamedly, "If there is anything I can do so that you will forgive me a little…"

The glance he bent on her, looking sidewise up, was sharp, appraising, and surprisingly alive.

"Perhaps you can," he murmured softly, so the huntsmen ahead might not hear. "As you must know, your father will have me tortured to death. You will be asked to watch it. Do just that. Keep your eyes riv-eted on mine the whole time. Sit close beside your father. Keep your hand on his arm. Aye, kiss him too. Above all, show no sign of fright or revulsion. Be like a statue carved of marble. Watch to the end. One other thing—wear, if you can, a gown of your mother's, or if not a gown, then some article of her clothing." He smiled at her thinly. "Do this and I will at least have the consolation of watching you flinch—and flinch—and flinch!"

"No mumbling charms now!" cried the hunts-man suddenly, jerking Mouse's horse ahead.

Ivrian reeled as if she had been struck in the face. She had thought her misery could go no deeper, but Mouse's words had beaten it down a final notch. At that instant the cavalcade came into the open, and the stronghold loomed up ahead—a great horned and jag-crested blot on the sunrise. Never before had it seemed so much like a hideous monster. Ivrian felt that its high gates were the iron jaws of death.

Janarrl, striding into the torture chamber deep below his stronghold, experienced a hot wave of exultation, as when he and his huntsmen closed in around an animal for the kill. But atop the wave was a very faint foam of fear. His feelings were a little like those of a ravenously hungry man invited to a sumptuous banquet, but who has been warned by a fortuneteller to fear death by poison. He was haunted by the feverish frightened face of the man arm-wounded by the wizardling's corroded bronze sword. His eyes met those of Glavas Rho's apprentice, whose half-naked body was stretched—though not yet painfully so—upon the rack, and the Duke's sense of fear sharpened. They were too searching, those eyes, too cold and menacing, too suggestive of magical powers.

He told himself angrily that a little pain would soon change their look to one of trapped panic. He told himself that it was natural that he should still be on edge from last night's horrors, when his life had almost been pried from him by dirty sorceries. But deep in his heart he knew that fear was always with him—fear of anything or anyone that some day might be stronger than he and hurt him as he had hurt others—fear of the dead he had harmed and could hurt no longer—fear of his dead wife, who had indeed been stronger and crueler than he and who had humiliated him in a thousand ways that no one but he remembered.

But he also knew that his daughter would soon be here and that he could then shift off his fear on her; by forcing her to fear, he would be able to heal his own courage, as he had done innumerable times in the past.

So he confidently took his place and gave order that the torture begin.

As the great wheel creaked and the leathern wristlets and anklets began to tighten a little, Mouse felt a qualm of helpless panic run over his body. It centered in his joints—those little deep-set hinges of bone normally exempt from danger. There was yet no pain. His body was merely stretched a little, as if he were yawning.

The low ceiling was close to his face. The flickering light of the torches revealed the mortises in the stone and the dusty cobwebs. Toward his feet he could see the upper portion of the wheel, and the two large hands that gripped its spokes, dragging them down effortlessly, very slowly, stopping for twenty heartbeats at a time. By turning his head and eyes to the side he could see the big figure of the Duke—not wide as his doll of him, but wide—sitting in a carven wooden chair, two armed men standing behind him. The Duke's brown hands, their jeweled rings flashing fire, were closed over the knobs on the chair-arms. His feet were firmly planted. His jaw was set. Only his eyes showed any uneasiness or vulnerability. They kept shifting from side to side—rapidly, regularly, like the pivoted ones of a doll.

"My daughter should be here," he heard the Duke say abruptly in a flat voice. "Hasten her. She is not to be permitted to delay."

One of the men hurried away.

Then the twinges of pain commenced, striking at random in the forearm, the back, the knee, the shoulder. With an effort Mouse composed his features. He fixed his attention on the faces around him, surveying them in detail as if they formed a picture, noting the highlights on the cheeks and eyes and beards and the shadows, wavering with the torchflames, that their figures cast upon the low walls.

Then those low walls melted and, as if distance were no longer real, he saw the whole wide world he'd never visited beyond them: great reaches of forest, bright amber desert, and turquoise sea; the Lake of Monsters, the City of Ghouls, magnificent Lankhmar, the Land of the Eight Cities, the Trollstep Mountains, the fabulous Cold Waste and by some chance striding there an open-faced, hulking red-haired youth he'd glimpsed among the pirates and later spoken with—all places and persons he'd never now encounter, but showing in wondrous fine detail, as if carved and tinted by a master miniaturist.

With startling suddenness the pain returned and increased. The twinges became needle stabs—a cunning prying at his insides—fingers of force crawling up his arms and legs toward his spine—an unsettling at the hips. He desperately tensed his muscles against them.

Then he heard the Duke's voice, "Not so fast. Stop a while." Mouse thought he recognized the overtones of panic in the voice. He twisted his head despite the pangs it cost him and watched the uneasy eyes. They swung to and fro, like little pendulums.

Suddenly then, as if time were no longer real, Mouse saw another scene in this chamber. The Duke was there and his eyes swinging from side to side, but he was younger and there was open panic and horror in his face. Close beside him was a boldly handsome woman in a dark red dress cut low in the bosom and with slashes inset with yellow silk. Stretched upon the rack itself in Mouse's place was a strappingly beautiful but now pitifully whimpering maid, whom the woman in red was questioning, with great coldness and insistence on detail, about her amorous encounters with the Duke and her attempt on the life of herself, the Duke's wife, by poison.

Footsteps broke that scene, as stones destroy a reflection in water, and brought the present back. Then a voice: "Your daughter comes, oh Duke."

Mouse steeled himself. He had not realized how much he dreaded this meeting, even in his pain. He felt bitterly certain that Ivrian would not have heeded his words. She was not evil, he knew, and she had not meant to betray him, but by the same token she was without courage. She would come whimpering, and her anguish would eat at what little self-control he could muster and doom his last wild wishful schemings.

Lighter footsteps were approaching now— hers. There was something curiously measured about them.

It meant added pain for him to turn his head so he could see the doorway; yet he did so, watching her figure define itself as it entered the region of ruddy light cast by the torches.

Then he saw the eyes. They were wide and staring. They were fixed straight on him. And they did not turn away. The face was pale, calm with a deadly serenity.

He saw she was dressed in a gown of dark red, cut low in the bosom and with slashes inset with yellow silk.

And then the soul of Mouse exulted, for he knew that she had done what he had bidden her. Glavas Rho had said, "The sufferer can hurl his suffering back upon his oppressor, if only his oppressor can be tempted to open a channel for his hate." Now there was a channel open for him, leading to Janarrl's inmost being.

Hungrily, Mouse fastened his gaze on Ivrian's unblinking eyes, as if they were pools of black magic in a cold moon. Those eyes, he knew, could receive what he could give.

He saw her seat herself by the Duke. He saw the Duke peer sidewise at his daughter and start up as if she were a ghost. But Ivrian did not look toward him, only her hand stole out and fastened on his wrist, and the Duke sank shuddering back into his chair.

"Proceed!" he heard the Duke call out to the torturers, and this time the panic in the Duke's voice was very close to the surface.

The wheel turned. Mouse heard himself groan piteously. But there was something in him now that could ride on top of the pain and that had no part in the groan. He felt that there was a path between his eyes and Ivrian's—a rock-walled channel through which the forces of human spirit and of more than human spirit could be sent roaring like a mountain torrent. And still she did not turn away. No expression crossed her face when he groaned, only her eyes seemed to darken as she grew still more pale. Mouse sensed a shifting of feelings in his body. Through the scalding waters of pain, his hate rose to the surface, rode atop too. He pushed his hate down the rock-walled channel, saw Ivrian's face grow more deathlike as it struck her, saw her tighten her grip on her father's wrist, sensed the trembling that her father no longer could master.

The wheel turned. From far off Mouse heard a steady, heart-tearing whimpering. But a part of him was outside the room now—high, he felt, in the frosty emptiness above the world. He saw spread out below him a nighted panorama of wooded hills and valleys. Near the summit of one hill was a tight clump of tiny stone towers. But as if he were endowed with a magical vulture's eye, he could see through the walls and roofs of those towers into the very foundations beneath, into a tiny murky room in which men tinier than insects clustered and cowered together. Some were working at a mechanism which inflicted pain on a creature that might have been a bleached and writhing ant. And the pain of that creature, whose tiny thin cries he could faintly hear, had a strange effect on him at this height, strengthening his inward powers and tearing away a veil from his eyes—a veil that had hitherto hidden a whole black universe.

For he began to hear about him a mighty murmuring. The frigid darkness was beaten by wings of stone. The steely light of the stars cut into his brain like painless knives. He felt a wild black whirlpool of evil, like a torrent of black tigers, blast down upon him from above, and he knew that it was his to control. He let it surge through his body and then hurled it down the unbroken path that led to two points of darkness in the tiny room below—the two staring eyes of Ivrian, daughter of Duke Janarrl. He saw the black of the whirlwind's heart spread on her face like an inkblot, seep down her white arms and dye her fingers. He saw her hand tighten convulsively on her father's arm. He saw her reach her other hand toward the Duke and lift her open lips to his cheek.

Then, for one moment while the torch flames whipped low and blue in a physical wind that seemed to blow through the mortised stones of the buried chamber…for one moment while the torturers and guards dropped the tools of their trades…for one indelible moment of hate fulfilled and revenge accomplished, Mouse saw the strong, square face of Duke Janarrl shake in the agitation of ultimate terror, the features twisted like heavy cloth wrung between invisible hands, then crumpled in defeat and death.

The strand supporting Mouse snapped. His spirit dropped like a plummet toward the buried room.

An agonizing pain filled him, but it promised life, not death. Above him was the low stone ceiling. The hands on the wheel were white and slender. Then he knew that the pain was that of release from the rack.

Slowly Ivrian loosened the rings of leather from his wrists and ankles. Slowly she helped him down, supporting him with all her strength as they dragged their way across the room, from which everyone else had fled in terror save for one crumpled jeweled figure in a carven chair. They paused by that and he surveyed the dead thing with the cool, satisfied, masklike gaze of a cat. Then on and up they went, Ivrian and the Gray Mouser, through corridors emptied by panic, and out into the night.

FRITZ LEIBER'S
LANKhMAR

ILL MET IN LANKMAR

IV

SILENT AS SPECTERS, the tall and the fat thief edged past the dead, noose-strangled watch-leopard, out the thick, lock-picked door of Jengao the Gem Merchant, and strolled east on Cash Street through the thin black night-smog of Lankhmar, City of Sevenscore Thousand Smokes.

East on Cash it had to be, for west at the intersection of Cash and Silver was a police post with unbribed guardsmen in browned-iron cuirasses and helms, restlessly grounding and rattling their pikes, while Jengao's place had no alley entrance or even window in its stone walls three spans thick and the roof and floor almost as strong and without trap doors.

But tall, tight-lipped Slevyas, master thief candidate, and fat, darting-eyed Fissif, thief second class, brevetted first class for this operation, with a rating of talented in double-dealing, were not in the least worried. Everything was proceeding according to plan. Each carried thonged in his pouch a much smaller pouch of jewels of the first water only, for Jengao, now breathing stentoriously inside and senseless from the slugging he'd suffered, must be allowed, nay, nursed and encouraged, to build up his business again and so ripen it for another plucking. Almost the first law of the Thieves' Guild was never kill the hen that laid brown eggs with a ruby in the yolk, or white eggs with a diamond in the white.

The two thieves also had the relief of knowing that, with the satisfaction of a job well done, they were going straight home now, not to a wife, Aarth forbid!—or to parents and children, all gods forfend!—but to Thieves' House, headquarters and barracks of the all-mighty Guild which was father to them both and mother too, though no woman was allowed inside its ever-open portal on Cheap Street.

In addition there was the comforting knowledge that although each was armed only with his regulation silver-hilted thief's knife, a weapon seldom used except in rare intramural duels and brawls, in fact more a membership token than a weapon, they were nevertheless most strongly convoyed by three reliable and lethal bravos hired for the evening from the Slayers' Brotherhood, one moving well ahead of them as point, the other two well behind as rear guard and chief striking force, in fact almost out of sight—for it is never wise that such convoying be obvious, or so believed Krovas, Grandmaster of the Thieves' Guild.

And if all that were not enough to make Slevyas and Fissif feel safe and serene, there danced along soundlessly beside them in the shadow of the north curb a small, malformed or at any rate somewhat large-headed shape that might have been a small dog, a somewhat undersized cat, or a very big rat. Occasionally it scuttled familiarly and even encouragingly a little way toward their snugly felt-slippered feet, though it always scurried swiftly back into the darker dark.

True, this last guard was not an absolutely unalloyed reassurance. At that very moment, scarcely twoscore paces yet from Jengao's, Fissif tautly walked for a bit on tiptoe and strained his pudgy lips upward to whisper softly in Slevyas' long-lobed ear, "Damned if I like being dogged by that familiar of Hristomilo, no matter what security he's supposed to afford us. Bad enough that Krovas employs or lets himself be cowed into employing a sorcerer of most dubious, if dire, reputation and aspect, but that—"

"Shut your trap!" Slevyas hissed still more softly.

Fissif obeyed with a shrug and occupied himself even more restlessly and keenly than was his wont in darting his gaze this way and that, but chiefly ahead.

Some distance in that direction, in fact just short of the Gold Street intersection, Cash was bridged by an enclosed second-story passageway connecting the two buildings which made up the premises of the famous stone-masons and sculptors Rokkermas and Slaarg. The firm's buildings themselves were fronted by very shallow porticos supported by unnecessarily large pillars of varied shape and decoration, advertisements more than structural members.

From just beyond the bridge there came two low, brief whistles, signal from the point bravo that he had inspected that area for ambushes and discovered nothing suspicious and that Gold Street was clear.

Fissif was by no means entirely satisfied by the safety signal. To tell the truth, the fat thief rather enjoyed being apprehensive and even fearful, at least up to a point. A sense of strident panic overlaid with writhing calm made him feel more excitingly alive than the occasional woman he enjoyed. So he scanned most closely through the thin, sooty smog the frontages and overhangs of Rokkermas and Slaarg as his and Slevyas' leisurely seeming yet un-slow pace brought them steadily closer.

On this side the bridge was pierced by four small windows, between which were three large niches in which stood—another advertisement— three life-size plaster statues, somewhat eroded by years of weather and dyed varyingly tones of dark gray by as many years of smog. Approaching Jengao's before the burglary, Fissif had noted them with a swift but comprehensive overshoulder glance. Now it seemed to him that the statue to the right had indefinably changed. It was that of a man of medium height wearing cloak and hood, who gazed down with crossed arms and brooding aspect. No, not indefinably quite—the statue was a more uniform dark gray now, he fancied, cloak, hood, and face; it seemed somewhat sharper featured, less eroded; and he would almost swear it had grown shorter!

Just below the niche, moreover, there was a scattering of gray and raw white rubble which he didn't recall having been there earlier. He strained to remember if during the excitement of the burglary, with its lively leopard-slaying and slugging and all, the unsleeping watch-corner of his mind had recorded a distant crash, and now he believed it had. His quick imagination pictured the possibility of a hole or even door behind each statue, through which it might be given a strong push and so tumbled onto passersby, himself and Slevyas specifically, the right-hand statue having been crashed to test the device and then replaced with a near twin.

He would keep close watch on all three statues as he and Slevyas walked under. It would be easy to dodge if he saw one start to overbalance. Should he yank Slevyas out of harm's way when that happened? It was something to think about.

Without pause his restless attention fixed next on the porticos and pillars. The latter, thick and almost three yards tall, were placed at irregular intervals as well as being irregularly shaped and fluted, for Rokkermas and Slaarg were most modern and emphasized the unfinished look, randomness, and the unexpected.

Nevertheless it seemed to Fissif, his wariness wide awake now, that there was an intensification of unexpectedness, specifically that there was one more pillar under the porticos than when he had last passed by. He couldn't be sure which pillar was the newcomer, but he was almost certain there was one.

Share his suspicions with Slevyas? Yes, and get another hissed reproof and flash of contempt from the small, dull-seeming eyes.

The enclosed bridge was close now. Fissif glanced up at the right-hand statue and noted other differences from the one he'd recalled. Although shorter, it seemed to hold itself more strainingly erect, while the frown carved in its dark gray face was not so much one of philosophic brooding as sneering contempt, self-conscious cleverness, and conceit.

Still, none of the three statues toppled forward as he and Slevyas walked under the bridge. However, something else happened to Fissif at that moment. One of the pillars winked at him.

The Gray Mouser—for so Mouse now named himself to himself and Ivrian—turned around in the right-hand niche, leaped up and caught hold of the cornice, silently vaulted to the flat roof, and crossed it precisely in time to see the two thieves emerge below.

Without hesitation he leaped forward and down, his body straight as a crossbow bolt, the soles of his ratskin boots aimed at the shorter thief's fat buried shoulder blades, though leading him a little to allow for the yard he'd walk while the Mouser hurtled toward him.

In the instant that he leaped, the tall thief glanced up overshoulder and whipped out a knife, though making no move to push or pull Fissif out of the way of the human projectile speeding toward him.

The Mouser shrugged in full flight. He'd just have to deal with the tall thief faster after knocking down the fat one.

More swiftly than one would have thought he could manage, Fissif whirled around then and thinly screamed, "Slivikin!"

The ratskin boots took him high in the belly. It was like landing on a big cushion. Writhing aside from Slevyas' first thrust, the Mouser somersaulted forward, turning feet over head, and as the fat thief's skull hit a cobble with a dull bong he came to his feet with dirk in hand, ready to take on the tall one. But there was no need. Slevyas, his small eyes glazed, was toppling too.

One of the pillars had sprung forward, trailing a voluminous robe. A big hood had fallen back from a youthful face and long-haired head. Brawny arms had emerged from the long, loose sleeves that had been the pillar's topmost section, while the big fist ending one of the arms had dealt Slevyas a shrewd knockout punch on the chin.

Fafhrd and the Gray Mouser faced each other across the two thieves sprawled senseless. They were poised for attack, yet for the moment neither moved.

Each discerned something inexplicably familiar in the other.

Fafhrd said, "Our motives for being here seem identical."

"Seem? Surely must be!" the Mouser answered curtly, fiercely eyeing this potential new foe, who was taller by a head than the tall thief.

"You said?"

"I said, 'Seem? Surely must be!'"

"How civilized of you!" Fafhrd commented in pleased tones.

"Civilized?" the Mouser demanded suspiciously, gripping his dirk tighter.

"To care, in the eye of action, exactly what's said," Fafhrd explained. Without letting the Mouser out of his vision, he glanced down. His gaze traveled from the belt and pouch of one fallen thief to those of the other. Then he looked up at the Mouser with a broad, ingenuous smile.

"Sixty-sixty?" he suggested.

The Mouser hesitated, sheathed his dirk, and rapped out, "A deal!" He knelt abruptly, his fingers on the drawstrings of Fissif's pouch. "Loot you Slivikin," he directed.

It was natural to suppose that the fat thief had been crying his companion's name at the end. Without looking up from where he knelt, Fafhrd remarked, "That...ferret they had with them. Where did it go?"

"Ferret?" the Mouser answered briefly. "It was a marmoset!"

"Marmoset," Fafhrd mused. "That's a small tropical monkey, isn't it? Well, might have been, but I got the strange impression that—"

The silent, two-pronged rush which almost overwhelmed them at that instant really surprised neither of them. Each had been expecting it, but the expectation had dropped out of conscious thought with the startlement of their encounter.

The three bravos racing down upon them in concerted attack, two from the west and one from the east, all with swords poised to thrust, had assumed that the two highjackers would be armed at most with knives and as timid or at least cautious in weapons-combat as the general run of thieves and counter-thieves. So it was they who were surprised and thrown into confusion when with the lightning speed of youth the Mouser and Fafhrd sprang up, whipped out fearsomely long swords, and faced them back to back.

The Mouser made a very small parry in carte so that the thrust of the bravo from the east went past his left side by only a hair's breath. He instantly riposted. His adversary, desperately springing back, parried in turn in carte. Hardly slowing, the tip of the Mouser's long, slim sword dropped under that parry with the delicacy of a princess curtsying and then leaped forward and a little upward, the Mouser making an impossibly long-looking lunge for one so small, and went between two scales of the bravo's armored jerkin and between his ribs and through his heart and out his back as if all were angelfood cake.

Meanwhile Fafhrd, facing the two bravos from the west, swept aside their low thrusts with somewhat larger, down-sweeping parries in seconde and low prime, then flipped-up his sword, long as the Mouser's but heavier, so that it slashed through the neck of his right-hand adversary, half decapitating him. Then he, dropping back a swift step, readied a thrust for the other.

But there was no need. A narrow ribbon of bloodied steel, followed by a gray glove and arm, flashed past him from behind and transfixed the last bravo with the identical thrust the Mouser had used on the first.

The two young men wiped and sheathed their swords. Fafhrd brushed the palm of his open right hand down his robe and held it out. The Mouser pulled off right-hand gray glove and shook the other's big hand in his sinewy one. Without word exchanged, they knelt and finished looting the two unconscious thieves, se-

curing the small bags of jewels. With an oily towel and
then a dry one, the Mouser sketchily wiped from his
face the greasy ash-soot mixture which had darkened
it, next swiftly rolled up both towels and returned them
to his own pouch. Then, after only a questioning eye-
twitch east on the Mouser's part and a nod from Fafhrd,
they swiftly walked on in the direction Slevyas and Fissif
and their escort had been going.

After reconnoitering Gold Street, they
crossed it and continued east on Cash at Fafhrd's ges-
tured proposal.

"My woman's at the Golden Lamprey," he
explained.

"Let's pick her up and take her home to meet
my girl," the Mouser suggested.

"Home?" Fafhrd inquired politely, only the
barest hint of question in his voice.

"Dim Lane," the Mouser volunteered.

"Silver Eel?"

"Behind it. We'll have some drinks."

"I'll pick up a jug. Never have too much
juice."

"True. I'll let you."

Several squares farther on Fafhrd, after steal-
ing a number of looks at his new comrade, said with
conviction, "We've met before."

The Mouser grinned at him. "Beach by the
Mountains of Hunger?"

"Right! When I was a pirate's ship-boy."

"And I was a wizard's apprentice."

Fafhrd stopped, again wiped right hand on
robe, and held it out. "Name's Fafhrd. Ef ay ef aitch ar
dee."

Again the Mouser shook it. "Gray Mouser,"
he said a touch defiantly, as if challenging anyone to

laugh at the sobriquet. "Excuse me, but how exactly do you pronounce that? Faf-hrud?"

"Just Faf-erd."

"Thank you." They walked on.

"Gray Mouser, eh?" Fafhrd remarked. "Well, you killed yourself a couple of rats tonight."

"That I did." The Mouser's chest swelled and he threw back his head. Then with a comic twitch of his nose and a sidewise half-grin he admitted, "You'd have got your second man easily enough. I stole him from you to demonstrate my speed. Besides, I was excited."

Fafhrd chuckled. "You're telling me? How do you suppose I was feeling?"

Later, as they were crossing Pimp Street, he asked, "Learn much magic from your wizard?"

Once more the Mouser threw back his head. He flared his nostrils and drew down the corners of his lips, preparing his mouth for boastful, mystifying speech. But once more he found himself twitching his nose and half grinning. What the deuce did this big fellow have that kept him from putting on his usual acts? "Enough to tell me it's damned dangerous stuff. Though I still fool with it now and then."

Fafhrd was asking himself a similar question. All his life he'd mistrusted small men, knowing his height awakened their instant jealousy. But this clever little chap was somehow an exception. Quick thinker and brilliant swordsman too, no argument. He prayed to Kos that Vlana would like him.

On the northeast corner of Cash and Whore a slow-burning torch shaded by a broad gilded hoop cast a cone of light up into the thickening black night-smog and another cone down on the cobbles before the tavern door. Out of the shadows into the second cone stepped Vlana, handsome in a narrow black velvet dress and red stockings, her only ornaments a silver-sheathed and hilted dagger and a silver-worked black pouch, both on a plain black belt.

Fafhrd introduced the Gray Mouser, who behaved with an almost fawning courtesy, obsequiously gallant. Vlana studied him boldly, then gave him a tentative smile. Fafhrd opened under the torch the small pouch he'd taken off the tall thief. Vlana looked down into it. She put her arms around Fafhrd, hugged him tight, and kissed him soundly. Then she thrust the jewels into the pouch on her belt.

When that was done, he said, "Look, I'm going to buy a jug. You tell her what happened, Mouser."

When he came out of the Golden Lamprey he was carrying four jugs in the crook of his left arm and wiping his lips on the back of his right hand. Vlana was frowning. He grinned at her. The Mouser smacked his lips at the jugs. They continued east on Cash. Fafhrd realized that the frown was for more than the jugs and the prospect of stupidly drunken male revelry. The Mouser tactfully walked ahead, ostensibly to lead the way. When his figure was little more than a blob in the thickening smog, Vlana whispered harshly, "You had two members of the Thieves' Guild knocked out cold and you didn't cut their throats?"

"We slew three bravos," Fafhrd protested by way of excuse.

"My quarrel is not with the Slayers' Brotherhood, but that abominable Guild. You swore to me that whenever you had the chance—"

"Vlana! I couldn't have the Gray Mouser thinking I was an amateur counter-thief consumed by hysteria and blood lust."

"You already set great store by him, don't you?"

"He possibly saved my life tonight."

"Well, he told me that *he'd* have slit their throats in a wink, if he'd known I wanted it that way."

"He was only playing up to you from courtesy."

"Perhaps and perhaps not. But *you* knew and you didn't—"

"Vlana, shut up!"

Her frown became a rageful glare, then suddenly she laughed wildly, smiled twitchingly as if she were about to cry, mastered herself and smiled more lovingly. "Pardon me, darling," she said. "Sometimes you must think I'm going mad and sometimes I believe I am."

"Well, don't," he told her shortly. "Think of the jewels we've won instead. And behave yourself with our new friends. Get some wine inside you and relax. I mean to enjoy myself tonight. I've earned it."

She nodded and clutched his arm in agreement and for comfort and sanity. They hurried to catch up with the dim figure ahead.

The Mouser, turning left, led them a half square north on Cheap Street to where a narrower way went east again. The black mist in it looked solid.

"Dim Lane," the Mouser explained.

Fafhrd nodded that he knew.

Vlana said, "Dim's too weak—too *transparent* a word for it tonight," with an uneven laugh in which there were still traces of hysteria and which ended in a fit of strangled coughing. When she could swallow again, she gasped out, "Damn Lankhmar's night-smog! What a hell of a city."

"It's the nearness here of the Great Salt Marsh," Fafhrd explained. And he did indeed have part of the answer. Lying low betwixt the Marsh, the Inner Sea, the River Hlal, and the flat southern grain fields watered by canals fed by the Hlal, Lankhmar with its innumerable smokes was the prey of fogs and sooty smogs. No wonder the citizens had adopted the black toga as their formal garb. Some averred the toga had originally been white or pale brown, but so swiftly soot-blackened, necessitating endless laundering, that a thrifty Overlord had ratified and made official what nature or civilization's arts decreed.

About halfway to Carter Street, a tavern on the north side of the lane emerged from the murk. A gape-jawed serpentine shape of pale metal crested with soot hung high for a sign. Beneath it they passed a door curtained with begrimed leather, the slit in which spilled out noise, pulsing torchlight, and the reek of liquor.

Just beyond the Silver Eel the Mouser led them through an inky passageway outside the tavern's east wall. They had to go single file, feeling their way along rough, slimily bemisted brick and keeping close together.

"Mind the puddle," the Mouser warned. "It's deep as the Outer Sea."

The passageway widened. Reflected torch-light filtering down through the dark mist allowed them to make out only the most general shape of their surroundings. To the right was more window-less, high wall. To the left, crowding close to the back of the Silver Eel, rose a dismal, rickety building of darkened brick and blackened, ancient wood. It looked utterly deserted to Fafhrd and Vlana until they had craned back their heads to gaze at the fourth-story attic under the ragged-guttered roof. There faint lines and points of yellow light shone around and through three tightly-latticed windows. Beyond, crossing the T of the space they were in, was a narrow alley.

"Bones Alley," the Mouser told them in somewhat lofty tones. "I call it Ordure Boulevard."

"I can smell that," Vlana said.

By now she and Fafhrd could see a long, narrow wooden outside stairway, steep yet sagging and without a rail, leading up to the lighted attic. The Mouser relieved Fafhrd of the jugs and went up it quite swiftly.

"Follow me when I've reached the top," he called back. "I think it'll take your weight, Fafhrd, but best one of you at a time."

Fafhrd gently pushed Vlana ahead. With another hysteria-tinged laugh and a pause midway up for another fit of choked coughing, she mounted to the Mouser where he now stood in an open doorway, from which streamed yellow light that died swiftly in the night-smog. He was lightly resting a hand on a big, empty, wrought-iron lamp-hook firmly set in a stone section of the outside wall. He bowed aside, and she went in.

Fafhrd followed, placing his feet as close as he could to the wall, his hands ready to grab for support. The whole stairs creaked ominously and each step gave a little as he shifted his weight onto it. Near the top, one gave way with the muted crack of half-rotted wood. Gently as he could, he sprawled himself hand and knee on as many steps as he could reach, to distribute his weight, and cursed sulfurously.

"Don't fret, the jugs are safe," the Mouser called down gayly.

Fafhrd crawled the rest of the way, a somewhat sour look on his face, and did not get to his feet until he was inside the doorway. When he had done so, he almost gasped with surprise. It was like rubbing the verdigris from a cheap brass ring and finding a rainbow-fired diamond of the first water set in it. Rich drapes, some twinkling with embroidery of silver and gold, covered the walls except where the shuttered windows were—and the shutters of those were gilded. Similar but darker fabrics hid the low ceiling, making a gorgeous canopy in which the flecks of gold and silver were like stars. Scattered about were plump cushions and low tables, on which burned a multitude of candles. On shelves against the walls were neatly stacked like small logs a vast reserve of candles, numerous scrolls, jugs, bottles, and enameled boxes. A low vanity table was backed by a mirror of honed silver and thickly scattered over with jewels and cosmetics. In a large fireplace was set a small metal stove, neatly blacked, with an ornate fire-pot. Also set beside the stove were a tidy pyramid of thin, resinous torches with frayed ends—fire-kindlers— and other pyramids of short-handled brooms and mops, small, short logs, and gleamingly black coal.

On a low dais by the fireplace was a wide, short-legged, high-backed couch covered with cloth of gold. On it sat a thin, pale-faced, delicately handsome girl clad in a dress of thick violet silk worked with silver and belted with a silver chain. Her slippers were of white snow-serpent fur. Silver pins headed with amethysts held in place her high-piled black hair. Around her shoulders was drawn a white ermine wrap. She was leaning forward with uneasy-seeming graciousness and extending a narrow, white hand which shook a little to Vlana, who knelt before her and now gently took the proffered hand and bowed her head over it, her own glossy, straight, dark-brown hair making a canopy, and pressed the other girl's hand's back to her lips.

Fafhrd was happy to see his woman playing up properly to this definitely odd though delightful situation. Then looking at Vlana's long, red-stockinged leg stretched far behind her as she knelt on the other, he noted that the floor was everywhere strewn—to the point of double, treble, and quadruple overlaps—with thick-piled, close-woven, many-hued rugs of the finest imported from the Eastern Lands. Before he knew it, his thumb had shot toward the Gray Mouser.

"You're the Rug Robber!" he proclaimed. "You're the Carpet Crimp!—and the Candle Corsair too," he continued, referring to two series of unsolved thefts which had been on the lips of all Lankhmar when he and Vlana had arrived a moon ago.

The Mouser shrugged impassive-faced at Fafhrd, then suddenly grinned, his slitted eyes a-twinkle, and broke into an impromptu dance which carried him whirling and jigging around the room and left him behind Fafhrd, where he deftly reached down the hooded and long-sleeved huge robe from the latter's stooping shoulders, shook it out, carefully folded it, and set it on a pillow.

After a long, uncertain pause, the girl in violet nervously patted with her free hand the cloth of gold beside her and Vlana seated herself there, carefully not too close, and the two women spoke together in low voices, Vlana taking the lead, though not obviously.

The Mouser took off his own gray, hooded cloak, folded it almost fussily, and laid it beside Fafhrd's. Then they unbelted their swords, and the Mouser set them atop folded robe and cloak.

Without those weapons and bulking garments, the two men looked suddenly like youths, both with clear, close-shaven faces, both slender despite the swelling muscles of Fafhrd's arms and calves, he with long red-gold hair falling down his back and about his shoulders, the Mouser with dark hair cut in bangs, the one in brown leather tunic worked with copper wire, the other in jerkin of coarsely woven gray silk.

They smiled at each other. The feeling each had of having turned boy all at once made their smiles for the first time a bit embarrassed. The Mouser cleared his throat and, bowing a little, but looking still at Fafhrd, extended a loosely spread-fingered arm toward the golden couch and said with a preliminary stammer, though otherwise smoothly enough, "Fafhrd, my good friend, permit me to introduce you to my princess. Ivrian, my dear, receive Fafhrd graciously if you please, for tonight he and I fought back to back against three and we conquered."

Fafhrd advanced, stooping a little, the crown of his red-gold hair brushing the bestarred canopy, and knelt before Ivrian exactly as Vlana had. The slender hand extended to him looked steady now, but was still quiveringly a-tremble, he discovered as soon as he touched it. He handled it as if it were silk woven of the white spider's gossamer, barely brushing it with his lips, and still felt nervous as he mumbled some compliments.

He did not sense, at least at the moment, that the Mouser was quite as nervous as he, if not more so, praying hard that Ivrian would not overdo her princess part and snub their guests, or collapse in trembling or tears or run to him or into the next room, for Fafhrd and Vlana were literally the first beings, human or animal, noble, freeman, or slave, that he had brought or allowed into the luxurious nest he had created for his aristocratic beloved—save the two love birds that twittered in a silver cage hanging to the other side of the fireplace from the dais.

Despite his shrewdness and new-found cynicism it never occurred to the Mouser that it was chiefly his charming but preposterous coddling of Ivrian that was keeping doll-like and even making more so the potentially brave and realistic girl who had fled with him from her father's torture chamber four moons ago.

But now as Ivrian smiled at last and Fafhrd gently returned her her hand and cautiously backed off, the Mouser relaxed with relief, fetched two silver cups and two silver mugs, wiped them needlessly with a silken towel, carefully selected a bottle of violet wine, then with a grin at Fafhrd uncorked instead one of the jugs the Northerner had brought, and near-brimmed the four gleaming vessels and served them all four. With another preliminary clearing of throat, but no trace of stammer this time, he toasted, "To my greatest theft to date in Lankhmar, which willy-nilly I must share sixty-sixty with"—he couldn't resist the sudden impulse—"with this great, longhaired, barbarian lout here!" And he downed a quarter of his mug of pleasantly burning wine fortified with brandy.

Fafhrd quaffed off half of his, then toasted back, "To the most boastful and finical little civilized chap I've ever deigned to share loot with," quaffed off the rest, and with a great smile that showed white teeth held out his empty mug.

The Mouser gave him a refill, topped off his own, then set that down to go to Ivrian and pour into her lap from their small pouch the gems he'd filched from Fissif. They gleamed in their new, enviable location like a small puddle of rainbow-hued quicksilver.

Ivrian jerked back a-tremble, almost spilling them, but Vlana gently caught her arm, steadying it, and leaned in over the jewels with a throaty gasp of wonder and admiration, slowly turned an envious gaze on the pale girl, and began rather urgently but smilingly to whisper to her. Fafhrd realized that Vlana was acting now, but acting well and effectively, since Ivrian was soon nodding eagerly and not long after that beginning to whisper back. At her direction, Vlana fetched a blue-enameled box inlaid with silver, and the two of them transferred the jewels from Ivrian's lap into its blue velvet interior. Then Ivrian placed the box close beside her and they chatted on.

As he worked through his second mug in smaller gulps, Fafhrd relaxed and began to get a deeper feeling of his surroundings. The dazzling wonder of the first glimpse of this throne room in a slum, its colorful luxury intensified by contrast with the dark and mud and slime and rotten stairs and Ordure Boulevard just outside, faded, and he began to note the rickettiness and rot under the grand overlay.

Black, rotten wood and dry, cracked wood too showed here and there between the drapes and also loosed their sick, ancient stinks. The whole floor sagged under the rugs, as much as a span at the center of the room. A large cockroach was climbing down a gold-worked drape, another toward the couch. Threads of night-smog were coming through the shutters, making evanescent black arabesques against the gilt. The stones of the large fireplace had been scrubbed and varnished, yet most of the mortar was gone from between them; some sagged, others were missing altogether.

The Mouser had been building a fire there in the stove. Now he pushed in all the way the yellow flaring kindler he'd lit from the fire-pot, hooked the little black door shut over the mounting flames, and turned back into the room. As if he'd read Fafhrd's mind, he took up several cones of incense, set their peaks a-smolder at the fire-pot, and placed them about the room in gleaming, shallow, brass bowls—stepping hard on the one cockroach by the way and surreptitiously catching and crushing the other in the base of his flicked fist. Then he stuffed silken rags in the widest shutter-cracks, took up his silver mug again, and for a moment gave Fafhrd a very hard look, as if daring him to say just one word against the delightful yet faintly ridiculous doll's house he'd prepared for his princess.

Next moment he was smiling and lifting his mug to Fafhrd, who was doing the same. Need of refills brought them close together. Hardly moving his lips, the Mouser explained *sotto voce*, "Ivrian's father was a duke. I slew him, by black magic, I believe, while he was having me done to death on the torture rack. A most cruel man, cruel to his daughter too, yet a duke, so that Ivrian is wholly unused to fending or caring for herself. I pride myself that I maintain her in grander state than ever her father did with all his serving men and maids."

Suppressing the instant criticisms he felt of this attitude and program, Fafhrd nodded and said amiably, "Surely you've thieved together a most charming little palace, quite worthy of Lankhmar's

Overlord Karstak Ovartamortes, or the King of Kings at Horborixen."

From the couch Vlana called in her husky contralto, "Gray Mouser, your princess would hear an account of tonight's adventure. And might we have more wine?"

Ivrian called, "Yes, please, Mouse."

Wincing almost imperceptibly at that earlier nickname, the Mouser looked to Fafhrd for the go-ahead, got the nod, and launched into his story. But first he served the girls wine. There wasn't enough for their cups, so he opened another jug and after a moment of thought uncorked all three, setting one by the couch, one by Fafhrd where he sprawled now on the pillowy carpets, and reserving one for himself. Ivrian looked wide-eyed apprehensive at this signal of heavy drinking ahead, Vlana cynical with a touch of anger, but neither voiced their criticism.

The Mouser told the tale of counter-thievery well, acting it out in part, and with only the most artistic of embellishments—the ferret-marmoset before escaping ran up his back and tried to scratch out his eyes—and he was interrupted only twice.

When he said, "And so with a whish and a snick I bared Scalpel—" Fafhrd remarked, "Oh, so you've nicknamed your sword as well as yourself?"

The Mouser drew himself up. "Yes, and I call my dirk Cat's Claw. Any objections? Seem childish to you?"

"Not at all. I call my own sword Graywand. All weapons are in a fashion alive, civilized and nameworthy. Pray continue."

And when he mentioned the beastie of uncertain nature that had gamboled along with the thieves (and attacked his eyes!), Ivrian paled and said with a shudder, "Mouse! That sounds like a witch's familiar!"

"Wizard's," Vlana corrected. "Those gutless Guild villains have no truck with women, except as fee'd or forced vehicles for their lust. But Krovas, their current king, though superstitious, is noted for taking *all* precautions, and might well have a warlock in his service."

"That seems most likely; it harrows me with dread," the Mouser agreed with ominous gaze and sinister voice. He really didn't believe or feel what he said—he was about as harrowed as virgin prairie—in the least, but he eagerly accepted any and all atmospheric enhancements of his performance.

When he was done, the girls, eyes flashing and fond, toasted him and Fafhrd for their cunning and bravery. The Mouser bowed and eye-twinklingly smiled about, then sprawled him down with a weary sigh, wiping his forehead with a silken cloth and downing a large drink.

After asking Vlana's leave, Fafhrd told the adventurous tale of their escape from Cold Corner— he from his clan, she from an acting troupe—and of their progress to Lankhmar, where they lodged now in an actors' tenement near the Plaza of Dark Delights. Ivrian hugged herself to Vlana and shivered large-eyed at the witchy parts—at least as much in delight as fear of Fafhrd's tale, he thought. He told himself it was natural that a doll-girl should love ghost stories, though he wondered if her pleasure would have been as great if she had known that his ghost stories were truly true. She seemed to live in worlds of imagination—once more at least half the Mouser's doing, he was sure.

The only proper matter he omitted from his account was Vlana's fixed intent to get a monstrous revenge on the Thieves' Guild for torturing to death her accomplices and harrying her out of Lankhmar when she'd tried freelance thieving in the city, with miming as a cover. Nor of course did he mention his own promise—foolish, he thought now—to help her in this bloody business.

After he'd done and got his applause, he found his throat dry despite his skald's training, but when he sought to wet it, he discovered that his mug was empty and his jug too, though he didn't feel in the least drunk; he had talked all the liquor out of him, he told himself, a little of the stuff escaping in each glowing word he'd spoken.

The Mouser was in like plight and not drunk either—though inclined to pause mysteriously and peer toward infinity before answering question or making remark. This time he suggested, after a particularly long infinity-gaze, that Fafhrd accompany him to the Eel while he purchased a fresh supply.

"But we've a lot of wine left in *our* jug," Ivrian protested. "Or at least a little," she amended. It did sound empty when Vlana shook it. "Besides, you've wine of all sorts here."

"Not this sort, dearest, and first rule is never mix 'em," the Mouser explained, wagging a finger. "That way lies unhealth, aye, and madness."

"My dear," Vlana said, sympathetically patting Ivrian's wrist, "at some time in any good party all the men who are really men simply have to go out. It's extremely stupid, but it's their nature and can't be dodged, believe me."

"But, Mouse, I'm scared. Fafhrd's tale frightened me. So did yours—I'll hear that big-headed, black, ratty familiar a-scratch at the shutters when you're gone, I know I will!"

It seemed to Fafhrd she was not afraid at all, only taking pleasure in frightening herself and in demonstrating her power over her beloved.

"Darlingest," the Mouser said with a small...hiccup, "there is all the Inner Sea, all the Land of the Eight Cities, and to boot all the Trollstep Mountains in their sky-scraping grandeur between you and Fafhrd's frigid specters or—pardon me, my comrade, but it could be—hallucinations admixed with coincidences. As for familiars, pish! They've never in the world been anything but the loathy, all-too-natural pets of stinking old women and womanish old men."

"The Eel's but a step, Lady Ivrian," Fafhrd said, "and you'll have beside you my dear Vlana, who slew my chiefest enemy with a single cast of that dagger she now wears."

With a glare at Fafhrd that lasted no longer than a wink, but conveyed "What a way to reassure a frightened girl!" Vlana said merrily, "Let the sillies go, my dear. 'Twill give us chance for a private chat, during which we'll take 'em apart from wine-fumy head to restless foot."

So Ivrian let herself be persuaded and the Mouser and Fafhrd slipped off, quickly shutting the door behind them to keep out the night-smog. Their rather rapid steps down the stairs could clearly be heard from within. There were faint creakings and groanings of the ancient wood outside the wall, but no sound of another tread breaking or other mishap.

Waiting for the four jugs to be brought up from the cellar, the two newly met comrades ordered a mug each of the same fortified wine, or one near

enough, and ensconced themselves at the least noisy
end of the long serving counter in the tumultuous tavern. The Mouser deftly kicked a rat that thrust black
head and shoulders from his hole.

After each had enthusiastically complimented
the other on his girl, Fafhrd said diffidently, "Just between ourselves, do you think there might be anything
to your sweet Ivrian's notion that the small dark creature with Slivikin and the other Guild-thief was a wizard's
familiar, or at any rate the cunning pet of a sorcerer,
trained to act as go-between and report disasters to his
master or to Krovas or to both?"

The Mouser laughed lightly. "You're building bugbears—formless baby ones unlicked by
logic—out of nothing, dear barbarian brother, if I
may say so. *Imprimis*, we don't really know the beastie
was connected with the Guild-thieves at all. May
well have been a stray catling or a big bold rat—like
this damned one!" He kicked again. "But, *secundus*,
granting it to be the creature of a wizard employed
by Krovas, how could it make useful report? I don't
believe in animals that talk—except for parrots and
such birds, which only...parrot—or ones having an
elaborate sign language men can share. Or perhaps
you envisage the beastie dipping its paddy paw in a
jug of ink and writing its report in big on a floor-
spread parchment?

"Ho, there, you back of the counter! Where
are my jugs? Rats eaten the boy who went for them
days ago? Or he simply starved to death while on his
cellar quest? Well, tell him to get a swifter move on
and meanwhile brim us again!

"No, Fafhrd, even granting the beastie to be
directly or indirectly a creature of Krovas, and that it
raced back to Thieves' House after our affray, what

could it tell them there? Only that something had gone wrong with the burglary at Jengao's. Which they'd soon suspect in any case from the delay in the thieves' and bravos' return."

Fafhrd frowned and muttered stubbornly, "The furry slinker might, nevertheless, convey our appearances to the Guild masters, and they might recognize us and come after us and attack us in our homes. Or Slivikin and his fat pal, revived from their bumps, might do likewise."

"My dear friend," the Mouser said condolingly, "once more begging your indulgence, I fear this potent wine is addling your wits. If the Guild knew our looks or where we lodge, they'd have been nastily on our necks days, weeks, nay, months ago. Or conceivably you don't know that their penalty for freelance or even unassigned thieving within the walls of Lankhmar and for three leagues outside them is nothing less than death, after torture if happily that can be achieved."

"I know all about that and my plight is worse even than yours," Fafhrd retorted, and after pledging the Mouser to secrecy told him the tale of Vlana's vendetta against the Guild and her deadly serious dreams of an all-encompassing revenge.

During his story the four jugs came up from the cellar, but the Mouser only ordered that their earthenware mugs be refilled.

Fafhrd finished, "And so, in consequence of a promise given by an infatuated and unschooled boy in a southern angle of the Cold Waste, I find myself now as a sober—well, at other times—man being constantly asked to make war on a power as great as that of Karstak Ovartamortes, for as you may know, the Guild has locals in all other cities and major towns of this land, not to mention agreements including powers of extradition with robber and bandit organizations in other countries. I love Vlana dearly, make no mistake about that, and she is an experienced thief herself, without whose guidance I'd hardly have survived my first week in Lankhmar, but on this one topic she has a kink in her brains, a hard knot neither logic nor persuasion can even begin to loosen. And I, well, in the month I've been here I've learned that the only way to survive in civilization is to abide by its unwritten rules—far more important than its laws chiseled in stone—and break them only at peril, in deepest secrecy, and taking all precautions. As I did tonight—not my first hijacking, by the by."

        "Certes t'would be insanity to assault the Guild direct, your wisdom's perfect there," the Mouser commented. "If you cannot break your most handsome girl of this mad notion, or coax her from it—and I can see she's a fearless, self-willed one—then you must stoutly refuse e'en her least request in that direction."

        "Certes I must," Fafhrd agreed, adding somewhat accusingly, "though I gather you told her you'd have willingly slit the throats of the two we struck senseless."

        "Courtesy merely, man! Would you have had me behave ungraciously to your girl? 'Tis measure of the value I was already setting then on your goodwill. But only a woman's man may cross her. As you must, in this instance."

        "Certes I must," Fafhrd repeated with great emphasis and conviction. "I'd be an idiot taking on the Guild. Of course if they should catch me they'd kill me in any case for freelancing and highjacking. But wantonly to assault the Guild direct, kill one

Guild-thief needlessly, only behave as if I might—lunacy entire!"

"You'd not only be a drunken, drooling idiot, you'd questionless be stinking in three nights at most from that emperor of diseases, Death. Malicious attacks on her person, blows directed at the organization, the Guild requites tenfold what she does other rule-breakings. All planned robberies and other thefts would be called off and the entire power of the Guild and its allies mobilized against you alone. I'd count your chances better to take on single-handed the host of the King of Kings rather than the Thieves' Guild's subtle minions. In view of your size, might, and wit you're a squad perhaps, or even a company, but hardly an army. So, no least giving-in to Vlana in this one matter."

"Agreed!" Fafhrd said loudly, shaking the Mouser's iron-thewed hand in a near crusher grip.

"And now we should be getting back to the girls," the Mouser said.

"After one more drink while we settle the score. Ho, boy!"

"Suits." The Mouser dug into his pouch to pay, but Fafhrd protested vehemently. In the end they tossed coin for it, and Fafhrd won and with great satisfaction clinked out his silver smerduks on the stained and dinted counter also marked with an infinitude of mug circles, as if it had been once the desk of a mad geometer. They pushed themselves to their feet, the Mouser giving the rathole one last light kick for luck.

At this, Fafhrd's thoughts looped back and he said, "Grant the beastie can't paw-write, or talk by mouth or paw, it still could have followed us at distance, marked down your dwelling, and then returned to Thieves' House to lead its masters down on us like a hound!"

"Now you're speaking shrewd sense again," the Mouser said. "Ho, boy, a bucket of small beer to go! On the instant!" Noting Fafhrd's blank look, he explained, "I'll spill it outside the Eel to kill our scent and all the way down the passageway. Yes, and splash it high on the walls too."

Fafhrd nodded wisely. "I thought I'd drunk my way past the addled point."

Vlana and Ivrian, deep in excited talk, both started at the pounding rush of footsteps up the stairs. Racing behemoths could hardly have made more noise. The creaking and groaning were prodigious and there were the crashes of two treads breaking, yet the pounding footsteps never faltered. The door flew open and their two men rushed in through a great mushroom top of night-smog which was neatly sliced off its black stem by the slam of the door.

"I told you we'd be back in a wink," the Mouser cried gayly to Ivrian, while Fafhrd strode forward, unmindful of the creaking floor, crying, "Dearest heart, I've missed you sorely," and caught up Vlana despite her voiced protests and pushings-off and kissed and hugged her soundly before setting her back on the couch again.

Oddly, it was Ivrian who appeared to be angry at Fafhrd then, rather than Vlana, who was smiling fondly if somewhat dazedly.

"Fafhrd, sir," she said boldly, little fists set on her narrow hips, her tapered chin held high, her dark eyes blazing, "my beloved Vlana has been telling me about the unspeakably atrocious things the Thieves' Guild did to her and to her dearest friends. Pardon my frank speaking to one I've only met, but I think it quite unmanly of you to refuse her the just revenge she desires and fully deserves. And that goes for you too, Mouse, who boasted to Vlana of what you would have done had you but known, who in like case did not scruple to slay my very own father—or reputed father—for his cruelties!"

It was clear to Fafhrd that while he and the Gray Mouser had idly boozed in the Eel, Vlana had been giving Ivrian a doubtless empurpled account of her grievances against the Guild and playing mercilessly on the naive girl's bookish, romantic sympathies and high concept of knightly honor. It was also clear to him that Ivrian was more than a little drunk. A three-quarters empty flask of violet wine of far Kiraay sat on the low table next them.

Yet he could think of nothing to do but spread his big hands helplessly and bow his head, more than the low ceiling made necessary, under Ivrian's glare, now reinforced by that of Vlana. After all, they *were* in the right. He *had* promised.

So it was the Mouser who first tried to rebut.

"Come now, pet," he cried lightly as he danced about the room, silk-stuffing more cracks against the thickening night-smog and stirring up and feeding the fire in the stove, "and you too, beauteous Lady Vlana. For the past month Fafhrd has been hitting the Guild-thieves where it hurts them most—in their purses a-dangle between their legs. His highjackings of the loot of their robberies have been like so many fierce kicks in their groins. Hurts worse, believe me, than robbing them of life with a swift, near painless sword slash or thrust. And tonight I helped him in his worthy purpose—and will eagerly do so again. Come, drink we up all." Under his handling, one of the new jugs came uncorked

with a pop and he darted about brimming silver cups
and mugs.

"A merchant's revenge!" Ivrian retorted with
scorn, not one whit appeased, but rather angered anew.
"Ye both are at heart true and gentle knights, I know,
despite all current backsliding. At the least you must
bring Vlana the head of Krovas!"

"What would she *do* with it? What *good*
would it be except to spot the carpets?" the Mouser
plaintively inquired, while Fafhrd, gathering his wits
at last and going down on one knee, said slowly,
"Most respected Lady Ivrian, it is true I solemnly
promised my beloved Vlana I would help her in her
revenge, but that was while I was still in barbarous
Cold Corner, where blood-feud is a commonplace,
sanctioned by custom and accepted by all the clans
and tribes and brotherhoods of the savage Northerners of the Cold Waste. In my naïveté I thought of
Vlana's revenge as being of that sort. But here in
civilization's midst, I discover all's different and rules
and customs turned upside-down. Yet—Lankhmar or
Cold Corner—one must seem to observe rule and
custom to survive. Here cash is all-powerful, the idol
placed highest, whether one sweat, thieve, grind others down, or scheme for it. Here feud and revenge
are outside all rules and punished worse than vio-
lent lunacy. Think, Lady Ivrian, if Mouse and I should
bring Vlana the head of Krovas, she and I would have
to flee Lankhmar on the instant, every man's hand
against us; while you infallibly would lose this fairy-
land Mouse has created for love of you and be forced
to do likewise, be with him a beggar on the run for
the rest of your natural lives."

It was beautifully reasoned and put…and no
good whatsoever. While Fafhrd spoke, Ivrian snatched

up her new-filled cup and drained it. Now she stood up straight as a soldier, her pale face flushed, and said scathingly to Fafhrd kneeling before her, "*You count the cost!* You speak to me of *things*"—she waved at the many-hued splendor around her—"of mere property, however costly, when *honor* is at stake. You gave Vlana *your word.* Oh, is knighthood wholly dead? And that applies to you, too, Mouse, who swore you'd slit the miserable throats of two noisome Guild-thieves."

"I didn't swear *to,*" the Mouser objected feebly, downing a big drink. "I merely said I *would have,*" while Fafhrd could only shrug again and writhe inside and gulp a little easement from his silver mug. For Ivrian was speaking in the same guilt-showering tones and using the same unfair yet heart-cleaving womanly arguments as Mor his mother might have, or Mara, his deserted Snow Clan sweetheart and avowed wife, big-bellied by now with his child.

In a master stroke, Vlana tried gently to draw Ivrian down to her golden seat again. "Softly, dearest," she pleaded. "You have spoken nobly for me and my cause, and believe me, I am most grateful. Your words revived in me great, fine feelings dead these many years. But of us here, only you are truly an aristocrat attuned to the highest proprieties. We other three are naught but thieves. Is it any wonder some of us put safety above honor and word-keeping, and most prudently avoid risking our lives? Yes, we are three thieves and I am outvoted. So please speak no more of honor and rash, dauntless bravery, but sit you down and—"

"You mean they're both *afraid* to challenge the Thieves' Guild, don't you?" Ivrian said, eyes wide and face twisted by loathing. "I always thought my Mouse was a nobleman first and a thief second.

Thieving's nothing. My father lived by cruel thievery done on rich wayfarers and neighbors less powerful than he, yet he was an aristocrat. Oh, you're *cowards*, both of you! *Poltroons!*" she finished, turning her eyes flashing with cold scorn first on the Mouser, then on Fafhrd.

The latter could stand it no longer. He sprang to his feet, face flushed, fists clenched at his sides, quite unmindful of his down-clattered mug and the ominous creak his sudden action drew from the sagging floor.

"*I am not a coward!*" he cried. "I'll dare Thieves' House and fetch you Krovas' head and toss it with blood a-drip at Vlana's feet. I swear that, witness me, Kos the god of dooms, by the brown bones of Nalgron my father and by his sword Graywand here at my side!"

He slapped his left hip, found nothing there but his tunic, and had to content himself with pointing tremble-armed at his belt and scabbarded sword where they lay atop his neatly folded robe—and then picking up, refilling splashily, and draining his mug.

The Gray Mouser began to laugh in high, delighted, tuneful peals. All stared at him. He came dancing up beside Fafhrd, and still smiling widely, asked, "*Why not?* Who speaks of fearing the Guildthieves? Who becomes upset at the prospect of this ridiculously easy exploit, when all of us know that all of them, even Krovas and his ruling clique, are but pygmies in mind and skill compared to me or Fafhrd here? A wondrously simple, foolproof scheme has just occurred to me for penetrating Thieves' House, every closet and cranny. Stout Fafhrd and I will put it into effect at once. Are you with me, Northerner?"

"Of course I am," Fafhrd responded gruffly, at the same time frantically wondering what madness had gripped the little fellow.

"Give me a few heartbeats to gather needed props, and we're off!" the Mouser cried. He snatched from a shelf and unfolded a stout sack, then raced about, thrusting into it coiled ropes, bandage rolls, rags, jars of ointment and unction and unguent, and other oddments.

"But you can't go *tonight*," Ivrian protested, suddenly grown pale and uncertain-voiced. "You're both…in no condition to."

"You're both *drunk*," Vlana said harshly. "Silly drunk—and that way you'll get naught in Thieves' House but your deaths. Fafhrd, where's that heartless reason you employed to slay or ice-veined see slain a clutch of mighty rivals and win me at Cold Corner and in the chilly, sorcery-webbed depths of Trollstep Canyon? Revive it! And infuse some into your skipping gray friend."

"Oh, no," Fafhrd told her as he buckled on his sword. "You wanted the head of Krovas heaved at your feet in a great splatter of blood, and that's what you're going to get, like it or not!"

"Softly, Fafhrd," the Mouser interjected, coming to a sudden stop and drawing tight the sack's mouth by its strings. "And softly you too, Lady Vlana, and my dear princess. Tonight I intend but a scouting expedition. No risks run, only the information gained needful for planning our murderous strike tomorrow or the day after. So no head-choppings whatsoever tonight, Fafhrd, you hear me? Whatever mayhap, hist's the word. And don your hooded robe."

Fafhrd shrugged, nodded, and obeyed.

Ivrian seemed somewhat relieved. Vlana too, though she said, "Just the same you're both drunk."

"All to the good!" the Mouser assured her with a mad smile. "Drink may slow a man's sword-arm and soften his blows a bit, but it sets his wits ablaze and fires his imagination, and those are the qualities we'll need tonight. Besides," he hurried on, cutting off some doubt Ivrian was about to voice, "drunken men are supremely cautious! Have you ever seen a staggering sot pull himself together at sight of the guard and walk circumspectly and softly past?"

"Yes," Vlana said, "and fall flat on his face just as he comes abreast 'em."

"Pish!" the Mouser retorted and, throwing back his head, grandly walked toward her along an imaginary straight line. Instantly he tripped over his own foot, plunged forward, suddenly without touching floor did an incredible forward flip, heels over head, and landed erect and quite softly—toes, ankles, and knees bending just at the right moment to soak up impact—directly in front of the girls. The floor barely complained.

"You see?" he said, straightening up and unexpectedly reeling backward. He tripped over the pillow on which lay his cloak and sword, but by a wrenching twist and a lurch stayed upright and began rapidly to accouter himself.

Under cover of this action Fafhrd made quietly yet swiftly to fill once more his and the Mouser's mugs, but Vlana noted it and gave him such a glare that he set down mugs and uncorked jug so swiftly his robe swirled, then stepped back from the drinks table with a shrug of resignation and toward Vlana a grimacing nod.

The Mouser shouldered his sack and

drew open the door. With a casual wave at the girls, but no word spoken, Fafhrd stepped out on the tiny porch. The night-smog had grown so thick he was almost lost to view. The Mouser waved four fingers at Ivrian, softly called, "Bye-bye, Misling," then followed Fafhrd.

"Good fortune go with you," Vlana called heartily.

"Oh be careful, Mouse," Ivrian gasped.

The Mouser, his figure slight against the loom of Fafhrd's, silently drew shut the door.

Their arms automatically gone around each other, the girls waited for the inevitable creaking and groaning of the stairs. It delayed and delayed. The night-smog that had entered the room dissipated and still the silence was unbroken. "What can they be doing out there?" Ivrian whispered. "Plotting their course?"

Vlana, scowling, impatiently shook her head, then disentangled herself, tiptoed to the door, opened it, descended softly a few steps, which creaked most dolefully, then returned, shutting the door behind her.

"They're gone," she said in wonder, her eyes wide, her hands spread a little to either side, palms up.

"I'm frightened!" Ivrian breathed and sped across the room to embrace the taller girl.

Vlana hugged her tight, then disengaged an arm to shoot the door's three heavy bolts.

In Bones Alley the Mouser returned to his pouch the knotted line by which they'd descended from the lamp-hook. He suggested, "How about stopping at the Silver Eel?"

"You mean and just *tell* the girls we've been to Thieves' House?" Fafhrd asked, not too indignantly.

"Oh, no," the Mouser protested. "But you missed your stirrup cup upstairs and so did I."

At the word "stirrup" he looked down at his ratskin boots and then crouching began a little gallop in one place, his boot-soles clopping softly on the cobbles. He flapped imaginary reins—"Giddap!"—and quickened his gallop, but leaning sharply back pulled to a stop—"Whoa!"—when with a crafty smile Fafhrd drew from his robe two full jugs.

"Palmed 'em, as 'twere, when I set down the mugs. Vlana sees a lot, but not all."

"You're a prudent, far-sighted fellow, in addition to having some skill at sword taps," the Mouser said admiringly. "I'm proud to call you comrade."

Each uncorked and drank a hearty slug. Then the Mouser led them west, they veering and stumbling only a little. Not so far as Cheap Street, however, but turning north into an even narrower and more noisome alley.

"Plague Court," the Mouser said. Fafhrd nodded.

After several preliminary peepings and peerings, they staggered swiftly across wide, empty Crafts Street and into Plague Court again. For a wonder it was growing a little lighter. Looking upward, they saw stars. Yet there was no wind blowing from the north. The air was deathly still.

In their drunken preoccupation with the project at hand and mere locomotion, they did not look behind them. There the night-smog was thicker than ever. A high-circling nighthawk would have seen the stuff converging from all sections of Lankhmar, north, east, south, west—from the Inner Sea, from the Great Salt Marsh, from the many-ditched grain lands, from the River Hlal—in swift-moving black rivers and rivulets, heaping, eddying, swirling, dark and reeking essence of Lankhmar from its branding irons, braziers, bonfires, bonefires, kitchen fires and warmth fires, kilns, forges, breweries, distilleries, junk and garbage fires innumerable, sweating alchemists' and sorcerers' dens, crematoriums, charcoal burners' turfed mounds, all those and many more…converging purposefully on Dim Lane and particularly on the Silver Eel and perhaps especially on the ricketty house behind it, untenanted except for attic. The closer to that center it got, the more substantial the smog became, eddy-strands and swirl-tatters tearing off and clinging to rough stone corners and scraggly-surfaced brick like black cobwebs.

But the Mouser and Fafhrd merely exclaimed in mild, muted amazement at the stars, muggily mused as to how much the improved visibility would increase the risk of their quest, and cautiously crossing the Street of the Thinkers, called Atheist Avenue by moralists, continued to Plague Court until it forked.

The Mouser chose the left branch, which trended northwest.

"Death Alley."

Fafhrd nodded.

After a curve and recurve, Cheap Street swung into sight about thirty paces ahead. The Mouser stopped at once and lightly threw his arm against Fafhrd's chest.

Clearly in view across Cheap Street was a wide, low, open doorway, framed by grimy stone blocks. There led up to it two steps hollowed by the treadings of centuries. Orange-yellow light spilled out from bracketed torches inside. They couldn't see very far in because of Death Alley's angle. Yet as far as they *could* see, there was no porter or guard in sight, nor anyone at all, not a watchdog on a chain. The effect was ominous.

"Now how do we get into the damn place?" Fafhrd demanded in a hoarse whisper. "Scout Murder Alley for a back window that can be forced. You've pries in that sack, I trow. Or try the roof? You're a roof man, I know already. Teach me the art. I know trees and mountains, snow, ice, and bare rock. See this wall here?" He backed off from it, preparing to go up it in a rush.

"Steady on, Fafhrd," the Mouser said, keeping his hand against the big young man's chest. "We'll hold the roof in reserve. Likewise all walls. And I'll take it on trust you're a master climber. As to how we get in, we walk straight through that doorway." He frowned. "Tap and hobble, rather. Come on, while I prepare us."

As he drew the skeptically grimacing Fafhrd back down Death Alley until all Cheap Street was again cut off from view, he explained, "We'll pretend to be beggars, members of *their* guild, which is but a branch of the Thieves' Guild and houses with it, or at any rate reports in to the Beggarmasters at Thieves' House. We'll be new members, who've gone out by day, so it'll not be expected that the Night Beggarmaster and any night watchmen know our looks."

"But we don't look like beggars," Fafhrd protested. "Beggars have awful sores and limbs all a-twist or lacking altogether."

"That's just what I'm going to take care of now," the Mouser chuckled, drawing Scalpel. Ignoring Fafhrd's backward step and wary glance, the Mouser gazed puzzledly at the long tapering strip of steel he'd bared, then with a happy nod unclipped from his belt Scalpel's scabbard furbished with ratskin, sheathed the sword and swiftly wrapped it up, hilt and all, in a spiral, with the wide ribbon of a bandage roll dug from his sack.

"There!" he said, knotting the bandage ends. "Now I've a tapping cane."

"What's that?" Fafhrd demanded. "And why?"

"Because I'll be blind, that's why." He took a few shuffling steps, tapping the cobbles ahead with wrapped sword—gripping it by the quillons, or cross guard, so that the grip and pommel were up his sleeve—and groping ahead with his other hand. "That look all right to you?" he asked Fafhrd as he turned back. "Feels perfect to me. Bat-blind, eh? Oh, don't fret, Fafhrd—the rag's but gauze. I can see through it fairly well. Besides, I don't have to convince anyone inside Thieves' House I'm actually blind. Most Guild-beggars fake it, as you must know. Now what to do with you? Can't have you blind also—too obvious, might wake suspicion." He uncorked his jug and sucked inspiration. Fafhrd copied this action, on principle.

The Mouser smacked his lips and said, "I've got it! Fafhrd, stand on your right leg and double up your left behind you at the knee. Hold! Don't fall on me! Avaunt! But steady yourself by my shoulder. That's right. Now get that left foot higher. We'll disguise your sword like mine, for a crutch cane—it's thicker and'll look just right. You can also steady yourself with your other hand on my shoulder as you hop—the halt leading the blind, always good for a tear, always good theater! But higher with that left foot! No, it just doesn't come off—I'll have to rope it. But first unclip your scabbard."

Soon the Mouser had Graywand and its scabbard in the same state as Scalpel and was tying Fafhrd's left ankle to his thigh, drawing the rope cruelly tight, though Fafhrd's wine-anesthetized nerves hardly registered it. Balancing himself with his steel-cored crutch cane as the Mouser worked, he swigged from his jug and pondered deeply. Ever since joining forces with Vlana, he'd been interested in the theater, and the atmosphere of the actors' tenement had fired that interest further, so that he was delighted at the prospect of acting a part in real life. Yet brilliant as the Mouser's plan undoubtedly was, there did seem to be drawbacks to it. He tried to formulate them.

"Mouser," he said, "I don't know as I like having our swords tied up, so we can't draw 'em in emergency."

"We can still use 'em as clubs," the Mouser countered, his breath hissing between his teeth as he drew the last knot hard. "Besides, we'll have our knives. Say, pull your belt around until yours is behind your back, so your robe will hide it sure. I'll do the same with Cat's Claw. Beggars don't carry weapons, at least in view, and we must maintain dramatic consistency in every detail. Stop drinking now; you've had enough. I myself need only a couple swallows more to reach my finest pitch."

"And I don't know as I like going hobbled into that den of cutthroats. I can hop amazingly fast, it's true, but not as fast as I can run. Is it really wise, think you?"

"You can slash yourself loose in an instant," the Mouser hissed with a touch of impatience and anger. "Aren't you willing to make the least sacrifice for art's sake?"

"Oh, very well," Fafhrd said, draining his jug and tossing it aside. "Yes, of course I am."

"Your complexion's too hale," the Mouser said, inspecting him critically. He touched up Fafhrd's features and hands with pale gray greasepaint, then added wrinkles with dark. "And your garb's too tidy." He scooped dirt from between the cobbles and smeared it on Fafhrd's robe, then tried to put a rip in it, but the material resisted. He shrugged and tucked his lightened sack under his belt.

"So's yours," Fafhrd observed, and stooping on his right leg got a good handful of muck himself, ordure in it by its feel and stink. Heaving himself up with a mighty effort, he wiped the stuff off on the Mouser's cloak and gray silken jerkin too.

The small man got the odor and cursed, but, "Dramatic consistency," Fafhrd reminded him. "It's well we stink. Beggars do—that's one reason folk give 'em coins: to get rid of 'em. And no one at Thieves' House will be eager to inspect us close. Now come on, while our fires are still high." And grasping hold of the Mouser's shoulder, he propelled himself rapidly toward Cheap Street, setting his bandaged sword between cobbles well ahead and taking mighty hops.

"Slow down, idiot," the Mouser cried softly, shuffling along with the speed almost of a skater to keep up, while tapping his (sword) cane like mad. "A cripple's supposed to be *feeble*—that's what draws the sympathy."

Fafhrd nodded wisely and slowed somewhat. The ominous empty doorway slid again into view. The Mouser tilted his jug to get the last of his wine, swallowed awhile, then choked sputteringly. Fafhrd snatched and drained the jug, then tossed it over shoulder to shatter noisily.

They hop-shuffled into Cheap Street, halting almost at once for a richly clad man and woman to pass. The richness of the man's garb was sober and he was on the fat and oldish side, though hard-featured. A merchant doubtless, and with money in the Thieves' Guild—protection money, at least—to take this route at this hour.

The richness of the woman's garb was garish though not tawdry and she was beautiful and young, and looked still younger. A competent courtesan, almost certainly.

The man started to veer around the noisome and filthy pair, his face averted, but the girl swung toward the Mouser, concern growing in her eyes with hothouse swiftness. "Oh, you poor boy! Blind. What tragedy," she said. "Give us a gift for him, lover."

"Keep away from those stinkards, Misra, and come along," he retorted, the last of his speech vibrantly muffled, for he was holding his nose.

She made him no reply, but thrust white hand into his ermine pouch and swiftly pressed a coin against the Mouser's palm and closed his fingers on it, then took his head between her palms and kissed him sweetly on the lips before letting herself be dragged on.

"Take good care of the little fellow, old man," she called fondly back to Fafhrd while her companion grumbled muffled reproaches at her, of which only "perverted bitch" was intelligible.

The Mouser stared at the coin in his palm, then sneaked a long look after his benefactress. There was a dazed wonder in his voice as he whispered to Fafhrd, "Look. *Gold.* A golden coin and a beautiful woman's sympathy. Think you we should give over this rash project and for a profession take up beggary?"

"Buggery even, rather!" Fafhrd answered harsh and low. That "old man" rankled. "Onward we, bravely!"

They upped the two worn steps and went through the doorway, noting the exceptional thickness of the wall. Ahead was a long, straight, high-ceilinged corridor ending in a stairs and with doors spilling light at intervals and wall-set torches adding their flare, but empty all its length.

They had just got through the doorway when cold steel chilled the neck and pricked a shoulder of each of them. From just above, two voices commanded in unison, "Halt!"

Although fired—and fuddled—by fortified wine, they each had wit enough to freeze and then very cautiously look upward.

Two gaunt, scarred, exceptionally ugly faces, each topped by a gaudy scarf binding back hair, looked down at them from a big, deep niche just above the doorway and helping explain its lowness. Two bent, gnarly arms thrust down the swords that still pricked them.

"Gone out with the noon beggar-batch, eh?" one of them observed. "Well, you'd better have a high take to justify your tardy return. The Night Beggarmaster's on a Whore Street furlough. Report above to Krovas. Gods, you stink! Better clean up first, or Krovas will have you bathed in live steam. Begone!"

The Mouser and Fafhrd shuffled and hobbled forward at their most authentic. One niche-guard cried after them, "Relax, boys! You don't have to put it on here."

"Practice makes perfect," the Mouser called back in a quavering voice. Fafhrd's finger-ends dug his shoulder warningly. They moved along somewhat more naturally, so far as Fafhrd's tied-up leg allowed.

"Gods, what an easy life the Guild-beggars have," the other niche-guard observed to his mate.

"What slack discipline and low standards of skill! Perfect, my sacred butt! You'd think a child could see through those disguises."

"Doubtless some children do," his mate retorted. "But their dear mothers and fathers only drop a tear and a coin or give a kick. Grown folk go blind, lost in their toil and dreams, unless they have a profession such as thieving which keeps them mindful of things as they really are."

Resisting the impulse to ponder this sage philosophy, and glad they would not have to undergo a Beggarmaster's shrewd inspection—truly, thought Fafhrd, Kos of the Dooms seemed to be leading him direct to Krovas and perhaps head-chopping *would* be the order of the night—he and the Mouser went watchfully and slowly on. And now they began to hear voices, mostly curt and clipped ones, and other noises.

They passed some doorways they'd liked to have paused at, to study the activities inside, yet the most they dared do was slow down a bit more. Fortunately most of the doorways were wide, permitting a fairly long view.

Very interesting were some of those activities. In one room young boys were being trained to pick pouches and slit purses. They'd approach from behind an instructor, and if he heard scuff of bare foot or felt touch of dipping hand—or, worst, heard *clunk* of dropped leaden mock-coin—that boy would be thwacked. Others seemed to be getting training in group tactics: the jostle in front, the snatch from behind, the swift passing of lifted items from youthful thief to confederate.

In a second room, from which pushed air heavy with the reeks of metal and oil, older student thieves were doing laboratory work in lock picking. One group was being lectured by a grimy-handed graybeard, who was taking apart a most complex lock piece by weighty piece. Others appeared to be having their skill, speed, and ability to work soundlessly tested—they were probing with slender picks the keyholes in a half dozen doors set side by side in an otherwise purposeless partition, while a supervisor holding a sandglass watched them keenly.

In a third, thieves were eating at long tables. The odors were tempting, even to men full of booze. The Guild did well by its members.

In a fourth, the floor was padded in part and instruction was going on in slipping, dodging, ducking, tumbling, tripping, and otherwise foiling pursuit. These students were older too. A voice like a sergeant-major's rasped, "Nah, nah, nah! You couldn't give your crippled grandmother the slip. I said duck, not genuflect to holy Aarth. Now this time—"

"Grif's used grease," an instructor called.

"He has, eh? To the front, Grif!" the rasping voice replied as the Mouser and Fafhrd moved somewhat regretfully out of sight, for they realized much was to be learned here: tricks that might stand them in good stead even tonight. "Listen, all of you!" the rasping voice continued, so far-carrying it followed them a surprisingly long way. "Grease may be very well on a night job—by day its glisten shouts its user's profession to all Nehwon! But in any case it makes a thief overconfident. He comes to depend on it and then in a pinch he finds he's forgot to apply it. Also its aroma can betray him. Here we work always dry-skinned—save for natural sweat!—as all of you were told first night. Bend over, Grif. Grasp your ankles. Straighten your knees."

More thwacks, followed by yelps of pain, distant now, since the Mouser and Fafhrd were half-way up the end-stairs, Fafhrd vaulting somewhat laboriously as he grasped curving banister and swaddled sword.

The second floor duplicated the first, but was as luxurious as the other had been bare. Down the long corridor lamps and filigreed incense pots pendant from the ceiling alternated, diffusing a mild light and spicy smell. The walls were richly draped, the floor thick-carpeted. Yet this corridor was empty too and, moreover, *completely* silent. After a glance at each other, they started off boldly. The first door, wide open, showed an untenanted room full of racks of garments, rich and plain, spotless and filthy, also wig stands, shelves of beards and such, and several wall mirrors faced by small tables crowded with cosmetics and with stools before them. A disguising room, clearly.

After a look and listen either way, the Mouser darted in and out to snatch up a large green flask from the nearest table. He unstoppered and sniffed it. A rotten-sweet gardenia-reek contended with the nose-sting of spirits of wine. The Mouser sloshed his and Fafhrd's fronts with this dubious perfume.

"Antidote to ordure," he explained with the pomp of a physician, stoppering the flask. "Don't want to be parboiled by Krovas. No, no, no."

Two figures appeared at the far end of the corridor and came toward them. The Mouser hid the flask under his cloak, holding it between elbow and side, and he and Fafhrd continued onward—to turn back would look suspicious, both drunkenly judged.

The next three doorways they passed were shut by heavy doors. As they neared the fifth, the two approaching figures, coming on arm-in-arm, yet taking long strides, moving more swiftly than the hobble-shuffle, became distinct. Their clothing was that of noblemen, but their faces those of thieves. They were frowning with indignation and suspicion too at the Mouser and Fafhrd.

Just then—from somewhere between the two man-pairs, it sounded—a voice began to speak words in a strange tongue, using the rapid monotone priests employ in a routine service, or some sorcerers in their incantations.

The two richly clad thieves slowed at the seventh doorway and looked in. Their progress ceased altogether. Their necks strained, their eyes widened. They visibly paled. Then of a sudden they hastened onward, almost running, and bypassed Fafhrd and the Mouser as if they were furniture. The incantory voice drummed on without missing a beat.

The fifth doorway was shut, but the sixth was open. The Mouser peeked in with one eye, his nose brushing the jamb. Then he stepped forward and gazed inside with entranced expression, pushing the black rag up onto his forehead for better vision. Fafhrd joined him.

It was a large room, empty so far as could be told of human and animal life, but filled with most interesting things. From knee-height up, the entire far wall was a map of the city of Lankhmar and its immediate surrounds. Every building and street seemed depicted, down to the meanest hovel and narrowest court. There were signs of recent erasure and redrawing at many spots, and here and there little colored hieroglyphs of mysterious import.

The floor was marble, the ceiling blue as lapis lazuli. The side walls were thickly hung, by ring and padlock. One was covered with all manner of thieves' tools, from a huge thick pry-bar that looked

as if it could unseat the universe, or at least the door
of the Overlord's treasure-vault, to a rod so slim it
might be an elf-queen's wand and seemingly designed
to telescope out and fish from distance for precious
gauds on milady's spindle-legged, ivory-topped vanity
table; the other wall had on it all sorts of quaint, gold-
gleaming and jewel-flashing objects, evidently
mementos chosen for their oddity from the spoils of
memorable burglaries, from a female mask of thin gold,
breathlessly beautiful in its features and contours, but
thickly set with rubies simulating the spots of the pox
in its fever-stage, to a knife whose blade was wedge-
shaped diamonds set side by side and this diamond
cutting-edge looking razor-sharp.

All about were tables set chiefly with models
of dwelling houses and other buildings, accurate to
the last minutia, it looked, of ventilation hole under
roof gutter and ground-level drain hole, of creviced
wall and smooth. Many were cut away in partial or
entire section to show the layout of rooms, closets,
strongrooms, doorways, corridors, secret passages,
smoke-ways, and air-ways in equal detail.

In the center of the room was a bare round-
table of ebony and ivory squares. About it were set
seven straight-backed but well-padded chairs, the one
facing the map and away from the Mouser and Fafhrd
being higher backed and wider armed than the others—a chief's chair, likely that of Krovas.

The Mouser tiptoed forward, irresistibly
drawn, but Fafhrd's left hand clamped down on his
shoulder like the iron mitten of a Mingol cataphract
and drew him irresistibly back.

Scowling his disapproval, the Northerner
brushed down the black rag over the Mouser's eyes

again, and with his crutch-hand thumbed ahead; then set off in that direction in most carefully calculated, silent hops. With a shrug of disappointment the Mouser followed.

As soon as they had turned away from the doorway, but before they were out of sight, a neatly black-bearded, crop-haired head came like a serpent's around the side of the highest-backed chair and gazed after them from deep-sunken yet glinting eyes. Next a snake-supple, long hand followed the head out, crossed thin lips with ophidian forefinger for silence, and then finger-beckoned the two pairs of dark-tunicked men who were standing to either side of the doorway, their backs to the corridor wall, each of the four gripping a curvy knife in one hand and a dark leather, lead-weighted bludgeon in the other.

When Fafhrd was halfway to the seventh doorway, from which the monotonous yet sinister recitation continued to well, there shot out through it a slender, whey-faced youth, his narrow hands clapped over his mouth, under terror-wide eyes, as if to shut in screams or vomit, and with a broom clamped in an armpit, so that he seemed a bit like a young warlock about to take to the air. He dashed past Fafhrd and the Mouser and away, his racing footsteps sounding rapid-dull on the carpeting and hollow-sharp on the stairs before dying away.

Fafhrd gazed back at the Mouser with a grimace and shrug, then squatting one-legged until the knee of his bound-up leg touched the floor, advanced half his face past the doorjamb. After a bit, without otherwise changing position, he beckoned the Mouser to approach. The latter slowly thrust half his face past the jamb, just above Fafhrd's.

What they saw was a room somewhat smaller than that of the great map and lit by central lamps that burned blue-white instead of customary yellow. The floor was marble, darkly colorful and complexly whorled. The dark walls were hung with astrological and anthropomantic charts and instruments of magic and shelved with cryptically labeled porcelain jars and also with vitreous flasks and glass pipes of the oddest shapes, some filled with colored fluids, but many gleamingly empty. At the foot of the walls, where the shadows were thickest, broken and discarded stuff was irregularly heaped, as if swept out of the way and forgot, and here and there opened a large rathole.

In the center of the room and brightly illuminated by contrast was a long table with thick top and many stout legs. The Mouser thought fleetingly of a centipede and then of the bar at the Eel, for the tabletop was densely stained and scarred by many a spilled elixir and many a deep black burn by fire or acid or both.

In the midst of the table an alembic was working. The lamp's flame—deep blue, this one—kept a-boil in the large crystal cucurbit a dark, viscid fluid with here and there diamond glints. From out of the thick, seething stuff, strands of a darker vapor streamed upward to crowd through the cucurbit's narrow mouth and stain—oddly, with bright scarlet—the transparent head and then, dead black now, flow down the narrow pipe from the head into a spherical crystal receiver, larger even than the cucurbit, and there curl and weave about like so many coils of living black cord—an endless, skinny, ebon serpent.

Behind the left end of the table stood a tall, yet hunchbacked man in black robe and hood which shadowed more than hid a face of which the most prominent features were a long, thick, pointed nose with out-jutting, almost chinless mouth just below. His complexion was sallow-gray like clay and a short-haired bristly, gray beard grew high on his wide cheeks. From under a receding forehead and bushy gray brows, wide-set eyes looked intently down at an age-browned scroll, which his disgustingly small clubhands, knuckles big, short backs gray-bristled, ceaselessly unrolled and rolled up again. The only move his eyes ever made, besides the short side-to-side one as he read the lines he was rapidly intoning, was an occasional farther sidewise glance at the alembic.

On the other end of the table, beady eyes darting from the sorcerer to the alembic and back again, crouched a small black beast, the first glimpse of which made Fafhrd dig fingers painfully into the Mouser's shoulder and the latter almost gasp, not from the pain. It was most like a rat, yet it had a higher forehead and closer-set eyes than either had ever seen in a rat, while its forepaws, which it constantly rubbed together in what seemed restless glee, looked like tiny copies of the sorcerer's clubhands.

Simultaneously yet independently, Fafhrd and the Mouser each became certain it was the beast which had gutter-escorted Slivikin and his mate, then fled, and each recalled what Ivrian had said about a witch's familiar and Vlana about the likelihood of Krovas employing a warlock.

What with the ugliness of the clubhanded man and beast and between them the ropy black vapor coiling and twisting in the great receiver and head, like a black umbilical cord, it was a most horrid sight. And the similarities, save for size, between the two creatures were even more disquieting in their implications.

The tempo of the incantation quickened, the blue-white flames brightened and hissed audibly, the fluid in the cucurbit grew thick as lava, great bubbles formed and loudly broke, the black rope in the receiver writhed like a nest of snakes; there was an increasing sense of invisible presences, the supernatural tension grew almost unendurable, and Fafhrd and the Mouser were hard put to keep silent the open-mouthed gasps by which they now breathed, and each feared his heartbeat could be heard cubits away.

Abruptly the incantation peaked and broke off, like a drum struck very hard, then instantly silenced by palm and fingers outspread against the head. With a bright flash and dull explosion, cracks innumerable appeared in the cucurbit; its crystal became white and opaque, yet it did not shatter or drip. The head lifted a span, hung there, fell back. While two black nooses appeared among the coils in the receiver and suddenly narrowed until they were only two big black knots.

The sorcerer grinned, rolling up the end of the parchment with a snap, and shifted his gaze from the receiver to his familiar, while the latter chittered shrilly and bounded up and down in rapture.

"Silence, Slivikin! Comes now your time to race and strain and sweat," the sorcerer cried, speaking pidgin Lankhmarese now, but so rapidly and in so squeakingly high-pitched a voice that Fafhrd and the Mouser could barely follow him. They did, however, both realize they had been completely mistaken as to the identity of Slivikin. In moment of disaster, the fat thief had called to the witch-beast for help rather than to his human comrade.

"Yes, master," Slivikin squeaked back no less clearly, in an instant revising the Mouser's opinions about talking animals. He continued in the same fifelike, fawning tones, "Harkening in obedience, Hristomilo."

Now they knew the sorcerer's name too.

Hristomilo ordered in whiplash pipings, "To your appointed work! See to it you summon an ample sufficiency of feasters! I want the bodies stripped to skeletons, so the bruises of the enchanted smog and all evidence of death by suffocation will be vanished utterly. But forget not the loot! On your mission, now—depart!"

Slivikin, who at every command had bobbed his head in manner reminiscent of his bouncing, now squealed, "I'll see it done!" and gray-lightninglike leaped a long leap to the floor and down an inky rathole.

Hristomilo, rubbing together his disgusting clubhands much as Slivikin had his, cried chucklingly, "What Slevyas lost, my magic has rewon!"

Fafhrd and the Mouser drew back out of the doorway, partly with the thought that since neither his incantation and his alembic, nor his familiar now required his unblinking attention, Hristomilo would surely look up and spot them; partly in revulsion from what they had seen and heard; and in poignant if useless pity for Slevyas, whoever he might be, and for the other unknown victims of the ratlike and conceivably rat-related sorcerer's death spells, poor strangers already dead and due to have their flesh eaten from their bones.

Fafhrd wrested the green bottle from the Mouser and, though almost gagging on the rotten-flowery reek, gulped a large, stinging mouthful. The Mouser couldn't quite bring himself to do the same, but was comforted by the spirits of wine he inhaled during this byplay.

Then he saw, beyond Fafhrd, standing before the doorway to the map room, a richly clad man with gold-hilted knife jewel-scabbarded at his side. His sunken-eyed face was prematurely wrinkled by responsibility, overwork, and authority, framed by neatly cropped black hair and beard. Smiling, he silently beckoned them.

The Mouser and Fafhrd obeyed, the latter returning the green bottle to the former, who recapped it and thrust it under his left elbow with well-concealed irritation.

Each guessed their summoner was Krovas, the Guild's Grandmaster. Once again Fafhrd marveled, as he hobbledehoyed along, reeling and belching, how Kos or the Fates were guiding him to his target tonight. The Mouser, more alert and more apprehensive too, was reminding himself that they had been directed by the niche-guards to report to Krovas, so that the situation, if not developing quite in accord with his own misty plans, was still not deviating disastrously.

Yet not even his alertness, nor Fafhrd's primeval instincts, gave him forewarning as they followed Krovas into the map room.

Two steps inside, each of them was shoulder-grabbed and bludgeon-menaced by a pair of ruffians further armed with knives tucked in their belts.

They judged it wise to make no resistance, on this one occasion at least bearing out the Mouser's mouthings about the supreme caution of drunken men.

"All secure, Grandmaster," one of the ruffians rapped out.

Krovas swung the highest-backed chair around and sat down, eyeing them coolly yet searchingly.

"What brings two stinking, drunken beggar-Guildsmen into the top-restricted precincts of the masters?" he asked quietly.

The Mouser felt the sweat of relief bead his forehead. The disguises he had brilliantly conceived were still working, taking in even the head man, though he had spotted Fafhrd's tipsiness. Resuming his blind-man manner, he quavered, "We were directed by the guard above the Cheap Street door to report to you in person, great Krovas, the Night Beggarmaster being on furlough for reasons of sexual hygiene. To-night we've made good haul!" And fumbling in his purse, ignoring as far as possible the tightened grip on his shoulders, he brought out the golden coin given him by the sentimental courtesan and displayed it tremble-handed.

"Spare me your inexpert acting," Krovas said sharply. "I'm not one of your marks. And take that rag off your eyes."

The Mouser obeyed and stood to attention again insofar as his pinioning would permit, and smiling the more seeming carefree because of his reawakening uncertainties. Conceivably he wasn't doing quite as brilliantly as he'd thought.

Krovas leaned forward and said placidly yet piercingly, "Granted you were so ordered—and most improperly so; that door-guard will suffer for his stupidity!—why were you spying into a room beyond this one when I spotted you?"

"We saw brave thieves flee from that room," the Mouser answered pat. "Fearing that some danger threatened the Guild, my comrade and I investigated, ready to scotch it."

"But what we saw and heard only perplexed us, great sir," Fafhrd appended quite smoothly.

"I didn't ask you, sot. Speak when you're spoken to," Krovas snapped at him. Then, to the Mouser, "You're an overweening rogue, most presumptuous for your rank."

In a flash the Mouser decided that further insolence, rather than fawning, was what the situation required. "That I am, sir," he said smugly. "For example, I have a master plan whereby you and the Guild might gain more wealth and power in three months than your predecessors have in three millennia."

Krovas' face darkened. "Boy!" he called. Through the curtains of an inner doorway, a youth with dark complexion of a Kleshite and clad only in a black loincloth sprang to kneel before Krovas, who ordered, "Summon first my sorcerer, next the thieves Slevyas and Fissif," whereupon the dark youth dashed into the corridor.

Then Krovas, his face its normal pale again, leaned back in his great chair, lightly rested his sinewy arms on its great padded ones, and smilingly directed at the Mouser, "Speak your piece. Reveal to us this master plan."

Forcing his mind *not* to work on the surprising news that Slevyas was not victim but thief and not sorcery-slain but alive and available—why did Krovas want him *now*?—the Mouser threw back his head and, shaping his lips in a faint sneer, began, "You may laugh merrily at me, Grandmaster, but I'll warrant that in less than a score of heartbeats you'll be straining sober-faced to hear my least word. Like lightning, wit can strike anywhere, and the best of you in Lankhmar have age-honored blind spots for things obvious to us of outland birth. My master plan is but this: let Thieves' Guild under your iron autocracy seize supreme power in

Lankhmar City, then in Lankhmar Land, next over all Nehwon, after which who knows what realms undreamt will know your suzerainty!"

The Mouser had spoken true in one respect: Krovas was no longer smiling. He was leaning forward a little and his face was darkening again, but whether from interest or anger it was too soon to say.

The Mouser continued, "For centuries the Guild's had more than the force and intelligence needed to make a *coup d'etat* a nine-finger certainty; today there's not one hair's chance in a bushy head of failure. It is the proper state of things that thieves rule other men. All Nature cries out for it. No need slay old Karstak Ovartamortes, merely overmaster, control, and so rule through him. You've already fee'd informers in every noble or wealthy house. Your post's better than the King of Kings'. You've a mercenary striking force permanently mobilized, should you have need of it, in the Slayers' Brotherhood. We Guild-beggars are your foragers. O great Krovas, the multitudes know that thievery rules Nehwon, nay, the universe, nay, more, the highest gods' abode! And the multitudes accept this, they balk only at the hypocrisy of the present arrangement, at the pretense that things are otherwise. Oh, give them their decent desire, great Krovas! Make it all open, honest and aboveboard, with thieves ruling in name as well as fact."

The Mouser spoke with passion, for the moment believing all he said, even the contradictions. The four ruffians gaped at him with wonder and not a little awe. They slackened their holds on him and on Fafhrd too.

But leaning back in his great chair again and smiling thinly and ominously, Krovas said coolly, "In *our* Guild intoxication is no excuse for folly, rather grounds for the extremest penalty. But I'm well aware your organized beggars operate under a laxer discipline. So I'll deign to explain to you, you wee drunken dreamer, that we thieves know well that, behind the scenes, we already rule Lankhmar, Nehwon, all life in sooth—for what is life but greed in action? But to make this an open thing would not only force us to take on ten thousand sorts of weary work others now do for us, it would also go against another of life's deep laws: illusion. Does the sweetmeats hawker show you his kitchen? Does a whore let average client watch her enamel-over her wrinkles and hoist her sagging breasts in cunning gauzy slings? Does a conjurer turn out for you his hidden pockets? Nature works by subtle, secret means—man's invisible seed, spider bite, the viewless spores of madness and of death, rocks that are born in earth's unknown bowels, the silent stars a-creep across the sky—and we thieves copy her."

"That's good enough poetry, sir," Fafhrd responded with undertone of angry derision, for he had himself been considerably impressed by the Mouser's master plan and was irked that Krovas should do insult to his new friend by disposing of it so lightly. "Closet kingship may work well enough in easy times. But"—he paused histrionically—"will it serve when Thieves' Guild is faced with an enemy determined to obliterate it forever, a plot to wipe it entirely from the earth?"

"What drunken babble's this?" Krovas demanded, sitting up straight. "*What* plot?"

"'Tis a most *secret* one," Fafhrd responded grinning, delighted to pay this haughty man in his own coin and thinking it quite just that the thief-king sweat a little before his head was removed for convey-ance to Vlana. "I know naught of it, except that many a master thief is marked down for the knife—and your head doomed to fall!"

Fafhrd merely sneered his face and folded his arms, the still slack grip of his captors readily permit-ting it, his (sword) crutch hanging against his body from his lightly gripping hand. Then he scowled as there came a sudden shooting pain in his numbed, bound-up left leg, which he had forgotten for a space.

Krovas raised a clenched fist and himself half out of his chair, in prelude to some fearsome com-mand—likely that Fafhrd be tortured. The Mouser cut in hurriedly with, "The Secret Seven, they're called, are its leaders. None in the outer circles of the con-spiracy know their names, though rumor has it that they're secret Guild-thief renegades representing, one for each, the cities of Ool Hrusp, Kvarch Nar, Ilthmar, Horborixen, Tisilinilit, far Kiraay and Lankhmar's very self...It's thought they're moneyed by the merchants of the East, the priests of Wan, the sorcerers of the Steppes and half the Mingol leadership too, legended Quarmall, Aarth's Assassins in Sarheenmar, and also no lesser man than the King of Kings."

Despite Krovas' contemptuous and then an-gry remarks, the ruffians holding the Mouser continued to harken to their captive with interest and respect, and they did not retighten their grip on him. His col-orful revelations and melodramatic delivery held them, while Krovas' dry, cynical, philosophic observations largely went over their heads.

Hristomilo came gliding into the room then, his feet presumably taking swift, but very short steps, at any rate his black robe hung undisturbed to the marble floor despite his slithering speed.

There was a shock at his entrance. All eyes in the map room followed him, breaths were held, and the Mouser and Fafhrd felt the horny hands that gripped them shake just a little. Even Krovas' all-confident, world-weary expression became tense and guardedly uneasy. Clearly the sorcerer of the Thieves' Guild was more feared than loved by his chief employer and by the beneficiaries of his skills.

Outwardly oblivious to this reaction to his appearance, Hristomilo, smiling thin-lipped, halted close to one side of Krovas' chair and inclined his hood-shadowed rodent face in the ghost of a bow.

Krovas held palm toward the Mouser for silence. Then, wetting his lips, he asked Hristomilo sharply yet nervously, "Do you know these two?"

Hristomilo nodded decisively. "They just now peered a befuddled eye each at me," he said, "whilst I was about that business we spoke of. I'd have shooed them off, reported them, save such action might have broken my spell, put my words out of time with the alembic's workings. The one's a Northerner, the other's features have a southern cast—from Tovilyis or near, most like. Both younger than their now-looks. Freelance bravos, I'd judge 'em, the sort the Brotherhood hires as extras when they get at once several big guard and escort jobs. Clumsily disguised now, of course, as beggars."

Fafhrd by yawning, the Mouser by pitying head shake tried to convey that all this was so much poor guesswork.

"That's all I can tell you without reading their minds," Hristomilo concluded. "Shall I fetch my lights and mirrors?"

"Not yet." Krovas turned face and shot a finger at the Mouser. "How do you know these things you rant about?—Secret Seven and all. Straight simplest answer now—no rodomontades."

The Mouser replied most glibly: "There's a new courtesan dwells on Pimp Street—Tyarya her name, tall, beauteous, but hunchbacked, which oddly delights many of her clients. Now Tyarya loves me 'cause my maimed eyes match her twisted spine, or from simple pity of my blindness—*she* believes it!—and youth, or from some odd itch, like her clients' for her, which that combination arouses in her flesh.

"Now one of her patrons, a trader newly come from Kleg Nar—Mourph, he's called—was impressed by my intelligence, strength, boldness, and close-mouthed tact, and those same qualities in my comrade too. Mourph sounded us out, finally asking if we hated the Thieves' Guild for its control of the Beggars' Guild. Sensing a chance to aid the Guild, we played up, and a week ago he recruited us into a cell of three in the outermost strands of the conspiracy web of the Seven."

"You presumed to do all of this on your own?" Krovas demanded in freezing tones, sitting up straight and gripping hard the chair arms.

"Oh, no," the Mouser denied guilelessly. "We reported our every act to the Day Beggarmaster and he approved them, told us to spy our best and gather every scrap of fact and rumor we could about the Sevens' conspiracy."

"And he told me not a word about it!" Krovas rapped out. "If true, I'll have Bannat's head for this! But you're lying, aren't you?"

As the Mouser gazed with wounded eyes at Krovas, meanwhile preparing a most virtuous denial, a portly man limped past the doorway with help of a gilded staff. He moved with silence and aplomb. But

Krovas saw him. "Night Beggarmaster!" he called sharply. The limping man stopped, turned, came crippling majestically through the door. Krovas stabbed finger at the Mouser, then Fafhrd. "Do you know these two, Flim?"

The Night Beggarmaster unhurriedly studied each for a space, then shook his head with its turban of cloth of gold. "Never seen either before. What are they? Fink beggars?"

"But Flim wouldn't know us," the Mouser explained desperately, feeling everything collapsing in on him and Fafhrd. "All our contacts were with Bannat alone."

Flim said quietly, "Bannat's been abed with the swamp ague this past ten-day. Meanwhile I have been Day Beggarmaster as well as Night."

At that moment Slevyas and Fissif came hurrying in behind Flim. The tall thief bore on his jaw a bluish lump. The fat thief's head was bandaged above his darting eyes. He pointed quickly at Fafhrd and the Mouser and cried, "There are the two that slugged us, took our Jengao loot, and slew our escort."

The Mouser lifted his elbow and the green bottle crashed to shards at his feet on the hard marble. Gardenia-reek sprang swiftly through the air.

But more swiftly still the Mouser, shaking off the careless hold of his startled guards, sprang toward Krovas, clubbing his wrapped-up sword. If he could only overpower the King of Thieves and hold Cat's Claw at his throat, he'd be able to bargain for his and Fafhrd's lives. That is unless the other thieves wanted their master killed, which wouldn't surprise him at all.

With startling speed Flim thrust out his gilded staff, tripping the Mouser, who went heels over head, midway seeking to change his involuntary somersault into a voluntary one.

Meanwhile Fafhrd lurched heavily against his left-hand captor, at the same time swinging bandaged Graywand strongly upward to strike his right-hand captor under the jaw. Regaining his one-legged balance with a mighty contortion, he hopped for the loot-wall behind him.

Slevyas made for the wall of thieves' tools, and with a muscle-cracking effort wrenched the great pry-bar from its padlocked ring.

Scrambling to his feet after a poor landing in front of Krovas' chair, the Mouser found it empty and the Thief King in a half-crouch behind it, gold-hilted dagger drawn, deep-sunk eyes coldly battle-wild. Spinning around, he saw Fafhrd's guards on the floor, the one sprawled senseless, the other starting to scramble up, while the great Northerner, his back against the wall of weird jewelry, menaced the whole room with wrapped-up Graywand and with his long knife, jerked from its scabbard behind him.

Likewise drawing Cat's Claw, the Mouser cried in trumpet voice of battle, "Stand aside, all! He's gone mad! I'll hamstring his good leg for you!" And racing through the press and between his own two guards, who still appeared to hold him in some awe, he launched himself with flashing dirk at Fafhrd, praying that the Northerner, drunk now with battle as well as wine and poisonous perfume, would recognize him and guess his stratagem.

Graywand slashed well above his ducking head. His new friend not only guessed, but was playing up—and not just missing by accident, the Mouser hoped. Stooping low by the wall, he cut the lashings on Fafhrd's left leg. Graywand and Fafhrd's long knife continued to spare him. Springing up, he headed for the corridor, crying overshoulder to Fafhrd, "Come on!"

Hristomilo stood well out of his way, quietly observing. Fissif scuttled toward safety. Krovas stayed behind his chair, shouting, "Stop them! Head them off!"

The three remaining ruffian guards, at last beginning to recover their fighting-wits, gathered to oppose the Mouser. But menacing them with swift feints of his dirk, he slowed them and darted between—and then just in the nick of time knocked aside with a downsweep of wrapped-up Scalpel Flim's gilded staff, thrust once again to trip him.

All this gave Slevyas time to return from the tools-wall and aim at the Mouser a great swinging blow with the massive pry-bar. But even as that blow started, a very long, bandaged sword on a very long arm thrust over the Mouser's shoulder and solidly and heavily poked Slevyas high on the chest, jolting him backward, so that the pry-bar's swing was short and whistled past harmlessly.

Then the Mouser found himself in the corridor and Fafhrd beside him, though for some weird reason still only hopping. The Mouser pointed toward the stairs. Fafhrd nodded, but delayed to reach high, still on one leg only, and rip off the nearest wall a dozen cubits of heavy drapes, which he threw across the corridor to baffle pursuit.

They reached the stairs and started up the next flight, the Mouser in advance. There were cries behind, some muffled.

"Stop hopping, Fafhrd!" the Mouser ordered querulously. "You've got two legs again."

"Yes, and the other's still dead," Fafhrd complained. "Ahh! Now feeling begins to return to it."

A thrown knife whisked between them and dully clinked as it hit the wall point-first and stone-powder flew. Then they were around the bend.

Two more empty corridors, two more curving flights, and then they saw above them on the last landing a stout ladder mounting to a dark, square hole in the roof. A thief with hair bound back by a colorful handkerchief—it appeared to be a door guards' identification—menaced the Mouser with drawn sword, but when he saw that there were two of them, both charging him determinedly with shining knives and strange staves or clubs, he turned and ran down the last empty corridor.

The Mouser, followed closely by Fafhrd, rapidly mounted the ladder and without pause vaulted up through the hatch into the star-crusted night.

He found himself near the unrailed edge of a slate roof which slanted enough to have made it look most fearsome to a novice roof-walker, but safe as houses to a veteran.

Crouched on the long peak of the roof was another kerchiefed thief holding a dark lantern. He was rapidly covering and uncovering, presumably in some code, the lantern's bull's eye, whence shot a faint green beam north to where a red point of light winked dimly in reply—as far away as the sea wall, it looked, or perhaps the masthead of a ship beyond, riding in the Inner Sea. Smuggler?

Seeing the Mouser, this one instantly drew sword and, swinging the lantern a little in his other hand, advanced menacingly. The Mouser eyed him warily—the dark lantern with its hot metal, concealed flame, and store of oil would be a tricky weapon.

But then Fafhrd had clambered out and was standing beside the Mouser, on both feet again at last. Their adversary backed slowly away toward the north end of the roof ridge. Fleetingly the Mouser wondered if there was another hatch there.

Turning back at a bumping sound, he saw Fafhrd prudently hoisting the ladder. Just as he got it free, a knife flashed up close past him out of the hatch. While following its flight, the Mouser frowned, involuntarily admiring the skill required to hurl a knife vertically with any accuracy.

It clattered down near them and slid off the roof. The Mouser loped south across the slates and was halfway from the hatch to that end of the roof when the faint chink came of the knife striking the cobbles of Murder Alley.

Fafhrd followed more slowly, in part perhaps from a lesser experience of roofs, in part because he still limped a bit to favor his left leg, and in part because he was carrying the heavy ladder balanced on his right shoulder.

"We won't need that," the Mouser called back.

Without hesitation Fafhrd heaved it joyously over the edge. By the time it crashed in Murder Alley, the Mouser was leaping down two yards and across a gap of one to the next roof, of opposite and lesser pitch. Fafhrd landed beside him.

The Mouser led them at almost a run through a sooty forest of chimneys, chimney pots, ventilators with tails that made them always face the wind, black-legged cisterns, hatch covers, bird houses, and pigeon traps across five roofs, four progressively a little lower, the fifth regaining a yard of the altitude they'd lost— the spaces between the buildings easy to leap, none more than three yards, no ladder-bridge required, and only one roof with a somewhat greater pitch than that of Thieves' House—until they reached the Street of the Thinkers at a point where it was crossed by a roofed passageway much like the one at Rokkermas and Slaarg's.

While they crossed it at a crouching lope, something hissed close past them and clattered ahead. As they leaped down from the roof of the bridge, three more somethings hissed over their heads to clatter beyond. One rebounded from a square chimney almost to the Mouser's feet. He picked it up, expecting a stone, and was surprised by the greater weight of a leaden ball big as two doubled-up fingers.

"They," he said, jerking thumb overshoulder, "lost no time in getting slingers on the roof. When roused, they're good."

Southeast then through another black chimney-forest to a point on Cheap Street where upper stories overhung the street so much on either side that it was easy to leap the gap. During this roof-traverse, an advancing front of night-smog, dense enough to make them cough and wheeze, had engulfed them and for perhaps sixty heartbeats the Mouser had had to slow to a shuffle and feel his way, Fafhrd's hand on his shoulder. Just short of Cheap Street they had come abruptly and completely out of the smog and seen the stars again, while the black front had rolled off northward behind them.

"Now what the devil was that?" Fafhrd had asked and the Mouser had shrugged.

A nighthawk would have seen a vast thick hoop of black night-smog blowing out in all directions from a center near the Silver Eel, growing ever greater and greater in diameter and circumference.

East of Cheap Street the two comrades soon made their way to the ground, landing back in Plague Court behind the narrow premises of Nattick Nimblefingers the Tailor.

Then at last they looked at each other and their trammeled swords and their filthy faces and clothing made dirtier still by roof-soot, and they laughed and laughed and laughed, Fafhrd roaring still as he bent over to massage his left leg above and below knee. This hooting and wholly unaffected self-mockery continued while they unwrapped their swords—the Mouser as if his were a surprise package— and clipped their scabbards once more to their belts. Their exertions had burned out of them the last mote and atomy of strong wine and even stronger stenchful perfume, but they felt no desire whatever for more drink, only the urge to get home and eat hugely and guzzle hot, bitter gahveh, and tell their lovely girls at length the tale of their mad adventure.

They loped on side by side, at intervals glancing at each other and chuckling, though keeping a normally wary eye behind and before for pursuit or interception, despite their expecting neither.

Free of night-smog and drizzled with starlight, their cramped surroundings seemed much less stinking and oppressive than when they had set out. Even Ordure Boulevard had a freshness to it.

Only once for a brief space did they grow serious.

Fafhrd said, "You were a drunken idiot-genius indeed tonight, even if I was a drunken clodhopper. Lashing up my leg! Tying up our swords so we couldn't use 'em save as clubs!"

The Mouser shrugged. "Yet that sword-tying

doubtless saved us from committing a number of murders tonight."

Fafhrd retorted, a little hotly, "Killing in fight isn't murder."

Again the Mouser shrugged. "Killing is murder, no matter what nice names you give. Just as eating is devouring, and drinking guzzling. Gods, I'm dry, famished, and fatigued! Come on, soft cushions, food, and steaming gahveh!"

They hastened up the long, creaking, broken-treaded stairs with an easy carefulness and when they were both on the porch, the Mouser shoved at the door to open it with surprise-swiftness.

It did not budge.

"Bolted," he said to Fafhrd shortly. He noted now there was hardly any light at all coming through the cracks around the door, or noticeable through the lattices—at most, a faint orange-red glow. Then with sentimental grin and in a fond voice in which only the ghost of uneasiness lurked, he said, "They've gone to sleep, the unworrying wenches!" He knocked loudly thrice and then cupping his lips shouted softly at the door crack, "Hola, Ivrian! I'm home safe. Hail, Vlana! Your man's done you proud, felling Guild-thieves innumerable with one foot tied behind his back!"

There was no sound whatever from inside—that is, if one discounted a rustling so faint it was impossible to be sure of it. Fafhrd was wrinkling his nostrils. "I smell smoke."

The Mouser banged on the door again. Still no response.

Fafhrd motioned him out of the way, hunching his big shoulder to crash the portal.

The Mouser shook his head and with a deft tap, slide, and tug removed a brick that a moment

before had looked a firm-set part of the wall beside
the door. He reached in all his arm. There was the
scrape of a bolt being withdrawn, then another, then
a third. He swiftly recovered his arm and the door
swung fully inward at a touch.

But neither he nor Fafhrd rushed in at once,
as both had intended to, for the indefinable scent of
danger and the unknown came puffing out along with
an increased reek of smoke and a slight sickening sweet
scent that though female was no decent female perfume, and a musty-sour animal odor.

They could see the room faintly by the orange glow coming from the small oblong of the open
door of the little, well-blacked stove. Yet the oblong
did not sit properly upright but was unnaturally a-tilt;
clearly the stove had been half overset and now leaned
against a side wall of the fireplace, its small door fallen
open in that direction.

By itself alone, that unnatural angle conveyed
the entire impact of a universe overturned.

The orange glow showed the carpets oddly
rucked up with here and there black circles a palm's
breadth across, the neatly stacked candles scattered
about below their shelves along with some of the jars
and enameled boxes, and, above all, two black, low,
irregular, longish heaps, the one by the fireplace, the
other half on the golden couch, half at its foot.

From each heap there stared at the Mouser
and Fafhrd innumerable pairs of tiny, rather widely
set, furnace-red eyes.

On the thickly carpeted floor on the other
side of the fireplace was a silver cobweb—a fallen silver cage, but no love birds sang from it.

There was a faint scrape of metal as Fafhrd
made sure Graywand was loose in his scabbard.

As if that tiny sound had beforehand been chosen as the signal for attack, each instantly whipped out sword and they advanced side by side into the room, warily at first, testing the floor with each step.

At the screech of the swords being drawn, the tiny furnace-red eyes had winked and shifted restlessly, and now with the two men's approach they swiftly scattered pattering, pair by red pair, each pair at the forward end of a small, low, slender, hairless-tailed black body, and each making for one of the black circles in the rugs, where they vanished.

Indubitably the black circles were ratholes newly gnawed up through the floor and rugs, while the red-eyed creatures were black rats.

Fafhrd and the Mouser sprang forward, slashing and chopping at them in a frenzy, cursing and human-snarling besides.

They sundered few. The rats fled with preternatural swiftness, most of them disappearing down holes near the walls and the fireplace.

Also Fafhrd's first frantic chop went through the floor and on his third step with an ominous crack and splintering his leg plunged through the floor to his hip. The Mouser darted past him, unmindful of further crackings.

Fafhrd heaved out his trapped leg, not even noting the splinter-scratches it got and as unmindful as the Mouser of the continuing creakings. The rats were gone. He lunged after his comrade, who had thrust a bunch of kindlers into the stove, to make more light.

The horror was that, although the rats were all gone, the two longish heaps remained, although considerably diminished and, as now shown clearly by the yellow flames leaping from the tilted black door, changed in hue—no longer were the heaps red-beaded black, but a mixture of gleaming black and dark brown, a sickening purple-blue, violet and velvet black and ermine white, and the reds of stockings and blood and bloody flesh and bone.

Although hands and feet had been gnawed bone naked, and bodies tunneled heart-deep, the two faces had been spared. That was not good, for they were the parts purple-blue from death by strangulation, lips drawn back, eyes bulging, all features contorted in agony. Only the black and very dark brown hair gleamed unchanged—that and the white, white teeth.

As each man stared down at his love, unable to look away despite the waves of horror and grief and rage washing higher and higher in him, each saw a tiny black strand uncurl from the black depression ringing each throat and drift off, dissipating, toward the open door behind them—two strands of night-smog.

With a crescendo of crackings the floor sagged fully three spans more in the center before arriving at a new temporary stability.

Edges of centrally tortured minds noted details: that Vlana's silver-hilted dagger skewered to the floor a rat, which, likely enough, overeager had approached too closely before the night-smog had done its magic work. That her belt and pouch were gone. That the blue-enameled box inlaid with silver, in which Ivrian had put the Mouser's share of the highjacked jewels, was gone too.

The Mouser and Fafhrd lifted to each other white, drawn faces which were quite mad, yet completely joined in understanding and purpose. No need to tell each other what must have happened here when the two nooses of black vapor had jerked tight in Hristomilo's receiver, or why Slivikin had bounced and squeaked in glee, or the significance of such phrases as "an ample sufficiency of feasters," or "forget not the loot," or "that business we spoke of." No need for Fafhrd to explain why he now stripped off his robe and hood, or why he jerked up Vlana's dagger, snapped the rat off it with a wrist-flick, and thrust it in his belt. No need for the Mouser to tell why he searched out a half dozen jars of oil and after smashing three of them in front of the flaming stove, paused, thought, and stuck the other three in the sack at his waist, adding to them the remaining kindlers and the fire-pot, brimmed with red coals, its top lashed down tight.

Then, still without word exchanged, the Mouser muffled his hand with a small rug and reaching into the fireplace deliberately tipped the flaming stove forward, so that it fell door-down on oil-soaked rugs. Yellow flames sprang up around him.

They turned and raced for the door. With louder crackings than any before, the floor collapsed. They desperately scrambled their way up a steep hill of sliding carpets and reached door and porch just before all behind them gave way and the flaming rugs and stove and all the firewood and candles and the golden couch and all the little tables and boxes and jars—and the unthinkably mutilated bodies of their first loves—cascaded into the dry, dusty, cobweb-choked room below, and the great flames of a cleansing or at least obliterating cremation began to flare upward.

They plunged down the stairs, which tore away from the wall and collapsed and dully crashed in the dark just as they reached the ground. They had to fight their way over the wreckage to get to Bones Alley.

By then flames were darting their bright lizard-tongues out of the shuttered attic windows and the boarded-up ones in the story just below. By the time they reached Plague Court, running side by side at top speed, the Silver Eel's fire-alarm was clanging cacophonously behind them.

They were still sprinting when they took the Death Alley fork. Then the Mouser grappled Fafhrd and forced him to a halt. The big man struck out, cursing insanely, and only desisted—his white face still a lunatic's—when the Mouser cried, panting, "Only ten heartbeats to arm us!"

He pulled the sack from his belt and, keeping tight hold of its neck, crashed it on the cobbles—hard enough to smash not only the bottles of oil, but also the fire-pot, for the sack was soon flaming a little at its base.

Then he drew gleaming Scalpel and Fafhrd Graywand and they raced on, the Mouser swinging his sack in a great circle beside him to fan its flames. It was a veritable ball of fire burning his left hand as they dashed across Cheap Street and into Thieves' House, and the Mouser, leaping high, swung it up into the great niche above the doorway and let go of it.

The niche-guards screeched in surprise and pain at the fiery invader of their hidey hole and had no time to do anything with their swords, or whatever weapons else they had, against the other two invaders.

Student thieves poured out of the doors ahead at the screeching and foot-pounding, and then poured back as they saw the fierce point of flames and the two demon-faced oncomers brandishing their long, shining swords.

One skinny little apprentice—he could hardly have been ten years old—lingered too long. Graywand thrust him pitilessly through as his big eyes bulged and his small mouth gaped in horror and plea to Fafhrd for mercy.

Now from ahead of them there came a weird, wailing call, hollow and hair-raising, and doors began to thus shut instead of spewing forth the armed guards they almost prayed would appear to be skewered by their swords. Also, despite the long, bracketed torches looking newly renewed, the corridor was dark.

The reason for this last became clear as they plunged up the stairs. Strands of night-smog were appearing in the well, materializing from nothing or the air.

The strands grew longer and more numerous and tangible. They touched and clung nastily. In the corridor above they were forming from wall to wall and from ceiling to floor, like a gigantic cobweb, and were becoming so substantial that the Mouser and Fafhrd had to slash them to get through, or so their two maniac minds believed. The black web muffled a little a repetition of the eerie, wailing call, which came from the seventh door ahead and this time ended in a gleeful chittering and cackling insane as the emotions of the two attackers.

Here too doors were thudding shut. In an ephemeral flash of rationality, it occurred to the Mouser that it was not he and Fafhrd the thieves feared, for they had not been seen yet, but rather Hristomilo and his magic, even though working in defense of Thieves' House.

Even the map room, whence counter-attack

would most likely erupt, was closed off by a huge oaken, iron-studded door.

They were now twice slashing black, clinging, rope-thick spiderweb for every single step they drove themselves forward. Midway between the map and magic rooms, there was forming on the inky web, ghostly at first but swiftly growing more substantial, a black spider big as a wolf.

The Mouser slashed heavy cobweb before it, dropped back two steps, then hurled himself at it in a high leap. Scalpel thrust through it, striking amidst its eight new-formed jet eyes, and it collapsed like a daggered bladder, loosing a vile stink.

Then he and Fafhrd were looking into the magic room, the alchemist's chamber. It was much as they had seen it before, except some things were doubled, or multiplied even further.

On the long table two blue-boiled cucurbits bubbled and roiled, their heads shooting out a solid, writhing rope more swiftly than moves the black swamp-cobra, which can run down a man—and not into twin receivers, but into the open air of the room (if any of the air in Thieves' House could have been called open then) to weave a barrier between their swords and Hristomilo, who once more stood tall though hunchbacked over his sorcerous, brown parchment, though this time his exultant gaze was chiefly fixed on Fafhrd and the Mouser, with only an occasional downward glance at the text of the spell he drummingly intoned.

At the other end of the table, in the web-free space, there bounced not only Slivikin, but also a huge rat matching him in size in all members except the head.

From the ratholes at the foot of the walls red eyes glittered and gleamed in pairs.

With a bellow of rage Fafhrd began slashing at the black barrier, but the ropes were replaced from the cucurbit heads as swiftly as he sliced them, while the cut ends, instead of drooping slackly, now began to strain hungrily toward him like constrictive snakes or strangle-vines.

He suddenly shifted Graywand to his left hand, drew his long knife and hurled it at the sorcerer. Flashing toward its mark, it cut through three strands, was deflected and slowed by a fourth and fifth, almost halted by a sixth, and ended hanging futilely in the curled grip of a seventh.

Hristomilo laughed cacklingly and grinned, showing his huge upper incisors, while Slivikin chittered in ecstasy and bounded the higher.

The Mouser hurled Cat's Claw with no better result—worse, indeed, since his action gave two darting smog-strands time to curl hamperingly around his sword-hand and stranglingly around his neck. Black rats came racing out of the big holes at the cluttered base of the walls.

Meanwhile other strands snaked around Fafhrd's ankles, knees and left arm, almost toppling him. But even as he fought for balance, he jerked Vlana's dagger from his belt and raised it over his shoulder, its silver hilt glowing, its blade brown with dried rat's-blood.

The grin left Hristomilo's face as he saw it. The sorcerer screamed strangely and importuningly then and drew back from his parchment and the table, and raised clawed clubhands to ward off doom.

Vlana's dagger sped unimpeded through the

black web—its strands even seemed to part for it—
and betwixt the sorcerer's warding hands, to bury itself
to the hilt in his right eye.

He screamed thinly in dire agony and clawed
at his face.

The black web writhed as if in death spasm.

The cucurbits shattered as one, spilling their
lava on the scarred table, putting out the blue flames
even as the thick wood of the table began to smoke a
little at the lava's edge. Lava dropped with *plops* on
the dark marble floor.

With a faint, final scream Hristomilo pitched
forward, hands still clutched to his eyes above his jutting nose, silver dagger-hilt still protruding between
his fingers.

The web grew faint, like wet ink washed with
a gush of clear water.

The Mouser raced forward and transfixed
Slivikin and the huge rat with one thrust of Scalpel
before the beasts knew what was happening. They too
died swiftly with thin screams, while all the other rats
turned tail and fled back down their holes swift almost as black lightning.

Then the last trace of night-smog or sorcery-
smoke vanished and Fafhrd and the Mouser found
themselves standing alone with three dead bodies and
a profound silence that seemed to fill not only this
room but all Thieves' House. Even the cucurbit-lava
had ceased to move, was hardening, and the wood of
the table no longer smoked.

Their madness was gone and all their rage
too—vented to the last red atomy and glutted to more
than satiety. They had no more urge to kill Krovas or
any other of the thieves than to swat flies. With hor-

rified inner eye Fafhrd saw the pitiful face of the child-thief he'd skewered in his lunatic anger.

Only their grief remained with them, diminished not one whit, but rather growing greater—that and an ever more swiftly growing revulsion from all that was around them: the dead, the disordered magic room, all Thieves' House, all of the city of Lankhmar to its last stinking alleyway and smog-wreathed spire.

With a hiss of disgust the Mouser jerked Scalpel from the rodent cadavers, wiped it on the nearest cloth, and returned it to its scabbard. Fafhrd likewise sketchily cleansed and sheathed Graywand. Then the two men picked up their knife and dirk from where they'd dropped to the floor when the web had dematerialized, though neither so much as glanced at Vlana's dagger where it was buried. But on the sorcerer's table they did notice Vlana's black velvet, silver-worked pouch and belt, the latter half overrun by the hardened black lava, and Ivrian's blue-enameled box inlaid with silver. From these they took the gems of Jengao.

With no more word than they had exchanged back at the Mouser's burned nest behind the Eel, but with a continuing sense of their unity of purpose, their identity of intent, and of their comradeship, they made their way with shoulders bowed and with slow, weary steps which only very gradually quickened out of the magic room and down the thick-carpeted corridor, past the map room's wide door still barred with oak and iron, and past all the other shut, silent doors—clearly the entire Guild was terrified of Hristomilo, his spells, and his rats; down the echoing stairs, their footsteps speeding a little; down the bare-floored lower corridor past its closed, quiet doors, their footsteps resounding loudly no matter how softly they sought to tread; under the deserted, black-scorched guard-niche, and so out into Cheap Street, turning left and north because that was the nearest way to the Street of the Gods, and there turning right and east—not a waking soul in the wide street except for one skinny, bent-backed apprentice lad unhappily swabbing the flagstones in front of a wine shop in the dim pink light beginning to seep from the east, although there were many forms asleep, a-snore and a-dream in the gutters and under the dark porticos—yes, turning right and east down the Street of the Gods, for that way was the Marsh Gate, leading to Causey Road across the Great Salt Marsh, and the Marsh Gate was the nearest way out of the great and glamorous city that was now loathsome to them, indeed, not to be endured for one more stabbing, leaden heartbeat than was necessary—a city of beloved, unfaceable ghosts.

FRITZ LEIBER'S
LANKHMAR

THE CIRCLE CURSE

V

A TALL SWORDSMAN and a small one strode out the Marsh Gate of Lankhmar and east along Causey Road. They were youths by their skin and suppleness, men by their expressions of deep-bitten grief and stony purpose.

The sleepy guardsmen in browned-iron cuirasses did not question them. Only madmen and fools willingly leave the grandest city in the world of Nehwon, especially at dawn and afoot. Besides, these two looked extremely dangerous.

Ahead the sky was bright pink, like the bubbling rim of a great crystal goblet brimmed with effervescent red wine for delight of the gods, while the paler pink glow rising therefrom drove the last stars west. But before the sun could glare one scarlet sliver above the horizon, a black storm came racing out of the north over the Inner Sea—a sea-squall making landfall. It grew almost as dark again as night, except when the lightning stabbed and the thunder shook his great iron shield. The stormwind carried the salty tang of the sea commingled with the foul reek of the marsh. It bent the green swords of the sea grass flat and lashed into writhing the arms of the thorn and seahawk trees. It pushed black swampwater a yard up the northern side of the narrow, serpentine, flat-topped ridge that was Causey Road. Then came pelting rain.

The two swordsmen made no comment to each other and did not alter their movements, except to lift their shoulders and faces a little and slant the latter north, as if they welcomed the storm's cleansing and sting and what tiny distraction it brought to some deep agony of mind and heart.

"Ho, Fafhrd!" a deep voice grated above the

thunder's growl and the wind's roar and the rattle of the rain.

The tall swordsman turned his head sharply south.

"Hist, Gray Mouser!"

The small swordsman did likewise.

Close by the southern side of the road a rather large, rounded hut stood on five narrow posts. The posts had to be tall, for Causey Road ran high here yet the floor of the hut's low, rounded doorway looked straight at the tall swordsman's head.

This was nothing very strange, except that all men know that none dwell in the venomous Great Salt Marsh, save for giant worms, poison eels, water cobras, pale spindle-legged swamp rats, and the like.

Blue lightning glared, revealing with great clarity a hooded figure crouched inside the low doorway. Each fold and twist of the figure's draperies stood out as precisely as in an iron engraving closely viewed.

But the lightning showed nothing whatsoever inside the hood, only inky blackness.

Thunder crashed.

Then from the hood the grating voice recited the following lines, harshly and humorlessly hammering out the words, so that what was light verse became a dismal and doomful incantation:

Ho, Fafhrd tall!
Hist, Mouser small!
Why leave you the city
Of marvelous parts?
It were a great pity
To wear out your hearts
And wear out the soles of your feet,
Treading all earth,

Foregoing all mirth,
Before you once more Lankhmar greet.
Now return, now return, now!

This doleful ditty was three-quarters done
before the two swordsmen realized that they were striding along steadily all this while and the hut still abreast
them. So it must be walking along with them on its
posts, or legs rather. And now that they were aware of
this, they could see those five thin wooden members
swinging and knee-bending.

When the grating voice ceased to speak on
that last great "now," Fafhrd halted.

So did the Mouser.

So did the hut.

The two swordsmen turned toward the low
doorway, facing it squarely.

Simultaneously with deafening thunderclap,
a great bolt of lightning struck close behind them. It
jolted their bodies, shocked their flesh thrillingly and
painfully, and it illumined the hut and its dweller
brighter than day, yet still revealed nothing inside the
dweller's hood.

If the hood had been empty, the draperies at
its back would have been shown clearly. But no, there
was only that oval of ebon darkness, which even the
levinbolt could not illumine.

As unmoved by this prodigy as by the thun-
der-stroke, Fafhrd bellowed above the storm toward
the doorway, his voice sounding tiny to himself in his
thunder-smitten ears, "Hear me, witch, wizard,
nightgaunt, whatever you are! I shall never in my life
enter again the foul city which has stolen from me my
dearest and only love, the incomparable and irreplace-
able Vlana, for whom I shall forever grieve and for

whose unspeakable death I shall forever feel guilt. The Thieves' Guild slew her for her freelance thieving— and we slew the slayers, though it profited us nothing at all."

"Likewise I shall never lift foot toward Lankhmar again," the Gray Mouser took up from beside him in a voice like an angry trumpet, "the loathy metropolis which horribly bereft me of my beloved Ivrian, even as Fafhrd was bereft and for similar reason, and left me loaded with an equal weight of sorrow and shame, which I shall bear forever, even past my perishing." A salt spider big as a platter sailed close by his ear in the grip of the gale, kicking its thick, corpse-white legs, and veered off past the hut, but the Mouser did not start in the least and there was no break whatever in his words as he continued, "Know, being of blackness, haunter of the dark, that we slew the foul wizard who murdered our loves and killed his two rodentine familiars and mauled and terrorized his employers at Thieves' House. But revenge is empty. It cannot bring back the dead. It cannot assuage by one atom the grief and guilt we shall feel forever for our darlings."

"Indeed it cannot," Fafhrd seconded loudly, "for we were drunk when our darlings died, and for that there is no forgiveness. We highjacked a small treasure in gems from thieves of the Guild, but we lost the two jewels beyond price and without compare. And we shall never return to Lankhmar!"

Lightning shone from beyond the hut and thunder crackled. The storm was moving inland, south from the road.

The hood that held darkness drew back a little and slowly shook from side to side, once, twice, thrice. The harsh voice intoned, fainter because

Fafhrd's and the Mouser's ears were still somewhat deafened and a-ring from that father of thunderstrokes:

> *Never and forever are neither for men.*
> *You'll be returning again and again.*

Then the hut was moving inland too on its five spindly legs. It turned around, so that its door faced away from them, and its speed increased, its legs moving nimbly as those of a cockroach, and was soon lost amongst the tangle of thorn and seahawk trees.

So ended the first encounter of the Mouser and his comrade Fafhrd with Sheelba of the Eyeless Face.

Later that day the two swordsmen waylaid an insufficiently guarded merchant Lankhmar-bound, depriving him of the best two of his four cart-horses—for thieving was first nature to them—and on these clumping mounts made their way out of the Great Salt Marsh and across the Sinking Land to the sinister hub-city of Ilthmar with its treacherous little inns and innumerable statues and bas-reliefs and other depictions of its rat-god. There they changed their clumsy horses for camels and were soon humping south across the desert, following the eastern shore of the turquoise Sea of the East. They crossed the River Tilth in dry season and continued on through the sands, bound for the Eastern Lands, where neither of them had previously traveled. They were searching for distraction in strangeness and intended first to visit Horborixen, citadel of the King of Kings and city second only to Lankhmar in size, antiquity, and baroque splendor.

For the next three years, the Years of Leviathan, the Roc, and the Dragon, they wandered the world of Nehwon south, east, north, and west, seeking forgetfulness of their first great loves and their first great guilts and finding neither. They ventured east past mystic Tisilinilit with its slender, opalescent spires, which always seemed newly crystallized out of its humid, pearly skies, to lands that were legends in Lankhmar and even Horborixen. One amongst many was the skeletally shrunken Empire of Eevamarensee, a country so decadent, so far-grown into the future, that all the rats and men are bald and even the dogs and cats hairless.

Returning by a northerly route through the Great Steppes, they narrowly escaped capture and enslavement by the pitiless Mingols. In the Cold Waste they sought for Fafhrd's Snow Clan, only to discover that it had been last year overwhelmed by a lemming horde of Ice Gnomes and, according to best rumor, massacred to the last person, which would have included Fafhrd's mother Mor, his deserted girl-bride Mara, and his first issue if any.

For a space they served Lithquil, the Mad Duke of Ool Hrusp, devising for him sprightly mock-duels, simulated murders, and other entertainments. Then they coasted south through the Outer Sea aboard a Sarheenmar trader to tropic Klesh, where they adventured a while in the jungle fringes. Then north again, circling past secretest Quarmall, that shadow realm, to the Lakes of Pleea that are the headwaters of the Hlal and to the beggar-city of Tovilyis, where the Gray Mouser believed he had been birthed, but was not sure, and when they left that lowly metropolis he was no surer. Crossing by grain barge the Sea of the East, they prospected for gold a while in the Moun-

tains of the Elder Ones, their last highjacked gems
having been long since gambled away or spent. Un-
successful in this quest, they wended their way west
again toward the Inner Sea and Ilthmar.

They lived by thievery, robbery, bodyguarding,
brief commissions as couriers and agents—commissions
they always, or almost always, fulfilled punctiliously—
and by showmanship, the Mouser entertaining by
legerdemain, juggling, and buffoonery, while Fafhrd
with his gift for tongues and training as a singing skald
excelled at minstrelsy, translating the legends of his
frigid homeland into many languages. They never
worked as cooks, clerks, carpenters, tree-fellers, or common servants and they never, never, never enlisted as
mercenary soldiers—their service to Lithquil having
been of a more personal nature.

They acquired new scars and skills, com-
prehensions and compassions, cynicisms and
secrecies—a laughter that lightly mocked and a cool
poise that tightly crusted all inner miseries and most
of the time hid the barbarian in Fafhrd and the slum
boy in the Mouser. They became outwardly merry,
uncaring, and cool, but their grief and guilt stayed
with them, the ghosts of Ivrian and Vlana haunt-
ing their sleeping and their waking dreams, so that
they had little commerce with other girls, and that
more a discomfort than a joy. Their comradeship
became firmer than a rock, stronger than steel, but
all other human relations were fleeting. Melancholy
was their commonest mood, though mostly hid even
from each other.

Came noon of the Day of the Mouse in the
Month of the Lion in the Year of the Dragon. They
were taking their siestas in the cool of a cave near
Ilthmar. Outside, heat shimmered above hard-baked

ground and scanty brown grass, but here was most pleasant. Their horses, a gray mare and a chestnut gelding, found shade in the cavern's mouth. Fafhrd had sketchily inspected the place for serpents, but discovered none. He loathed the cold scaly ones of the south, so different from the hot-blooded, fur-bearing snakes of the Cold Waste. He went a little way into a narrow, rocky corridor leading from the back of the cave under the small mountain in which it was set, but returned when light failed and he had found neither reptiles nor end.

They rested comfortably on their uncurled bedrolls. Sleep would not come to them, so idle talk did. By slow stages this talk became serious. Finally the Gray Mouser summed up the last trinity of years.

"We have searched the wide world over and not found forgetfulness."

"I dispute that," Fafhrd countered. "Not the latter part, for I am still as ghost-locked as you, but we have not crossed the Outer Sea and hunted over the great continent legend will have in the west."

"I believe we have," the Mouser disputed. "Not the former part, I'll agree, and what purpose in searching the sea? But when we went out farthest east and stood on the shore of that great ocean, deafened by its vast surf, I believe we stood on the western coast of the Outer Sea with nothing between us and Lankhmar but wild water."

"What great ocean?" Fafhrd demanded. "And what vast surf? It was a lake, a mere puddle with some ripples in it. I could readily see the opposite shore."

"Then you were seeing mirages, friend of mine, and languishing in one of those moods when all Nehwon seems but a small bubble you could burst with flick of fingernail."

"Perhaps," Fafhrd agreed. "Oh, how weary I am of this life."

There was a little cough, no more than a clearing of throat, in the dark behind them. They did not otherwise move, but their hair stirred at its roots, so close and intimate had been that tiny noise, and so indicative of intelligence rather than mere animality, because of a measuredly attention-asking quality about it.

Then as one they turned head over shoulder and looked at the black mouth of the rocky corridor. After a bit it seemed to each of them that he could see seven small, faint green glows swimming in the dark there and lazily changing position, like seven fireflies hovering, but with their light steadier and far more diffuse, as if each firefly wore a cloak made of several layers of gauze.

Then a voice sugary and unctuous, senescent though keen—a voice like a quavering flute—spoke from amidst those dimmest glows, saying, "Oh my sons, begging the question of that hypothetical western continent, on which I do not propose to enlighten you, there is yet one place in Nehwon you have not searched for forgetfulness since the cruel deaths of your beloved girls."

"And what place may that be?" the Mouser asked softly after a long moment and with slightest stammer. "And who are you?"

"The city of Lankhmar, my sons. Who I am, besides your spiritual father, is a private matter."

"We have sworn a great oath against ever returning to Lankhmar," Fafhrd growled after a bit, the growl low and just a shade defensive and perhaps even intimidated.

"Oaths are made to be kept only until their

purpose be fulfilled," the fluty voice responded. "Every geas is lifted at last, every self-set rule repealed. Otherwise orderliness in life becomes a limitation to growth; discipline, chains; integrity, bondage and evil-doing. You have learned what you can from the world. You have graduated from that huge portion of Nehwon. It now remains that you take up your post-graduate studies in Lankhmar, highest university of civilized life here."

The seven faint glows were growing still dimmer now and drawing together, as if retreating down the corridor.

"We won't go back to Lankhmar," Fafhrd and the Mouser replied speaking as one.

The seven glows faded altogether. So faintly the two men could barely hear it—yet hear it each did—the fluty voice inquired, "Are you afraid?" Then they heard a grating of rock, a very faint sound, yet somehow ponderous.

So ended the first encounter of Fafhrd and his comrade with Ningauble of the Seven Eyes.

After a dozen heartbeats, the Gray Mouser drew his slim, arm-and-a-half-long sword, Scalpel, with which he was accustomed to draw blood with surgical precision, and followed its glittering tip into the rocky corridor. He strode very deliberately, with a measured determination. Fafhrd went after, but more cautiously, with many a hesitation, holding the point of his heavier sword Graywand, which he yet handled most nimbly in strife, close to the stony floor and wagging it from side to side. The seven glows in their lazy swayings and bobbings had mightily suggested to him the heads of large cobras raised up to strike. He reasoned that cave cobras, if such existed, might well be phosphorescent like abyssal eels.

They had penetrated somewhat farther under the mountainside than Fafhrd had on his first inspection—their slow pace enabling their eyes to accommodate better to the relative darkness—when with a slight, high-pitched shiver, Scalpel jarred vertical rock. Waiting without a word where they stood, their cave vision improved to the point where it became indisputable, without any more sword-testing at all, that the corridor ended where they were, wanting hole big enough even for a speaking serpent to glide away, let alone a being rightfully capable of speech. The Mouser pressed and then Fafhrd threw his weight against the rock ahead at several points, but it held firm as purest mountain heart. Nor had they missed any side tracks, even of the narrowest, or any pits or roof-holes on the way—a point they doubly checked going out.

Back at their bedrolls, their horses still tranquilly nibbling brown grass at the cavern's mouth, Fafhrd said abruptly, "What we heard speak, it was an echo."

"How have an echo without a voice?" the Mouser demanded with peevish impatience. "As well have a tail without a cat. I mean, a living tail."

"A small snow snake greatly resembles the animated tail of a white house cat," Fafhrd replied imperturbably. "Aye, and has just such a high, quavering cry."

"Are you suggesting—?"

"Of course not. As I imagine you do, I think there was a door somewhere in the rock, fitted so well we could not discern the junctures. We heard it shut. But before that, he—she, it, they—went through it."

"Then why babble of echoes and snow

snakes?"

"It is well to consider all possibilities."

"He—she and so forth—named us sons," the Mouser mused.

"Some say the serpent is wisest, oldest, and even father of all," Fafhrd observed judiciously.

"Snakes again! Well, one thing's certain: all hold it rash folly for a man to take advice of a serpent, let alone seven."

"Yet he—consider the other pronouns spoken—had a point, Mouser. Mauger the indeterminate western continent, we have traveled all Nehwon in spiderweb wise. What's left but Lankhmar?"

"Damn your pronouns! We swore never to return. Have you forgotten that, Fafhrd?"

"No, but I'm dying of boredom. Times I have sworn never again to drink wine."

"I would choke to death on Lankhmar! Her day-smokes, her night-smogs, her rats, her filth!"

"At the moment, Mouser, I care little whether I live or die, and where or when or how."

"Now adverbs and conjunctions! Bah, you need a drink!"

"We seek a deeper forgetfulness. They say to lay a ghost, go where she died."

"Aye, and be worse haunted!"

"I could not be worse haunted than now."

"To let a serpent shame us by asking, were we afraid!"

"Are we, perhaps?"

And so the argument went, with the final foreseeable result that Fafhrd and the Mouser cantered past Ilthmar to a stony stretch of shore that was a curiously abraded low precipice, and waited there a day and a night for the Sinking Land to emerge with anomalous aqueous convulsions from the waters joining the Sea of the East to the Inner Sea. They swiftly and warily crossed its flinty, steaming expanse—for it was a hot, sunny day—and so again rode Causey Road, but this time back toward Lankhmar.

Distant, twin thunderstorms played to either side—north over the Inner Sea and south above the Great Salt Marsh—as they approached that monstrous city and as its towers, spires, fanes, and great crenelated wall emerged from its huge, customary cap of smoke, being somewhat silhouetted by the light of the setting sun, which was turned to a dull silver disk by the high fog and the smoke.

Once the Mouser and Fafhrd thought they saw a rounded, flat-floored shape on tall, invisible legs moving amongst the seahawk trees and faintly heard a harsh voice crying, "I told you. I told you. I told you," but both Sheelba's wizardly hut and voice, if they were those, remained distant as the storms.

In such wise Fafhrd and the Gray Mouser returned flat against their oaths to the city they despised, yet hankered after. They did not find forgetfulness there, the ghosts of Ivrian and Vlana were not laid, yet perhaps solely because of passage of time, the two heroes were a little less troubled by them. Nor were their hates, as of the Thieves' Guild, rekindled, but rather faded. And in any case Lankhmar seemed no worse than any other place in Nehwon and more interesting than most. So they stayed there for a space, making it once more the headquarters of their adventurings.

FRITZ LEIBER'S
LANKhMAR

The JEWELS IN The FOREST

IT WAS THE Year of the Behemoth, the Month of the Hedgehog, the Day of the Toad. A hot, late summer sun was sinking down toward evening over the somber, fertile land of Lankhmar. Peasants toiling in the endless grain fields paused for a moment and lifted their earth-stained faces and noted that it would soon be time to commence lesser chores. Cattle cropping the stubble began to move in the general direction of home. Sweaty merchants and shopkeepers decided to wait a little longer before enjoying the pleasures of the bath. Thieves and astrologers moved restlessly in their sleep, sensing that the hours of night and work were drawing near.

At the southernmost limit of the land of Lankhmar, a day's ride beyond the village of Soreev, where the grain fields give way to rolling forests of maple and oak, two horsemen cantered leisurely along a narrow, dusty road. They presented a sharp contrast. The larger wore a tunic of unbleached linen, drawn tight at the waist by a very broad leather belt. A fold of linen cloak was looped over his head as a protection against the sun. A longsword with a pomegranate-shaped golden pommel was strapped to his side. Behind his right shoulder a quiver of arrows jutted up. Half sheathed in a saddlecase was a thick yew bow, unstrung. His great, lean muscles, white skin, copper hair, green eyes, and above all the pleasant yet untamed expression of his massive countenance, all hinted at a land of origin colder, rougher, and more barbarous than that of Lankhmar.

Even as everything about the larger man suggested the wilderness, so the general appearance of the smaller man—and he was considerably smaller—spoke of the city. His dark face was that of a jester. Bright, black eyes, snub nose, and little lines of irony about the mouth. Hands of a conjurer. Something about the set of his wiry frame betokening exceptional competence in street fights and tavern brawls. He was clad from head to foot in garments of gray silk, soft and curiously loose of weave. His slim sword, cased in gray mouseskin, was slightly curved toward the tip. From his belt hung a sling and a pouch of missiles.

Despite their many dissimilarities, it was obvious that the two men were comrades, that they were united by a bond of subtle mutual understanding, woven of melancholy, humor, and many another strand. The smaller rode a dappled gray mare; the larger, a chestnut gelding.

They were nearing a point where the narrow road came to the end of a rise, made a slight turn and wound down into the next valley. Green walls of leaves pressed in on either side. The heat was considerable, but not oppressive. It brought to mind thoughts of satyrs and centaurs dozing in hidden glades.

Then the gray mare, slightly in the lead, whinnied. The smaller man tightened his hold on the reins, his black eyes darting quick, alert glances, first to one side of the road and then to the other. There was a faint scraping sound, as of wood on wood.

Without warning the two men ducked down, clinging to the side harness of their horses. Simultaneously came the musical twang of bowstrings, like the prelude of some forest concert, and several arrows buzzed angrily through the spaces that had just been vacated. Then the mare and the gelding were around the turn and galloping like the wind, their hooves striking up great puffs of dust.

From behind came excited shouts and answers as the pursuit got underway. There seemed to have been fully seven or eight men in the ambuscade—squat, sturdy rogues wearing chain-mail shirts and steel caps. Before the mare and the gelding had gone a stone's throw down the road, they were out and after, a black horse in the lead, a black-bearded rider second.

But those pursued were not wasting time. The larger man rose to a stand in his stirrups, whipping the yew bow from its case. With his left hand he bent it against the stirrup, with his right he drew the upper loop of the string into place. Then his left hand slipped down the bow to the grip and his right reached smoothly back over his shoulder for an arrow. Still guiding his horse with his knees, he rose even higher and turned in his saddle and sent an eagle-feathered shaft whirring. Meanwhile his comrade had placed a small leaden ball in his sling, whirled it twice about his head, so that it hummed stridently, and loosed his cast.

Arrow and missile sped and struck together. The one pierced the shoulder of the leading horseman and the other smote the second on his steel cap and tumbled him from his saddle. The pursuit halted abruptly in a tangle of plunging and rearing horses. The men who had caused this confusion pulled up at the next bend in the road and turned back to watch.

"By the Hedgehog," said the smaller, grinning wickedly, "but they will think twice before they play at ambuscades again!"

"Blundering fools," said the larger. "Haven't they even learned to shoot from their saddles? I tell you, Gray Mouser, it takes a barbarian to fight his horse properly."

"Except for myself and a few other people," replied the one who bore the feline nickname of Gray Mouser. "But look, Fafhrd, the rogues retreat bearing their wounded, and one gallops far ahead. *Tcha*, but I dinted black beard's pate for him. He hangs over his nag like a bag of meal. If he'd have known who we were, he wouldn't have been so hot on the chase."

There was some truth to this last boast. The names of the Gray Mouser and the Northerner Fafhrd were not unknown in the lands around Lankhmar—and in proud Lankhmar, too. Their taste for strange adventure, their mysterious comings and goings, and their odd sense of humor were matters that puzzled almost all men alike.

Abruptly Fafhrd unstrung his bow and turned forward in his saddle.

"This should be the very valley we are seeking," he said. "See, there are the two hills, each with two close-set humps, of which the document speaks. Let's have another look at it, to test my guess."

The Gray Mouser reached into his capacious leather pouch and withdrew a page of thick vellum, ancient and curiously greenish. Three edges were frayed and worn; the fourth showed a clean and recent cut. It was inscribed with the intricate hieroglyphs of Lankhmarian writing, done in the black ink of the squid. But it was not to these that the Mouser turned his attention, but to several faint lines of diminutive red script, written into the margin. These he read.

"Let kings stack their treasure houses ceiling-high, and merchants burst their vaults with hoarded coin, and fools envy them. I have a treasure that outvalues theirs. A diamond as big as a man's skull. Twelve rubies each as big as the skull of a cat. Seventeen emeralds each as big as the skull of a mole. And certain rods of crystal and bars of orichalcum. Let Overlords swagger jewel-bedecked and queens load themselves with gems, and fools adore them. I have a treasure that will outlast theirs. A treasure house have I builded for it in the far southern forest, where the two hills hump double, like sleeping camels, a day's ride beyond the village of Soreev.

"A great treasure house with a high tower, fit for a king's dwelling—yet no king may dwell there. Immediately below the keystone of the chief dome my treasure lies hid, eternal as the glittering stars. It will outlast me and my name, I, Urgaan of Angarngi. It is my hold on the future. Let fools seek it. They shall win it not. For although my treasure house be empty as air, no deadly creature in rocky lair, no sentinel outside anywhere, no pitfall, poison, trap, or snare, above and below the whole place bare, of demon or devil not a hair, no serpent lethal-fanged yet fair, no skull with mortal eye a-glare, yet have I left a guardian there. Let the wise read this riddle and forbear."

"The man's mind runs to skulls," muttered the Mouser. "He must have been a gravedigger or a necromancer."

"Or an architect," observed Fafhrd thoughtfully, "in those past days when graven images of the skulls of men and animals served to bedeck temples."

"Perhaps," agreed the Mouser. "Surely the writing and ink are old enough. They date at least as far back as the Century of the Wars with the East— five long lifespans."

The Mouser was an accomplished forger, both of handwriting and of objects of art. He knew what he was talking about.

Satisfied that they were near the goal of their quest, the two comrades gazed through a break in the foliage down into the valley. It was shaped like the inside of a pod—shallow, long, and narrow. They were viewing it from one of the narrow ends. The two peculiarly humped hills formed the long sides. The whole of the valley was green with maple and oak, save for a small gap toward the middle. That, thought the Mouser, might mark a peasant's dwelling and the cleared space around it.

Beyond the gap he could make out something dark and squarish rising a little above the treetops. He called his companion's attention to it, but they could not decide whether it was indeed a tower such as the document mentioned, or just a peculiar shadow, or perhaps even the dead, limbless trunk of a gigantic oak. It was too far away.

"Almost sufficient time has passed," said Fafhrd, after a pause, "for one of those rogues to have sneaked up through the forest for another shot at us. Evening draws near."

They spoke to their horses and moved on slowly. They tried to keep their eyes fixed on the thing that looked like a tower, but since they were descending, it almost immediately dropped out of sight below the treetops. There would be no further chance of seeing it until they were quite close at hand.

The Mouser felt a subdued excitement running through his flesh. Soon they would discover if there was a treasure to be had or not. A diamond as big as a man's skull...rubies...emeralds... He found an almost nostalgic delight in prolonging and savor-

ing to the full this last, leisurely stage of their quest.
The recent ambuscade served as a necessary spice.

He thought of how he had slit the interest-
ing-looking vellum page from the ancient book on
architecture that reposed in the library of the rapa-
cious and overbearing Lord Rannarsh. Of how, half in
jest, he had sought out and interrogated several ped-
dlers from the South. Of how he had found one who
had recently passed through a village named Soreev.
Of how that one had told him of a stone structure in
the forest south of Soreev, called by the peasants the
House of Angarngi and reputed to be long deserted.
The peddler had seen a high tower rising above the
trees. The Mouser recalled the man's wizened, cunning face and chuckled. And that brought to mind
the greedy, sallow face of Lord Rannarsh, and a new
thought occurred to him.

"Fafhrd," he said, "those rogues we just now
put to flight—what did you take them for?"

The Northerner grunted humorous contempt.

"Run-of-the-manger ruffians. Waylayers of fat
merchants. Pasture bravos. Bumpkin bandits!"

"Still, they were all well armed, and armed
alike—as if they were in some rich man's service. And
that one who rode far ahead. Mightn't he have been
hastening to report failure to some master?"

"What is your thought?"

The Mouser did not reply for some moments.

"I was thinking," he said, "that Lord Rannarsh
is a rich man and a greedy one, who slavers at the
thought of jewels. And I was wondering if he ever read
those faint lines of red lettering and made a copy of
them, and if my theft of the original sharpened his
interest."

The Northerner shook his head.

"I doubt it. You are oversubtle. But if he did, and if he seeks to rival us in this treasure quest, he'd best watch each step twice—and choose servitors who can fight on horseback."

They were moving so slowly that the hooves of the mare and the gelding hardly stirred up the dust. They had no fear of danger from the rear. A well-laid ambuscade might surprise them, but not a man or horse in motion. The narrow road wound along in a purposeless fashion. Leaves brushed their faces, and occasionally they had to swing their bodies out of the way of encroaching branches. The ripe scent of the late summer forest was intensified now that they were below the rim of the valley. Mingled with it were whiffs of wild berries and aromatic shrubs. Shadows imperceptibly lengthened.

"Nine chances out of ten," murmured the Mouser dreamily, "the treasure house of Urgaan of Angarngi was looted some hundred years ago, by men whose bodies are already dust."

"It may be so," agreed Fafhrd. "Unlike men, rubies and emeralds do not rest quietly in their graves."

This possibility, which they had discussed several times before, did not disturb them now, or make them impatient. Rather did it impart to their quest the pleasant melancholy of a lost hope. They drank in the rich air and let their horses munch random mouthfuls of leaves. A jay called shrilly from overhead and off in the forest a catbird was chattering, their sharp voices breaking in on the low buzzing and droning of the insects. Night was drawing near. The almost-horizontal rays of the sun gilded the treetops. Then Fafhrd's sharp ears caught the hollow lowing of a cow.

A few more turns brought them into the clearing they had spied. In line with their surmise, it proved to contain a peasant's cottage—a neat little low-eaved house of weathered wood, situated in the midst of an acre of grain. To one side was a bean patch; to the other, a woodpile which almost dwarfed the house. In front of the cottage stood a wiry old man, his skin as brown as his homespun tunic. He had evidently just heard the horses and turned around to look.

"Ho, father," called the Mouser, "it's a good day to be abroad in, and a good home you have here."

The peasant considered these statements and then nodded his head in agreement.

"We are two weary travelers," continued the Mouser.

Again the peasant nodded gravely.

"In return for two silver coins will you give us lodging for the night?"

The peasant rubbed his chin and then held up three fingers.

"Very well, you shall have three silver coins," said the Mouser, slipping from his horse. Fafhrd followed suit.

Only after giving the old man a coin to seal the bargain did the Mouser question casually, "Is there not an old, deserted place near your dwelling called the House of Angarngi?" The peasant nodded.

"What's it like?"

The peasant shrugged his shoulders.

"Don't you know?"

The peasant shook his head.

"But haven't you ever seen the place?" The Mouser's voice carried a note of amazement he did not bother to conceal.

He was answered by another head-shake.

"But, father, it's only a few minutes' walk from your dwelling, isn't it?"

The peasant nodded tranquilly, as if the whole business were no matter for surprise.

A muscular young man, who had come from behind the cottage to take their horses, offered a suggestion.

"You can see tower from other side the house. I can point her out."

At this the old man proved he was not completely speechless by saying in a dry, expressionless voice: "Go ahead. Look at her all you want."

And he stepped into the cottage. Fafhrd and the Mouser caught a glimpse of a child peering around the door, an old woman stirring a pot, and someone hunched in a big chair before a tiny fire.

The upper part of the tower proved to be barely visible through a break in the trees. The last rays of the sun touched it with deep red. It looked about four or five bowshots distant. And then, even as they watched, the sun dipped under and it became a featureless square of black stone.

"She's an old place," explained the young man vaguely. "I been all around her. Father, he's just never bothered to look."

"You've been inside?" questioned the Mouser.

The young man scratched his head.

"No. She's just an old place. No good for anything."

"There'll be a fairly long twilight," said Fafhrd, his wide green eyes drawn to the tower as if by a lodestone. "Long enough for us to have a closer look."

"I'd show the way," said the young man, "save I got water to fetch."

"No matter," replied Fafhrd. "When's supper?"

"When the first stars show."

They left him holding their horses and walked straight into the woods. Immediately it became much darker, as if twilight were almost over, rather than just begun. The vegetation proved to be somewhat thicker than they had anticipated. There were vines and thorns to be avoided. Irregular, pale patches of sky appeared and disappeared overhead.

The Mouser let Fafhrd lead the way. His mind was occupied with a queer sort of reverie about the peasants. It tickled his fancy to think how they had stolidly lived their toilsome lives, generation after generation, only a few steps from what might be one of the greatest treasure-troves in the world. It seemed incredible. How could people sleep so near jewels and not dream of them? But probably they never dreamed.

So the Gray Mouser was sharply aware of few things during the journey through the woods, save that Fafhrd seemed to be taking a long time—which was strange, since the barbarian was an accomplished woodsman.

Finally a deeper and more solid shadow loomed up through the trees, and in a moment they were standing in the margin of a small, boulder-studded clearing, most of which was occupied by the bulky structure they sought. Abruptly, even before his eyes took in the details of the place, the Mouser's mind was filled with a hundred petty perturbations. Weren't they making a mistake in leaving their horses with those strange peasants? And mightn't those rogues have followed them to the cottage? And wasn't this the Day of the Toad, an unlucky day for entering deserted houses? And shouldn't they have a short spear along, in case they met a leopard? And wasn't that a whippoorwill he heard crying on his left hand, an augury of ill omen?

The treasure house of Urgaan of Angarngi was a peculiar structure. The main feature was a large, shallow dome, resting on walls that formed an octagon. In front, and merging into it, were two lesser domes. Between these gaped a great square doorway. The tower rose asymmetrically from the rear part of the chief dome. The eyes of the Mouser sought hurriedly through the dimming twilight for the cause of the salient peculiarity of the structure, and decided it lay in the utter simplicity. There were no pillars, no outjutting cornices, no friezes, no architectural ornaments of any sort, skull-embellished or otherwise. Save for the doorway and a few tiny windows set in unexpected places, the House of Angarngi was a compact mass of uniformly dark gray stones most closely joined.

But now Fafhrd was striding up the short flight of terraced steps that led toward the open door, and the Mouser followed him, although he would have liked to spy around a little longer. With every step he took forward he sensed an odd reluctance growing within him. His earlier mood of pleasant expectancy vanished as suddenly as if he'd stepped into quicksand. It seemed to him that the black doorway yawned like a toothless mouth. And then a little shudder went through him, for he saw the mouth had a tooth—a bit of ghostly white that jutted up from the floor. Fafhrd was reaching down toward the object.

"I wonder whose skull this may be?" said the Northerner calmly.

The Mouser regarded the thing, and the scattering of bones and fragments of bone beside it. His feeling of uneasiness was fast growing toward a climax, and he had the unpleasant conviction that, once it did reach a climax, something would happen. What was the answer to Fafhrd's question? What form of death had struck down that earlier intruder? It was very dark inside the treasure house. Didn't the manuscript mention something about a guardian? It was hard to think of a flesh-and-blood guardian persisting for three hundred years, but there were things that were immortal or nearly immortal. He could tell that Fafhrd was not in the least affected by any premonitory disquietude, and was quite capable of instituting an immediate search for the treasure. That must be prevented at all costs. He remembered that the Northerner loathed snakes.

"This cold, damp stone," he observed casually. "Just the place for scaly, cold-blooded snakes."

"Nothing of the sort," replied Fafhrd angrily. "I'm willing to wager there's not a single serpent inside. Urgaan's note said, 'No deadly creature in rocky lair,' and to cap that, 'no serpent lethal-fanged yet fair.'"

"I am not thinking of guardian snakes Urgaan may have left here," the Mouser explained, "but only of serpents that may have wandered in for the night. Just as that skull you hold is not one set there by Urgaan 'with mortal eye a-glare,' but merely the braincase of some unfortunate wayfarer who chanced to perish here."

"I don't know," Fafhrd said, calmly eyeing the skull.

"Its orbits might glow phosphorescently in absolute dark."

A moment later he was agreeing it would be well to postpone the search until daylight returned, now that the treasure house was located. He carefully replaced the skull.

As they re-entered the woods, the Mouser heard a little inner voice whispering to him, *Just in time. Just in time.* Then the sense of uneasiness departed as suddenly as it had come, and he began to feel somewhat ridiculous. This caused him to sing a bawdy ballad of his own invention, wherein demons and other supernatural agents were ridiculed obscenely. Fafhrd chimed in good-naturedly on the choruses.

It was not as dark as they expected when they reached the cottage. They saw to their horses, found they had been well cared for, and then fell to the savory mess of beans, porridge, and pot herbs that the peasant's wife ladled into oak bowls. Fresh milk to wash it down was provided in quaintly carved oak goblets. The meal was a satisfying one and the interior of the house was neat and clean, despite its stamped earthen floor and low beams, which Fafhrd had to duck.

There turned out to be six in the family, all told. The father, his equally thin and leathery wife, the older son, a young boy, a daughter, and a mumbling grandfather, whom extreme age confined to a chair before the fire. The last two were the most interesting of the lot.

The girl was in the gawkish age of mid-adolescence, but there was a wild, coltish grace in the way she moved her lanky legs and slim arms with their prominent elbows. She was very shy, and gave the impression that at any moment she might dart out the door and into the woods.

In order to amuse her and win her confidence, the Mouser began to perform small feats of legerdemain, plucking copper coins out of the ears of the astonished peasant, and bone needles from the nose of his giggling wife. He turned beans into buttons and back again into beans, swallowed a large fork, made a tiny wooden manikin jig on the palm of his hand, and utterly bewildered the cat by pulling what seemed to be a mouse out of its mouth.

The old folks gaped and grinned. The little boy became frantic with excitement. His sister watched everything with concentrated interest, and even smiled warmly when the Mouser presented her with a square of fine, green linen he had conjured from the air, although she was still too shy to speak.

Then Fafhrd roared sea-chanteys that rocked the roof and sang lusty songs that set the old grandfather gurgling with delight. Meanwhile the Mouser fetched a small wineskin from his saddlebags, concealed it under his cloak, and filled the oak goblets as if by magic. These rapidly fuddled the peasants, who were unused to so potent a beverage, and by the time Fafhrd had finished telling a bloodcurdling tale of the frozen north, they were all nodding, save the girl and the grandfather.

The latter looked up at the merry-making adventurers, his watery eyes filled with a kind of impish, senile glee, and mumbled, "You two be right clever men. Maybe you be beast-dodgers." But before this remark could be elucidated, his eyes had gone vacant again, and in a few moments he was snoring.

Soon all were asleep, Fafhrd and the Mouser keeping their weapons close at hand, but only variegated snores and occasional snaps from the dying embers disturbed the silence of the cottage.

The Day of the Cat dawned clear and cool. The Mouser stretched himself luxuriously and, catlike, flexed his muscles and sucked in the sweet, dewy air. He felt exceptionally cheerful and eager to be up and doing. Was not this *his* day, the day of the Gray Mouser, a day in which luck could not fail him?

His slight movements awakened Fafhrd and together they stole silently from the cottage so as not to disturb the peasants, who were oversleeping with the wine they had taken. They refreshed their faces and hands in the wet grass and visited their horses. Then they munched some bread, washed it down with drafts of cool well water flavored with wine, and made ready to depart.

This time their preparations were well thought out. The Mouser carried a mallet and a stout iron pry-bar, in case they had to attack masonry, and made certain that candles, flint, wedges, chisels, and several other small tools were in his pouch. Fafhrd borrowed a pick from the peasant's implements and tucked a coil of thin, strong rope in his belt. He also took his bow and quiver of arrows.

The forest was delightful at this early hour. Bird cries and chatterings came from overhead, and once they glimpsed a black, squirrel-like animal scampering along a bough. A couple of chipmunks scurried under a bush dotted with red berries. What had been shadow the evening before was now a variety of green-leafed beauty. The two adventurers trod softly.

They had hardly gone more than a bowshot into the woods when they heard a faint rustling behind them. The rustling came rapidly nearer, and

suddenly the peasant girl burst into view. She stood
breathless and poised, one hand touching a
treetrunk, the other pressing some leaves, ready to
fly away at the first sudden move. Fafhrd and the
Mouser stood as stock-still as if she were a doe or a
dryad. Finally she managed to conquer her shyness
and speak.

"You go there?" she questioned, indicating the
direction of the treasure house with a quick, ducking
nod. Her dark eyes were serious.

"Yes, we go there," answered Fafhrd, smiling.

"Don't." This word was accompanied by a
rapid head-shake.

"But why shouldn't we, girl?" Fafhrd's voice
was gentle and sonorous, like an integral part of the
forest. It seemed to touch some spring within the girl
that enabled her to feel more at ease. She gulped a big
breath and began.

"Because I watch it from edge of the forest,
but never go close. Never, never, never. I say to myself there be a magic circle I must not cross. And I
say to myself there be a giant inside. Queer and fearsome giant." Her words were coming rapidly now,
like an undammed stream. "All gray he be, like the
stone of his house. All gray—eyes and hair and fingernails, too. And he has a stone club as big as a
tree. And he be big, bigger than you, twice as big."
Here she nodded at Fafhrd. "And with his club he
kills, kills, kills. But only if you go close. Every day,
almost, I play a game with him. I pretend to be going to cross the magic circle. And he watches from
inside the door, where I can't see him, and he thinks
I'm going to cross. And I dance through the forest
all around the house, and he follows me, peering

from the little windows. And I get closer and closer to the circle, closer and closer. But I never cross. And he be very angry and gnash his teeth, like rocks rubbing rocks, so that the house shakes. And I run, run, run away. But you mustn't go inside. Oh, you mustn't."

She paused, as if startled by her own daring. Her eyes were fixed anxiously on Fafhrd. She seemed drawn toward him. The Northerner's reply carried no overtone of patronizing laughter.

"But you've never actually seen the gray giant, have you?"

"Oh, no. He be too cunning. But I say to myself he must be there inside. I know he be inside. And that's the same thing, isn't it? Grandfather knows about him. We used to talk about him, when I was little. Grandfather calls him the beast. But the others laugh at me, so I don't tell."

Here was another astounding peasant-paradox, thought the Mouser with an inward grin. Imagination was such a rare commodity with them that this girl unhesitatingly took it for reality.

"Don't worry about us, girl. We'll be on the watch for your gray giant," he started to say, but he had less success than Fafhrd in keeping his voice completely natural or else the cadence of his words didn't chime so well with the forest setting.

The girl uttered one more warning. "Don't go inside, oh, please," and turned and darted away. The two adventurers looked at each other and smiled. Somehow the unexpected fairy tale, with its conventional ogre and its charmingly naive narrator added to the delight of the dewy morning. Without a comment they resumed their soft-stepping progress. And it was well that they went quietly, for when they had

gotten within a stone's throw of the clearing, they
heard low voices that seemed to be in grumbling argument. Immediately they cached the pick and pry-bar
and mallet under a clump of bushes, and stole forward,
taking advantage of the natural cover and watching
where they planted their feet.

On the edge of the clearing stood half a dozen
stocky men in black chain-mail shirts, bows on their
backs, shortswords at their sides. They were immediately recognizable as the rogues who had laid the
ambuscade. Two of them started for the treasure house,
only to be recalled by a comrade. Whereupon the argument apparently started afresh.

"That red-haired one," whispered the Mouser
after an unhurried look. "I can swear I've seen him in
the stables of Lord Rannarsh. My guess was right. It
seems we have a rival."

"Why do they wait, and keep pointing at the
house?" whispered Fafhrd. "Is it because some of their
comrades are already at work inside?"

The Mouser shook his head. "That cannot
be. See those picks and shovels and levers they have
rested on the ground? No, they wait for someone—
for a leader. Some of them want to examine the
house before he arrives. Others counsel against it.
And I will bet my head against a bowling ball that
the leader is Rannarsh himself. He is much too
greedy and suspicious to entrust a treasure quest to
any henchmen."

"What's to do?" murmured Fafhrd. "We cannot enter the house unseen, even if it were the wise
course, which it isn't. Once in, we'd be trapped."

"I've half a mind to loose my sling at them
right now and teach them something about the art of

ambuscade," replied the Mouser, slitting his eyes grimly. "Only then the survivors would flee into the house and hold us off until, mayhap, Rannarsh came, and more men with him."

"We might circle part way around the clearing," said Fafhrd, after a moment's pause, "keeping to the woods. Then we can enter the clearing unseen and shelter ourselves behind one of the small domes. In that way we become masters of the doorway, and can prevent their taking cover inside. Thereafter I will address them suddenly and try to frighten them off, you meanwhile staying hid and giving substance to my threats by making enough racket for ten men."

This seemed the handiest plan to both of them, and they managed the first part of it without a hitch. The Mouser crouched behind the small dome, his sword, sling, daggers, and a couple of sticks of wood laid ready for either noise-making or fight. Then Fafhrd strode briskly forward, his bow held carelessly in front of him, an arrow fitted to the string. It was done so casually that it was a few moments before Rannarsh's henchmen noticed him. Then they quickly reached for their own bows and as quickly desisted when they saw that the huge newcomer had the advantage of them. They scowled in irritated perplexity.

"Ho, rogues!" began Fafhrd. "We allow you just as much time as it will take you to make yourselves scarce, and no more. Don't think to resist or come skulking back. My men are scattered through the woods. At a sign from me they will feather you with arrows."

Meanwhile the Mouser had begun a low din and was slowly and artistically working it up in volume. Rapidly varying the pitch and intonation of his voice and making it echo first from some part of the building and then from the forest wall, he created the illusion of a squad of bloodthirsty bowmen. Nasty cries of "Shall we let fly?" "You take the redhead," and "Try for the belly shot; it's surest," kept coming now from one point and now another, until it was all Fafhrd could do to refrain from laughing at the woebegone, startled glances the six rogues kept darting around. But his merriment was extinguished when, just as the rogues were starting to slink shamefacedly away, an arrow arched erratically out of the woods, passing a spear's length above his head.

"Curse that branch!" came a deep, guttural voice the Mouser recognized as issuing from the throat of Lord Rannarsh. Immediately after, it began to bark commands.

"At them, you fools! It's all a trick. There are only the two of them. Rush them!"

Fafhrd turned without warning and loosed point-blank at the voice, but did not silence it. Then he dodged back behind the small dome and ran with the Mouser for the woods.

The six rogues, wisely deciding that a charge with drawn swords would be overly heroic, followed suit, unslinging their bows as they went. One of them turned before he had reached sufficient cover, nocking an arrow. It was a mistake. A ball from the Mouser's sling took him low in the forehead, and he toppled forward and was still.

The sound of that hit and fall was the last heard in the clearing for quite a long time, save for the inevitable bird cries, some of which were genuine, and some of which were communications between Fafhrd and the Mouser. The conditions of the death-dealing contest were obvious. Once it had fairly begun, no one dared enter the clearing, since he would become a fatally easy mark; and the Mouser was sure that none of the five remaining rogues had taken shelter in the treasure house. Nor did either side dare withdraw all its men out of sight of the doorway, since that would allow someone to take a commanding position in the top of the tower, providing the tower had a negotiable stair. Therefore it was a case of sneaking about near the edge of the clearing, circling and counter-circling, with a great deal of squatting in a good place and waiting for somebody to come along and be shot.

The Mouser and Fafhrd began by adopting the latter strategy, first moving about twenty paces nearer the point at which the rogues had disappeared. Evidently their patience was a little better than that of their opponents. For after about ten minutes of nerve-racking waiting, during which pointed seed pods had a queer way of looking like arrowheads, Fafhrd got the red-haired henchman full in the throat just as he was bending his bow for a shot at the Mouser. That left four besides Rannarsh himself. Immediately the two adventurers changed their tactics and separated, the Mouser circling rapidly around the treasure house and Fafhrd drawing as far back from the open space as he dared.

Rannarsh's men must have decided on the same plan, for the Mouser almost bumped into a scar-faced rogue as soft-footed as himself. At such close range, bow and sling were both useless—in their normal function. Scarface attempted to jab the barbed arrow he held into the Mouser's eye. The Mouser weaved his body to one side, swung his sling like a whip, and felled the man senseless with a blow from the horn handle. Then he retreated a few paces, thanked the Day of the Cat that there had not been two of them, and took to the trees as being a safer, though slower method of progress. Keeping to the middle heights, he scurried along with the sure-footedness of a rope walker, swinging from branch to branch only when it was necessary, making sure he always had more than one way of retreat open.

He had completed three-quarters of his circuit when he heard the clash of swords a few trees ahead. He increased his speed and was soon looking down on a sweet little combat. Fafhrd, his back to a great oak, had his broadsword out and was holding off two of Rannarsh's henchmen, who were attacking with their shorter weapons. It was a tight spot and the Northerner realized it. He knew that ancient sagas told of heroes who could best four or more men at swordplay. He also knew that such sagas were lies, providing the hero's opponents were reasonably competent.

And Rannarsh's men were veterans. They attacked cautiously but incessantly, keeping their swords well in front of them and never slashing wildly. Their breath whistled through their nostrils, but they were grimly confident, knowing the Northerner dared not lunge strongly at one of them because it would lay him wide open to a thrust by the other. Their game was to get one on each side of him and then attack simultaneously.

Fafhrd's counter was to shift position quickly and attack the nearer one murderously before the other could get back in range. In that way he managed to keep them side by side, where he could hold their blades in check by swift feints and crosswise sweeps. Sweat beaded his face and blood dripped from a scratch on his left thigh. A fearsome grin showed his white teeth, which occasionally parted to let slip a base, primitive insult.

The Mouser took in the situation at a glance, descended rapidly to a lower bough, and poised himself, aiming a dagger at the back of one of Fafhrd's adversaries. He was, however, standing very close to the thick trunk, and around this trunk darted a horny hand tipped with a short sword. The third henchman had also thought it wise to take to the trees. Fortunately for the Mouser, the man was uncertain of his footing and therefore his thrust, although well aimed, came a shade slow. As it was the little gray-clad man only managed to dodge by dropping off.

Thereupon he startled his opponent with a modest acrobatic feat. He did not drop to the ground, knowing that would put everyone at the mercy of the man in the tree. Instead, he grabbed hold of the branch on which he had been standing, swung himself smartly up again, and grappled. Steadying themselves now with one hand, now another, they drove for each other's throats, ramming with knees and elbows whenever they got a chance. At the first onset both dagger and sword were dropped, the latter sticking point-down in the ground directly between the two battling henchmen and startling them so that Fafhrd almost got home an attack.

The Mouser and his man surged and tee-tered along the branch away from the trunk, inflicting little damage on each other since it was hard to keep balance. Finally they slid off at the same time, but grabbed the branch with their hands. The puffing henchman aimed a vicious kick. The Mouser escaped it by yanking up his body and doubling up his legs. The latter he let fly violently, taking the henchman full in the chest, just where the ribs stop. The unfortunate retainer of Rannarsh fell to the ground, where he had the wind knocked out of him a second time.

At the same moment one of Fafhrd's opponents tried a trick that might have turned out well. When his companion was pressing the Northerner closely, he snatched for the shortsword sticking in the ground, intending to hurl it underhanded as if it were a javelin. But Fafhrd, whose superior endurance was rapidly giving him an advantage in speed, anticipated the movement and simultaneously made a brilliant counterattack against the other man. There were two thrusts, both lightninglike, the first a feint at the belly, the second a slicing stab that sheared through the throat to the spine. Then he whirled around and, with a quick sweep, knocked both weapons out of the hands of the first man, who looked up in bewilderment and promptly collapsed into a sitting position, panting in utter exhaustion, though with enough breath left to cry, "Mercy!"

To cap the situation, the Mouser dropped lightly down, as if out of the sky. Fafhrd automatically started to raise his sword, for a backhand swipe. Then he stared at the Mouser for as long a time as it took the man sitting on the ground to give three tremendous gasps. Then he began to laugh, first uncontrollable snickers and later thundering peals. It was a laughter in which the battle-begotten madness, completely sated anger, and relief at escape from death were equally mingled.

"Oh, by Glaggerk and by Kos!" he roared. "By the Behemoth! Oh, by the Cold Waste and the guts of the Red God! Oh! Oh! Oh!" Again the insane bellowing burst out. "Oh, by the Killer Whale and the Cold Woman and her spawn!" By degrees the laughter died away, choking in his throat. He rubbed his forehead with the palm of his hand and his face became starkly grave. Then he knelt beside the man he had just slain, and straightened his limbs, and closed his eyes, and began to weep in a dignified way that would have seemed ridiculous and hypocritical in anyone but a barbarian.

Meanwhile the Mouser's reactions were nowhere near as primitive. He felt worried, ironic, and slightly sick. He understood Fafhrd's emotions, but knew that he would not feel the full force of his own for some time yet, and by then they would be deadened and somewhat choked. He peered about anxiously, fearful of an anticlimactic attack that would find his companion helpless. He counted over the tally of their opponents. Yes, the six henchmen were all accounted for. But Rannarsh himself, where was Rannarsh? He fumbled in his pouch to make sure he had not lost his good-luck talismans and amulets. His lips moved rapidly as he murmured two or three prayers and cantrips. But all the while he held his sling ready, and his eyes never once ceased their quick shifting.

From the middle of a thick clump of bushes he heard a series of agonized gasps, as the man he had felled from the tree began to regain his wind. The henchman whom Fafhrd had disarmed, his face ashy pale from exhaustion rather than fright, was slowly edging back into the forest. The Mouser watched him carelessly, noting the comical way in

which the steel cap had slipped down over his forehead and rested against the bridge of his nose.
Meanwhile the gasps of the man in the bushes were
taking on a less agonized quality. At almost the same
instant, the two rose to their feet and stumbled off
into the forest.

The Mouser listened to their blundering retreat. He was sure that there was nothing more to
fear from them. They wouldn't come back. And
then a little smile stole into his face, for he heard
the sounds of a third person joining them in their
flight. That would be Rannarsh, thought the
Mouser, a man cowardly at heart and incapable of
carrying on single-handed. It did not occur to him
that the third person might be the man he had
stunned with his sling handle.

Mostly just to be doing something, he followed them leisurely for a couple of bowshots into the
forest. Their trail was impossible to miss, being marked
by trampled bushes and thorns bearing tatters of cloth.
It led in a beeline away from the clearing. Satisfied,
he returned, going out of his way to regain the mallet,
pick, and pry-bar.

He found Fafhrd tying a loose bandage around
the scratch on his thigh. The Northerner's emotions
had run their gamut and he was himself again. The
dead man for whom he had been somberly grieving
now meant no more to him than food for beetles and
birds. Whereas for the Mouser it continued to be a
somewhat frightening and sickening object.

"And now do we proceed with our interrupted business?" the Mouser asked.

Fafhrd nodded in a matter-of-fact manner and
rose to his feet. Together they entered the rocky clearing. It came to them as a surprise how little time the

fight had taken. True, the sun had moved somewhat higher, but the atmosphere was still that of early morning. The dew had not dried yet. The treasure house of Urgaan of Angarngi stood massive, featureless, grotesquely impressive.

"The peasant girl predicted the truth without knowing it," said the Mouser with a smile. "We played her game of 'circle-the-clearing and don't-cross-the-magic circle,' didn't we?"

The treasure house had no fears for him today. He recalled his perturbations of the previous evening, but was unable to understand them. The very idea of a guardian seemed somewhat ridiculous. There were a hundred other ways of explaining the skeleton inside the doorway.

So this time it was the Mouser who skipped into the treasure house ahead of Fafhrd. The interior was disappointing, being empty of any furnishings and as bare and unornamented as the outside walls. Just a large, low room. To either side square doorways led to the smaller domes, while to the rear a long hallway was dimly apparent, and the beginnings of a stair leading to the upper part of the main dome.

With only a casual glance at the skull and the broken skeleton, the Mouser made his way toward the stair.

"Our document," he said to Fafhrd, who was now beside him, "speaks of the treasure as resting just below the keystone of the chief dome. Therefore we must seek in the room or rooms above."

"True," answered the Northerner, glancing around. "But I wonder, Mouser, just what use this structure served. A man who builds a house solely to hide a treasure is shouting to the world that he has a treasure. Do you think it might have been a temple?"

The Mouser suddenly shrank back with a sibilant exclamation. Sprawled a little way up the stair was another skeleton, the major bones hanging together in lifelike fashion. The whole upper half of the skull was smashed to bony shards paler than those of a gray pot. "Our hosts are overly ancient and indecently naked," hissed the Mouser, angry with himself for being startled. Then he darted up the stairs to examine the grisly find. His sharp eyes picked out several objects among the bones. A rusty dagger, a tarnished gold ring that looped a knucklebone, a handful of horn buttons, and a slim, green-eaten copper cylinder. The last awakened his curiosity. He picked it up, dislodging hand-bones in the process, so that they fell apart, rattling dryly. He pried off the cap of the cylinder with his dagger point, and shook out a tightly rolled sheet of ancient parchment. This he gingerly unwound. Fafhrd and he scanned the lines of diminutive red lettering by the light from a small window on the landing above.

Mine is a secret treasure. Orichalcum have I, and crystal, and blood-red amber. Rubies and emeralds that demons would war for, and a diamond as big as the skull of a man. Yet none have seen them save I. I, Urgaan of Angarngi, scorn the flattery and the envy of fools. A fittingly lonely treasure house have I built for my jewels. There, hidden under the keystone, they may dream unperturbed until earth and sky wear away. A day's ride beyond the village of Soreev, in the valley of the two double-humped hills, lies that house, trebly-domed and single-towered. It is empty. Any fool may enter. Let him. I care not.

"The details differ slightly," murmured the Mouser, "but the phrases have the same ring as in our document."

"The man must have been mad," asserted Fafhrd, scowling. "Or else why should he carefully hide a treasure and then, with equal care, leave directions for finding it?"

"We thought our document was a memorandum or an oversight," said the Mouser thoughtfully. "Such a notion can hardly explain two documents." Lost in speculation, he turned toward the remaining section of the stair, only to find still another skull grinning at him from a shadowy angle. This time he was not startled, yet he experienced the same feeling that a fly must experience when, enmeshed in a spider's web, it sees the dangling, empty corpses of a dozen of its brothers. He began to speak rapidly.

"Nor can such a notion explain three or four or mayhap a dozen such documents. For how came these other questers here, unless each had found a written message? Urgaan of Angarngi may have been mad, but he sought deliberately to lure men here. One thing is certain: this house conceals—or did conceal—some deadly trap. Some guardian. Some giant beast, say. Or perhaps the very stones distill a poison. Perhaps hidden springs release sword blades which stab out through cracks in the walls and then return."

"That cannot be," answered Fafhrd. "These men were killed by great, bashing blows. The ribs and spine of the first were splintered. The second had his skull cracked open. And that third one there. See! The bones of his lower body are smashed."

The Mouser started to reply. Then his face broke into an unexpected smile. He could see the conclusion to which Fafhrd's arguments were unconsciously leading—and he knew that that conclusion was ridiculous. What thing would kill with

great, bashing blows? What thing but the gray giant
the peasant girl had told them about? The gray giant
twice as tall as a man, with his great stone club—a
giant fit only for fairy tales and fantasies.

And Fafhrd returned the Mouser's smile. It
seemed to him that they were making a great deal of
fuss about nothing. These skeletons were suggestive
enough, to be sure, but did they not represent men
who had died many, many years ago—centuries ago?
What guardian could outlast three centuries? Why,
that was a long enough time to weary the patience
of a demon! And there were no such things as demons, anyhow. And there was no earthly use in
mucking around about ancient fears and horrors that
were as dead as dust. The whole matter, thought
Fafhrd, boiled down to something very simple. They
had come to a deserted house to see if there was a
treasure in it.

Agreed upon this point, the two comrades
made their way up the remaining section of stair that
led to the dimmer regions of the House of Angarngi.
Despite their confidence, they moved cautiously and
kept sharp watch on the shadows lying ahead. This
was wise.

Just as they reached the top, a flash of steel
spun out of the darkness. It nicked the Mouser in the
shoulder as he twisted to one side. There was a metallic clash as it fell to the stone floor. The Mouser,
gripped by a sudden spasm of anger and fright, ducked
down and dashed rapidly through the door from which
the weapon had come, straight at the danger, whatever it was.

"Dagger-tossing in the dark, eh, you slick-bel-
lied worm?" Fafhrd heard the Mouser cry, and then
he, too, had plunged through the door.

Lord Rannarsh cowered against the wall, his rich hunting garb dusty and disordered, his black, wavy hair pushed back from his forehead, his cruelly handsome face a sallow mask of hate and extreme terror. For the moment the latter emotion seemed to predominate and, oddly enough, it did not appear to be directed toward the men he had just assailed, but toward something else, something unapparent.

"O gods!" he cried. "Let me go from here. The treasure is yours. Let me out of this place. Else I am doomed. The thing has played at cat and mouse with me. I cannot bear it. I cannot bear it!"

"So now we pipe a different tune, do we?" snarled the Mouser. "First dagger-tossing, then fright and pleas!"

"Filthy coward tricks," added Fafhrd. "Skulking here safe while your henchmen died bravely."

"Safe? Safe, you say? O gods!" Rannarsh almost screamed. Then a subtle change became apparent in his rigid-muscled face. It was not that his terror decreased. If anything, that became greater. But there was added to it, over and above, a consciousness of desperate shame, a realization that he had demeaned himself ineradicably in the eyes of these two ruffians. His lips began to writhe, showing tight-clenched teeth. He extended his left hand in a gesture of supplication.

"Oh, mercy, have mercy," he cried piteously, and his right hand twitched a second dagger from his belt and hurled it underhand at Fafhrd.

The Northerner knocked aside the weapon with a swift blow of his palm, then said deliberately, "He is yours, Mouser. Kill the man."

And now it was cat against cornered rat. Lord Rannarsh whipped a gleaming sword from its gold-worked scabbard and rushed in, cutting, thrusting, stabbing. The Mouser gave ground slightly, his slim blade flickering in a defensive counterattack that was wavering and elusive, yet deadly. He brought Rannarsh's rush to a standstill. His blade moved so quickly that it seemed to weave a net of steel around the man. Then it leaped forward three times in rapid succession. At the first thrust it bent nearly double against a concealed shirt of chain mail. The second thrust pierced the belly. The third transfixed the throat. Lord Rannarsh fell to the floor, spitting and gagging, his fingers clawing at his neck. There he died.

"An evil end," said Fafhrd somberly, "although he had fairer play than he deserved, and handled his sword well. Mouser, I like not this killing, although there was surely more justice to it than the others."

The Mouser, wiping his weapon against his opponent's thigh, understood what Fafhrd meant. He felt no elation at his victory, only a cold, queasy disgust. A moment before he had been raging, but now there was no anger left in him. He pulled open his gray jerkin and inspected the dagger wound in his left shoulder. A little blood was still welling from it and trickling down his arm.

"Lord Rannarsh was no coward," he said slowly. "He killed himself, or at least caused his own death, because we had seen him terrified and heard him cry in fright."

And at these words, without any warning whatsoever, stark terror fell like an icy eclipse upon the hearts of the Gray Mouser and Fafhrd. It was as if Lord Rannarsh had left them a legacy of fear, which passed to them immediately upon his death. And the unmanning thing about it was that they had no premonitory apprehension, no hint of its approach. It did not take root and grow gradually greater. It came all at once, paralyzing, overwhelming. Worse still, there was no discernible cause. One moment they were looking down with something of indifference upon the twisted corpse of Lord Rannarsh. The next moment their legs were weak, their guts were cold, their spines prickling, their teeth clicking, their hearts pounding, their hair lifting at the roots.

Fafhrd felt as if he had walked unsuspecting into the jaws of a gigantic serpent. His barbaric mind was stirred to the deeps. He thought of the grim god Kos brooding alone in the icy silence of the Cold Waste. He thought of the masked powers Fate and Chance, and of the game they play for the blood and brains of men. And he did not will these thoughts. Rather did the freezing fear seem to crystallize them, so that they dropped into his consciousness like snowflakes.

Slowly he regained control over his quaking limbs and twitching muscles. As if in a nightmare, he looked around him slowly, taking in the details of his surroundings. The room they were in was semicircular, forming half of the great dome. Two small windows, high in the curving ceiling, let in light.

An inner voice kept repeating, *Don't make a sudden move. Slowly. Slowly. Above all, don't run. The others did. That was why they died so quickly. Slowly. Slowly.*

He saw the Mouser's face. It reflected his own terror. He wondered how much longer this would last, how much longer he could stand it without running amuck, how much longer he could passively endure this feeling of a great invisible paw reaching out over him, span by span, implacably.

The faint sound of footsteps came from the room below. Regular and unhurried footsteps. Now they were crossing into the rear hallway below. Now they were on the stairs. And now they had reached the landing, and were advancing up the second section of the stairs.

The man who entered the room was tall and frail and old and very gaunt. Scant locks of intensely black hair straggled down over his high-domed forehead. His sunken cheeks showed clearly the outlines of his long jawbone, and waxy skin was pulled tight over his small nose. Fanatical eyes burned in deep, bony sockets. He wore the simple, sleeveless robe of a holy man. A pouch hung from the cord round his waist.

He fixed his eyes upon Fafhrd and the Gray Mouser.

"I greet you, you men of blood," he said in a hollow voice. Then his gaze fell with displeasure upon the corpse of Rannarsh.

"More blood has been shed. It is not well."

And with the bony forefinger of his left hand he traced in the air a curious triple square, the sign sacred to the Great God.

"Do not speak," his calm, toneless voice continued, "for I know your purposes. You have come to take treasure from this house. Others have sought to do the same. They have failed. You will fail. As for myself, I have no lust for treasure. For forty years I have lived on crusts and water, devoting my spirit to the Great God." Again he traced the curious sign. "The gems and ornaments of this world and the jewels and gauds of the world of demons cannot tempt or corrupt me. My purpose in coming here is to destroy an evil thing.

"I"—and here he touched his chest—"I am Arvlan of Angarngi, the ninth lineal descendant of Urgaan of Angarngi. This I always knew, and sorrowed for, because Urgaan of Angarngi was a man of evil. But not until fifteen days ago, on the Day of the Spider, did I discover from ancient documents that Urgaan had built this house, and built it to be an eternal trap for the unwise and venturesome. He has left a guardian here, and that guardian has endured.

"Cunning was my accursed ancestor, Urgaan, cunning and evil. The most skillful architect in all Lankhmar was Urgaan, a man wise in the ways of stone and learned in geometrical lore. But he scorned the Great God. He longed for improper powers. He had commerce with demons, and won from them an unnatural treasure. But he had no use for it. For in seeking wealth and knowledge and power, he lost his ability to enjoy any good feeling or pleasure, even simple lust. So he hid his treasure, but hid it in such a way that it would wreak endless evil on the world, even as he felt men and one proud, contemptuous, cruel woman—as heartless as this fane—had wreaked evil upon him. It is my purpose and my right to destroy Urgaan's evil.

"Seek not to dissuade me, lest doom fall upon you. As for me, no harm can befall me. The hand of the Great God is poised above me, ready to ward off any danger that may threaten his faithful servant. His will is my will. Do not speak, men of blood! I go to destroy the treasure of Urgaan of Angarngi."

And with these words, the gaunt holy man walked calmly on, with measured stride, like an apparition, and disappeared through the narrow doorway that led into the forward part of the great dome.

Fafhrd stared after him, his green eyes wide, feeling no desire to follow or to interfere. His terror had not left him but it was transmuted. He was still aware of a dreadful threat, but it no longer seemed to be directed against him personally.

Meanwhile, a most curious notion had lodged in the mind of the Mouser. He felt that he had just now seen, not a venerable holy man, but a dim reflection of the centuries-dead Urgaan of Angarngi. Surely Urgaan had that same high-domed forehead, that same secret pride, that same air of command. And those locks of youthfully black hair, which contrasted so ill with the aged face also seemed part of a picture looming from the past. A picture dimmed and distorted by time, but retaining something of the power and individuality of the ancient original.

They heard the footsteps of the holy man proceed a little way into the other room. Then for the space of a dozen heartbeats there was complete silence. Then the floor began to tremble slightly under their feet, as if the earth were quaking, or as if a giant were treading near. Then there came a single quavering cry from the next room, cut off in the middle by a single sickening crash that made them lurch. Then, once again, utter silence.

Fafhrd and the Mouser looked at one another in blank amazement—not so much because of what they had just heard but because, almost at the moment of the crash, the pall of terror had lifted from them completely. They jerked out their swords and hurried into the next room.

It was a duplicate of the one they had quitted, save that instead of two small windows, there were three, one of them near the floor. Also, there was but a single door, the one through which they had just entered. All else was closely mortised stone—floor, walls, and hemidomed ceiling.

Near the thick center wall, which bisected the dome, lay the body of the holy man. Only "lay" was not the right word. Left shoulder and chest were mashed against the floor. Life was fled. Blood puddled around.

Fafhrd's and the Mouser's eyes searched wildly for a being other than themselves and the dead man and found none—no, not one gnat hovering amongst the dust motes revealed by the narrow shafts of sunlight shooting down through the windows. Their imaginations searched as wildly and as much in vain for a being that could strike such a man-killing blow and vanish through one of the three tiny orifices of the windows. A giant, striking serpent with a granite head…

Set in the wall near the dead man was a stone about two feet square, jutting out a little from the rest. On this was boldly engraved, in antique Lankhmarian hieroglyphs: "Here rests the treasure of Urgaan of Angarngi."

The sight of that stone was like a blow in the face to the two adventurers. It roused every ounce of obstinacy and reckless determination in them. What matter that an old man sprawled smashed beside it? They had their swords! What matter they now had proof some grim guardian resided in the treasure house? They could take care of themselves! Run away and leave that stone unmoved, with its insultingly provocative inscription? No, by Kos, and the Behemoth! They'd see themselves in Nehwon's hell first!

Fafhrd ran to fetch the pick and the other large tools, which had been dropped on the stairs when Lord Rannarsh tossed his first dagger. The Mouser looked more closely at the jutting stone. The cracks around it were wide and filled with a dark, tarry mixture. It gave out a slightly hollow sound when he tapped it with his sword hilt. He calculated that the wall was about six feet thick at this point—enough to contain a sizable cavity. He tapped experimentally along the wall in both directions, but the hollow ring quickly ceased. Evidently the cavity was a fairly small one. He noted that the crevices between all the other stones were very fine, showing no evidence of any cementing substance whatsoever. In fact, he couldn't be sure that they weren't false crevices, superficial cuts in the surface of solid rock. But that hardly seemed possible. He heard Fafhrd returning, but continued his examination.

The state of the Mouser's mind was peculiar. A dogged determination to get at the treasure overshadowed other emotions. The inexplicably sudden vanishing of his former terror had left certain parts of his mind benumbed. It was as if he had decided to hold his thoughts in leash until he had seen what the treasure cavity contained. He was content to keep his mind occupied with material details, and yet make no deductions from them.

His calmness gave him a feeling of at least temporary safety. His experiences had vaguely convinced him that the guardian, whatever it was, which had smashed the holy man and played cat and mouse with Rannarsh and themselves, did not strike without first inspiring a premonitory terror in its victims.

Fafhrd felt very much the same way, except that he was even more single-minded in his determination to solve the riddle of the inscribed stone.

They attacked the wide crevices with chisel and mallet. The dark tarry mixture came away fairly easily, first in hard lumps, later in slightly rubbery, gouged strips. After they had cleared it away to the depth of a finger, Fafhrd inserted the pick and managed to move the stone slightly. Thus the Mouser was enabled to gouge a little more deeply on that side. Then Fafhrd subjected the other side of the stone to the leverage of the pick. So the work proceeded, with alternate pryings and gougings.

They concentrated on each detail of the job with unnecessary intensity, mainly to keep their imaginations from being haunted by the image of a man more than two hundred years dead. A man with high-domed forehead, sunken cheeks, nose of a skull—that is, if the dead thing on the floor was a true type of the breed of Angarngi. A man who had somehow won a great treasure, and then hid it away from all eyes, seeking to obtain neither glory nor material profit from it. Who said he scorned the envy of fools, and who yet wrote many provocative notes in diminutive red lettering in order to inform fools of his treasure and make them envious. Who seemed to be reaching out across the dusty centuries, like a spider spinning a web to catch a fly on the other side of the world.

And yet, he was a skillful architect, the holy man had said. Could such an architect build a stone automaton twice as tall as a tall man? A gray stone automaton with a great club? Could he make a hiding place from which it could emerge, deal death, and then return? No, no, such notions were childish, not to be entertained! Stick to the job in hand. First find what lay behind the inscribed stone. Leave thoughts until afterward.

The stone was beginning to give more easily to the pressure of the pick. Soon they would be able to get a good purchase on it and pry it out.

Meanwhile an entirely new sensation was growing in the Mouser—not one of terror at all, but of physical revulsion. The air he breathed seemed thick and sickening. He found himself disliking the texture and consistency of the tarry mixture gouged from the cracks, which somehow he could only liken to wholly imaginary substances, such as the dung of dragons or the solidified vomit of the behemoth. He avoided touching it with his fingers, and he kicked away the litter of chunks and strips that had gathered around his feet. The sensation of queasy loathing became difficult to endure.

He tried to fight it, but had no more success than if it had been seasickness, which in some ways it resembled. He felt unpleasantly dizzy. His mouth kept filling with saliva. The cold sweat of nausea beaded his forehead. He could tell that Fafhrd was unaffected, and he hesitated to mention the matter; it seemed ridiculously out of place, especially as it was unaccompanied by any fear or fright. Finally the stone itself began to have the same effect on him as the tarry mixture, filling him with a seemingly causeless, but none the less sickening revulsion. Then he could bear it no longer. With a vaguely apologetic nod to Fafhrd, he dropped his chisel and went to the low window for a breath of fresh air.

This did not seem to help matters much. He pushed his head through the window and gulped deeply. His mental processes were overshadowed by the general indifference of extreme nausea, and everything seemed very far away. Therefore when he saw that the peasant girl was standing in the middle of the clearing, it was some time before he began to consider the import of the fact. When he did, part of his sickness left him; or at least he was enabled to overpower it sufficiently to stare at her with gathering interest.

Her face was white, her fists were clenched, her arms held rigid at her sides. Even at the distance he could catch something of the mingled terror and determination with which her eyes were fixed on the great doorway. Toward this doorway she was forcing herself to move, one jerking step after another, as if she had to keep screwing her courage to a higher pitch. Suddenly the Mouser began to feel frightened, not for himself at all, but for the girl. Her terror was obviously intense, and yet she must be doing what she was doing—braving her "queer and fearsome gray giant"— for his sake and Fafhrd's. At all costs, he thought, she must be prevented from coming closer. It was wrong that she be subjected for one moment longer to such a horribly intense terror.

His mind was confused by his abominable nausea, yet he knew what he must do. He hurried toward the stairs with shaky strides, waving Fafhrd another vague gesture. Just as he was going out of the room he chanced to turn up his eyes, and spied something peculiar on the ceiling. What it was he did not fully realize for some moments.

Fafhrd hardly noticed the Mouser's movements, much less his gestures. The block of stone was rapidly yielding to his efforts. He had previously experienced a faint suggestion of the Mouser's nausea, but perhaps because of his greater single-mindedness, it had not become seriously bothersome. And now his attention was wholly concentrated on the stone. Persistent prying had edged it out a palm's breadth from the wall. Seizing it firmly in his two powerful hands, he tugged it from one side to the other, back and forth. The dark, viscous stuff clung to it tenaciously, but with each sidewise jerk it moved forward a little.

The Mouser lurched hastily down the stairs, fighting vertigo. His feet kicked bones and sent them knocking against the walls. What was it he had seen on the ceiling? Somehow, it seemed to mean something. But he must get the girl out of the clearing. She mustn't come any closer to the house. She mustn't enter.

Fafhrd began to feel the weight of the stone, and knew that it was nearly clear. It was damnably heavy—almost a foot thick. Two carefully gauged heaves finished the job. The stone overbalanced. He stepped quickly back. The stone crashed ponderously on the floor. A rainbow glitter came from the cavity that had been revealed. Fafhrd eagerly thrust his head into it.

The Mouser staggered toward the doorway. It was a bloody smear he had seen on the ceiling. And just above the corpse of the holy man. But why should that be? He'd been smashed against the floor, hadn't he? Was it blood splashed up from his lethal clubbing? But then why smeared? No matter. The girl. He must get to the girl. He must. There she was, almost at the doorway. He could see her. He felt the stone floor vibrating slightly beneath his feet. But that was his dizziness, wasn't it?

Fafhrd felt the vibration, too. But any thought he might have had about it was lost in his wonder at what he saw. The cavity was filled to a level just below the surface of the opening, with a heavy metallic liquid that resembled mercury, except that it was night-black. Resting on this liquid was a more astonishing group of gems than Fafhrd had ever dreamed of.

In the center was a titan diamond, cut with a myriad of oddly angled facets. Around it were two irregular circles, the inner formed of twelve rubies, each a decahedron, the outer formed of seventeen emeralds, each an irregular octahedron. Lying between these gems, touching some of them, sometimes connecting them with each other, were thin, fragile-looking bars of crystal, amber, greenish tourmaline, and honey-pale orichalchum. All these objects did not seem to be floating in the metallic liquid so much as resting upon it, their weight pressing down the surface into shallow depressions, some cup-shaped, others troughlike. The rods glowed faintly, while each of the gems glittered with a light that Fafhrd's mind strangely conceived to be refracted starlight.

His gaze shifted to the mercurous heavy fluid, where it bulged up between, and he saw distorted reflections of stars and constellations which he recognized, stars and constellations which would be visible now in the sky overhead, were it not for the concealing brilliance of the sun. An awesome wonder engulfed him. His gaze shifted back to the gems. There was something tremendously meaningful about their complex arrangement, something that seemed to speak of overwhelming truths in an alien symbolism. More, there was a compelling impression of inner movement, of sluggish thought, of inorganic consciousness. It was like what the eyes see when they close at night—not utter blackness, but a shifting, fluid pattern of many-colored points of light. Feeling that he was reaching impiously into the core of a thinking mind, Fafhrd gripped with his right hand for the diamond as big as a man's skull.

The Mouser blundered through the doorway. There could be no mistaking it now. The close-mortised stones were trembling. That bloody smear, as if the ceiling had champed down upon the holy man, crushing him against the floor, or as if the floor had struck upward. But there was the girl, her terror-wide eyes fastened upon him, her mouth open for a scream that did not come. He must drag her away, out of the clearing.

But why should he feel that a fearful threat was now directed at himself as well? Why should he feel that something was poised above him, threatening? As he stumbled down the terraced steps, he looked over his shoulder and up. The tower. The tower! It was falling. It was falling toward him. It was dipping at him over the dome. But there were no fractures along its length. It was not breaking. It was not falling. It was bending.

Fafhrd's hand jerked back, clutching the great, strangely faceted jewel, so heavy that he had difficulty in keeping his hold upon it. Immediately the surface of the metallic, star-reflecting fluid was disturbed. It bobbled and shook. Surely the whole house was shaking, too. The other jewels began to dart about erratically, like water insects on the surface of a puddle. The various crystalline and metallic bars began to spin, their tips attracted now to one jewel and now to another, as if the jewels were lodestone and the bars iron needles. The whole surface of the fluid was in a whirling, jerking confusion that suggested a mind gone mad because of loss of its chief part.

For an agonizing instant the Mouser stared up in amazement—frozen at the clublike top of the tower, hurling itself down upon him. Then he ducked and lunged forward at the girl, tackling her, rapidly rolling over and over with her. The tower top struck a sword's length behind them, with a thump that jolted them momentarily off the ground. Then it jerked itself up from the pitlike depression it had made.

Fafhrd tore his gaze away from the incredible, alien beauty of the jewel-confused cavity. His right hand was burning. The diamond was hot. No, it was cold beyond belief. By Kos, the room was changing shape! The ceiling was bulging downward at a point. He made for the door, then stopped dead in his tracks. The door was closing like a stony mouth. He turned and took a few steps over the quaking floor toward the small, low window. It snapped shut, like a sphincter. He tried to drop the diamond. It clung painfully to the inside of his hand. With a snap of his wrist he whipped it away from him. It hit the floor and began to bounce about, glaring like a living star.

The Mouser and the peasant girl rolled toward the edge of the clearing. The tower made two more tremendous bashes at them, but both went yards wide, like the blows of a blind madman. Now they were out of range. The Mouser lay sprawled on his side, watching a stone house that hunched and heaved like a beast, and a tower that bent double as it thumped grave-deep pits into the ground. It crashed into a group of boulders and its top broke off, but the jaggedly fractured end continued to beat the boulders in wanton anger, smashing them into fragments. The Mouser felt a compulsive urge to take out his dagger and stab himself in the heart. A man had to die when he saw something like that.

Fafhrd clung to sanity because he was threatened from a new direction at every minute and because he could say to himself, "I know. I know. The house is a beast, and the jewels are its mind. Now that mind is mad. I know. I know." Walls, ceiling, and floor quaked and heaved, but their movements did not seem to be directed especially at him. Occasional crashes almost deafened him. He staggered over rocky swells, dodging stony advances that were half bulges and half blows, but that lacked the speed and directness of the tower's first smash at the Mouser. The corpse of the holy man was jolted about in grotesque mechanical reanimation.

Only the great diamond seemed aware of Fafhrd. Exhibiting a fretful intelligence, it kept bounding at him viciously, sometimes leaping as high as his head. He involuntarily made for the door as his only hope. It was champing up and down with convulsive regularity.

Watching his chance, he dived at it just as it was opening, and writhed through. The diamond followed him, striking at his legs. The carcass of Rannarsh was flung sprawling in his path. He jumped over it, then slid, lurched, stumbled, fell down stairs in earthquake, where dry bones danced. Surely the beast must die, the house must crash and crush him flat. The diamond leaped for his skull, missed, hurtled through the air, and struck a wall. Thereupon it burst into a great puff of iridescent dust.

Immediately the rhythm of the shaking of the house began to increase. Fafhrd raced across the heaving floor, escaped by inches the killing embrace of the great doorway, plunged across the clearing—passing a dozen feet from the spot where the tower was beating boulders into crushed rock—and then leaped over two pits in the ground. His face was rigid and white. His eyes were vacant. He blundered bull-like into two or three trees, and only came to a halt because he knocked himself flat against one of them.

The house had ceased most of its random movements, and the whole of it was shaking like a huge dark jelly. Suddenly its forward part heaved up like a behemoth in death agony. The two smaller domes were jerked ponderously a dozen feet off the ground, as if they were the paws. The tower whipped into convulsive rigidity. The main dome contracted sharply, like a stupendous lung. For a moment it hung there, poised. Then it crashed to the ground in a heap of gigantic stone shards. The earth shook. The forest resounded. Battered atmosphere whipped branches and leaves. Then all was still. Only from the fractures in the stone a tarry, black liquid was slowly oozing, and here and there iridescent puffs of air suggested jewel-dust.

Along a narrow, dusty road two horsemen were cantering slowly toward the village of Soreev in the southernmost limits of the land of Lankhmar. They presented a somewhat battered appearance. The limbs of the larger, who was mounted on a chestnut gelding, showed several bruises, and there was a bandage around his thigh and another around the palm of his right hand. The smaller man, the one mounted on a gray mare, seemed to have suffered an equal number of injuries.

"Do you know where we're headed?" said the latter, breaking a long silence. "We're headed for a city. And in that city are endless houses of stone, stone towers without numbers, streets paved with stone, domes, archways, stairs. *Tcha*, if I feel then as I feel now, I'll never go within a bowshot of Lankhmar's walls."

His large companion smiled.

"What now, little man? Don't tell me you're afraid of earthquakes?"